POISON BRANCHES

by

Cynthia Raleigh

Copyright © 2016 by Cynthia Raleigh. All Rights Reserved.

Cover design by Colin Lawson

Poison Branches / Cynthia Raleigh: Second Edition

Paperback ISBN: 978-1539301523

Electronic ISBN: 978-1310660504

To my husband, Greg, for making it possible for me to have the time to write; to Debby: for all the years of shared experiences, without you, life would be much less exciting; and to my cousin, Chad, thank you for sharing your knowledge and love of genealogy.

There will be a very last time we see each person we know. Sometimes we realize it, sometimes we suspect it, but many times we have no inkling that we will never see this person again. Then there are the times we can only hope for it.

Chapter 1

The cemetery was dutifully quiet and sad. The rain had nearly stopped. Amy was aware of the irregular plop and slap of fat raindrops as they drooped and fell heavily from the leaves of the many surrounding trees to the leaves flattened to the ground during the storm. The sound made it feel cold to her even though it was near the end of August.

She focused her dull stare on the new grave. The sodden dirt, piled high in the center, had turned to muddy chunks. Stray pieces of grass flecked the mound, along with a dirty and torn artificial flower from another grave. It had to be from someone else's grave. This one didn't have flowers from a funeral home gathered around the mound protecting it from the elements. It was bare and stark; the body traveled straight from the mortuary to the cemetery. Only a temporary marker was in place. It was a cheap-looking, thin aluminum plate with the last name and year of death stamped in low relief. The black paint meant to highlight the letters and numbers was already smearing, as though it had been applied moments before the rain started. Amy wondered if there would be a headstone. Not likely, and in a few weeks, this cheap aluminum plate would be blowing out into the field beyond the cemetery, the mud would dry and settle, and eventually the grass and weeds would grow back over the turned earth.

Amy laid the small bunch of flowers she had picked up at a grocery store onto the center of the grave. A few simple flowers: a couple each of daisies, chrysanthemums, carnations, and what she thought might be zinnias. Was that right? She didn't know. It looked garish, wrapped in tissue paper in the color of green that seemed to appear mainly on golf courses and sports fields with fake turf. There was no vase to turn upright to hold the flowers, but that was alright, the vases were usually stuck from being jammed in crooked or the chains were tangled up in roots and mired in mud, and if they did come free of their subterranean home, they never seemed to fit straight in the toothed setting. But no, this grave didn't have that.

She glanced around the cemetery. It was rural, not consistently cared for, and had some areas that were wild and overgrown. It was surrounded by a mortarless stone wall, which continued through part of the cemetery interior. There was a Victorian style family plot enclosed by an iron fence. The fence was still standing but had a dull, powdery appearance and was brick red with rust. There were two obelisk type stones within the enclosure, one of which had toppled over and was strangled with vines. Blackberry bushes grew higher than the remaining upright stone and then bent over it preventing any intrusion by the curious who might want to read the names. The grass in the cemetery had been mown, but judging by the stacks of brown matted grass heaped throughout the cemetery and stuck to the surface of the lower stones, it had been the only time that season. The person responsible for the mowing had obviously hurried the job; there were long patches of grass at the edges of most stones where the mower had taken a sloppy turn and not bothered to go back for the missed parts.

She was surprised there were still interments being made here; most of the stones were pretty old. It looked like most of the ones in this section were from the 1930s.

But there it was, the grave of someone who was the same age as herself, whom she had known for three-fourths of her life. They had gone to school together, had been close friends at one time, even shared an apartment for a while between high school and the second year of college. Those days were long gone and seemed like someone else's memory. Not all of them were good.

Amy turned toward the cemetery road and her car. The road was gravel but most of it had scattered and the lane was rutted down into the hard clay. There was a ridge of scrubby grass growing in the center. She had pulled over partially onto the verge to park in case another car came through, not that it was likely. As she neared the passenger side of her car, she saw headlights in her peripheral vision. They weren't moving, so she continued to her car, rounded the back and up the side. As she pulled open her door, she glanced back to her right at the car. The lights were still on and she could just detect the silhouette of someone sitting in the driver's seat. It looked like an older car, long and ungainly; the type that had a hood nearly as long as her entire car. There were four round lights, two headlights and two smaller lights. It may have been tan, or beige, or some other nondescript color. It was hard to tell under the crusting of dirt and rust.

From her sideways viewpoint, not wanting to obviously stare at the driver, Amy couldn't be sure if it was a man or a woman, but they weren't moving, just sitting still and appeared to be staring straight ahead. Straight at her. She shivered just a bit and slid into the car, set her purse on the passenger seat, closed the door, and, glancing into her rearview mirror, locked the doors.

A cemetery can be a peaceful, reflective place when everything seems calm and normal. Let one thing get out of kilter and it becomes menacing and lonely. Amy looked down to buckle her seat belt which took a minute, having to retrieve the buckle end from between the seat and the console. Then she took a look into her outside mirror. The car was closer. It had been parked fully in the grass on a curve, backed under an overhanging clump of twisted cedar trees, but now was idling in the single lane of the road behind her. She could see the foggy exhaust slithering up and over the back fender of the car like someone with a cigarette letting the smoke escape lazily from their mouth and trail upward. There was lettering on the chrome frame, right above the grill: R E L S Y R H C. She could make out the shape of a person in a bulky coat and hat behind the wheel. Waiting.

Returning her gaze to the rear-view mirror, Amy pressed her foot on the brake and put the car in gear. As she moved her foot to the accelerator, the other car lunged toward her. She saw the front bumper lift slightly higher as the occupant gave it the gas. Her right hand jerked off the gear shift at the same time as her left hand came off the steering wheel in a start of surprise. She grappled for the wheel and slammed her foot on the accelerator. Her smooth-bottomed shoes were slick from the wet grass and her foot slipped off the left side of the accelerator and jarred on the floorboard. She again looked into the rearview mirror and saw the hulking car looming right behind her. Now she could hear the roar of the engine, along with her own panicked breathing as she tried to keep her foot on the pedal and push. Her hands gripped the steering wheel tightly and her arms were locked straight. Just as her foot found some purchase, her tires starting to spin and throw stray bits of gravel and clumps of mud, the old Chrysler slammed into the back of her car.

It was a huge car, the frame made of steel. As Amy fought to get a view over the top of the deployed airbag, the massive car pushed her comparatively tiny Focus forward smoothly and easily. She pulled down on the bag with both hands just enough to get a look. She was being pushed toward the stone wall that ran perpendicular to the section of road she was on. Just ahead, the road curved to the left and ran alongside the wall.

There was not a lot of time to analyze the situation, but Amy did wonder who this person was, why they were angry at her, and why they wanted to wreck her car. She tried to grab the wheel under or around the bag to turn the car but could only grasp the left side of the wheel with her left hand. She pulled down and moved the wheel a bit, which turned the car only a small amount. She pressed down with both feet on the brake, but the wheels locked and the car continued to shovel Amy's car along. The sound from the big car's engine increased as it pushed harder. The small and lightweight Ford reached the shoulder as the road turned left. It bumped over the accumulated rock and grassy border. The wall came to meet the front bumper as her car was rammed into it. The airbag began to deflate. The hood of the car was crumpled.

The Chrysler was backing up. Amy could see that a scarf or some other material was wrapped around the driver's face and the hat was pulled down low. She could see enough to have the impression it was a man. The dirty car reversed over the shoulder and back into the lane. Amy's hands were shaking and she tried to reach her purse for her phone to call for help. But the car wasn't leaving. It was shifting gears. She suddenly understood that it wasn't over and looked wildly around the cemetery for any sign of someone else. She tried to honk the horn but either the airbag blocked the way or the horn was no longer working. She scrabbled with the door handle to escape the car and get over the waist-high wall. The door opened about ten inches and stopped. The front of the door was caught behind the fender which had been shoved backward. She kicked at the door with both feet in terror and got it open a few more inches, just barely enough to squeeze out as the Chrysler came barreling back toward her.

Amy was still holding the edge of the door when the second impact crunched the Focus into the wall and lifted the back wheels off the ground. Her arm jerked forward and then flung backward, painfully wrenching her shoulder. The fiberglass panels of the fender cracked and fell, useless, to the soggy ground. The buckled hood lurched backward onto the cracked windshield. Amy fell onto her knees in a muddy puddle in the grass. As she struggled to her feet, she headed for the wall. The black-coated figure stepped out of the car as steam began to rise around the edges of the enormous hood, the radiator quietly hissing.

Amy grabbed the top of the wall and used the ruined fender to heft herself up. Once on top of the wall, she launched herself to the other side and made an awkward landing on the spongy moss, but didn't fall. Her mouth open, ragged breaths being sucked in and out, she didn't pause to get a good look, but she did see the man raise his arms, holding something long and dark. A strangled sound escaped her throat as she began a desperate sprint across the grass. She felt like she was running as swift as the wind but the scenery wasn't passing by very quickly, like one of those dreams where she was trying to run but couldn't. This part of the cemetery was very sparsely filled and the stones were infrequent or they were missing. Easier to avoid while running, but nowhere to hide quickly. And hiding behind a gravestone wasn't going to help.

Amy ran toward a decrepit looking mausoleum, frequently stepping hard down into a burrow entrance or a low spot over an old grave, the stone long gone. She heard a popping sound followed by a wet thud. She didn't turn around, but kept going. Almost to the mausoleum. She didn't remember tripping, but at the same time as the second pop, she felt her head burning and painful as though she had fallen and hit it on a stone. The sodden, weedy ground came up to meet her face very quickly. She didn't have time to wonder why.

Chapter 2

Perri Seamore peeped through her fingers just a bit so she could see the clock on the wall. Two p.m., an hour and a half to go. Too long for that "almost time" end of shift burst of energy and too little time to finish her charting. She hadn't even given all the meds yet. 'Oh, good grief, just get on with it,' she thought to herself. It was the last shift of her assignment to this hospital and she was not at all unhappy. As a prn nurse, one who takes temporary assignments for specified lengths of time, Perri had the freedom to take some time off when she needed to, and that is exactly what she was doing after today, when her contract would be fulfilled.

She had plopped down in the ergonomic chair at the nurse's station for a breather following an incident with an elderly patient who had removed every tube and line attached to him, slinging them this way and that, and then perched precariously in the middle of his bed systematically lobbing every movable item in his room toward the door, shouting as best his worn-out lungs would allow. The IV and feeding tubes had continued to pulse liquids out onto the floor and formed a slippery mess when mixed with the large Styrofoam cup of water and paper tub of vanilla ice cream that had previously occupied the over-the-bed table.

After dealing with the 'I don't want to be disturbed' physician and prying new orders out of him, the shift finally ended with the patient calmed, all tubes reinserted, tucked up in his bed and sleeping the quiet slumber of the medicated. Why these doctors could not see that they spent more time grumbling about being disturbed, for their own patient's welfare, than they spent just listening and giving new orders, Perri couldn't understand. She shook her head as she walked across the smelly blacktop parking lot. She hoped the nurse following her wouldn't be too miffed by her machine-gun style recorded report. "Oh well," she sighed aloud, "everyone does that anyway," as she opened the door of her car. She was glad to be done with this assignment.

It was another steamy, airless day in southern Indiana. After the car had baked in the back forty all day, the steering wheel was blazing hot. It felt sticky, like it was melting. She wanted to put the top of the convertible down, but didn't want the sun scorching her. "Just give me air conditioning." Perri allowed the furnace-like air to billow out of the car before settling in the seat. She waited for the a/c to kick in and cool the interior down a bit before she pulled out of the green-lined parking space designated for employees. She grumped aloud that even with the window shade in place, the merciless August sun made the inside of the car seem hot enough to fire ceramics. She didn't feel comfortable leaving her window cracked, even a small amount, since there had recently been some break-ins to cars parked at the hospital. Cameras everywhere, campus security patrolling around, and thieves still managed to break into cars and steal what they could without getting caught.

Finally, Perri was able to thread her way through the obstacle course of the hospital parking area, between islands of ornamental grasses and crusty looking begonias, to reach the main road leading away from Magnet Central Hospital. Why did they make parking lots like those maze puzzles in kids' magazines? As she approached the stoplight it turned green and she pushed down the accelerator with the joy that comes from leaving a particularly eventful shift knowing she had time off ahead of her and that the next three days would be relaxing and fun. She was relieved she didn't have to shut her phone off to avoid being called to come in on her days off for a while. Because no matter what, they will call. They always call.

The car cooled down about the time Perri pulled into her driveway. She eased into the one-car stall, avoiding the mower on one side and the assorted tools and stacked plastic storage containers on the other. She hadn't found a place for many of her belongings since she moved into this house a year ago following the break-up of her two-year marriage. Two whole years. It seemed longer than that in a way.

Perri hadn't spoken at any length to Alan since the divorce was finalized. She'd seen him with the Girlfriend du Jour here and there a few times. Alan seemed to want to be seen and acknowledged, as though she still cared, and Perri limited her communications to grunted hellos or a nod of her head followed by a smirk. He actually thought she felt hurt seeing him out with his flouncy girlfriends. True enough, it had hurt when they were married, but not now. Alan seemed to hang on to the opinion that Perri wouldn't be able to get along without him. 'Well,' she thought, 'we all have our disappointments.'

It was a relief to walk into her kitchen and shut the door on the week behind her. Perri slipped her shoes off right inside the door and carried them directly to the laundry room. She put the contents of her pockets in an old cast iron bowl on a shelf, peeled off her scrubs and tossed them into the washer, and left her shoes by the dryer. The shoes looked pretty bad. They never lasted very long. The nurses were required to wear white shoes, which is the least practical color to wear. She marveled at the numerous manufacturers who insisted on putting mesh on their shoes. It didn't serve as ventilation, but more of a catch-all for stuff you didn't want to bring home with you. Stuff got under the mesh, stained it, and made the shoe look nasty before it was worn out. She tossed them into the washer too. She added detergent that claimed to smell like a spring morning, set the cycle for hot water, and turned it on.

After changing into her jeans and t-shirt, Perri filled the electric kettle with hot water to make tea and flipped the switch on. She knew she was supposed to use cold water but it took longer. The water boiled and she poured it over the tea bag, stirred in plenty of creamer and some sugar. She flopped down in her favorite old armchair to review her plans for the upcoming trip, starting early the next morning.

To occupy her time and mind since her divorce, Perri had been working on her family tree in the evenings when she didn't have anything else lined up, which was almost every night. Joyce, a coworker, had suggested it, and since some of her stories about her experiences could be amusing, Perri decided to give it a try. At first it was merely a distraction, but then it became more meaningful as she uncovered more and more information.

No one else in her family seemed to have more than a passing interest in their history, which made getting information from those people difficult. Sometimes it seemed like the distant relatives she contacted to ask questions about their families were too bored and disinterested to even attempt to remember things. She had asked Mildred, a second cousin of her father's, if she could identify the three people in a photograph taken in front of her own childhood house, a photo Mildred was actually in, but she said she really didn't know who they were. Turns out, one of the women in the photo was Mildred's own mother. The others she had asked promised they would but then didn't respond. That was the last time she asked any of her extended family about photos. She didn't understand it. People kept boxes of photos but didn't know, or care, who was in them.

The thought of finding a treasure trove of courthouse records that answered all her brick wall questions got Perri thinking about making a trip for that. She had been planning this trip for quite a while. The actual travel itself was a minimal part of it and took the least amount of time. She and Nina, her longtime friend and frequent fellow traveler, hadn't seen each other much in the last few months. Nina was more than happy to go along and help, so Perri had decided to combine a research trip with a Girls' Weekend Away. They were heading for southern Kentucky in the morning. Perri had found a Bed & Breakfast within the county she needed to visit and booked a room for Friday and Saturday nights. They would need to leave early Friday morning and visit the County Clerk that day, then over the weekend they could take their time going to the cemeteries.

She only booked one room for the two of them. Truth be told, in all the years they had been doing this, one or other of them had always been at a point where money was an issue and sharing a room had been the best way to make sure they got to go on their trips. Now that this wasn't as much of a problem, they would miss the "sleepover" appeal if they had different rooms. The trips didn't always need to accomplish anything other than spending time together, catching up, drinking some wine, and retelling their favorite stories about each other until the wee hours of the morning.

The only somewhat complicated parts of the trip were getting to the County Clerk's office Friday with enough time to look through documents, and deciding what documents she needed to ask for once she was there. Then they could move on to the cemeteries, which was the part Perri was looking forward to the most. It seemed every county had different rules about how to get records, who could get them, and how much it would cost. Logan County seemed to be reasonable in both their prices and requirements for obtaining records.

Perri finished her tea and went to the bathroom to get ready for bed. She had already packed everything she could yesterday. All she had to do in the morning was to add her toiletries and hair dryer to the suitcase. She had packed her newer pajamas for the trip, so she pulled on her raggedy nightshirt, the threadbare one with the holes that she dearly loved and climbed into bed hoping she didn't lie awake for an hour first.

Chapter 3

Friday morning, Perri woke up at 5:56 a.m., four minutes before her alarm was set to go off. She wanted to get started on the trip. She knew Nina would probably be doing the same. Perri smiled and hummed as she showered and got dressed. She didn't take a lot of time to fool with her hair; they would be riding with the wind in their hair. She filled her travel thermos with her first cup of superhot coffee from the percolator she preferred to use and went about checking to make sure she had everything she needed.

Perri was typically a very organized person, and the uncertainties and loose ends and brick walls of this research business sometimes drove her nuts, but she was determined to get some answers. One of the cemeteries she wanted to visit, the oldest one on her list, was on private property. She had contacted the property owner by mail and then talked with him on the phone. He had obliged by mailing her his permission to be on the farmer's lands. She wanted a hard copy ready in case she needed it.

She also printed directions to the cemeteries that were supposed to have the graves of some of her ancestors, as well as the satellite images of the surrounding area. She had marked her chosen route with red marker. There was a separate sheet for each cemetery on the agenda with the names she was looking for and the graves' location if known. All the addresses and phone numbers for the clerk's office, courthouse, and the B&B were on paper along with maps.

Perri nodded to herself, "It looks like I have everything that I can think of for this trip." She put all her paperwork, pens, notebooks, maps, sticky notes, thumb drives, and a phone number list into a bulging zippered organizer that went into a satchel with straps so she could easily carry it. Next, she checked the contents of a freebie duffle bag she gotten from work. It had the hospital insignia on the side, but that didn't matter for her purpose. It contained her "cemetery kit": Graph paper, pencils, foil, a soft bristle brush on a handle, gloves, a small trowel, a flashlight, extra batteries, and a pair of "rods" that Joyce had given her to find graves, like a divining rod used for water. She wasn't sure about that, but she meant to try it out sometime. She wondered if she was overdoing it a bit and said aloud, "Perri, you might be getting a bit obsessed by this…but here goes."

After refilling her thermos with the rest of the coffee and checking twice that she had unplugged the pot, she tossed her bags in the back seat. She settled into the front seat and buckled her seatbelt. She flipped on the CD player and relaxed as she backed out of the narrow garage. This was going to be a great trip and she was blissfully happy to be getting away from the regular grind.

***

Perri pulled into the driveway at Nina's house twenty minutes later. As she got out of the car, she saw a hand wave briefly from the curtained window and the door was wide open by the time she reached it. Nina was buzzing around the living room gathering her bag, purse, and travel coffee cup. Perri could hear Aaron, Nina and Tom's toddler, babbling in the kitchen. Tom poked his head around the corner and said, "Have a good time, Thelma and Louise! Behave." Perri laughed and said, "Don't worry, I have a Bail Bond card and I promise I won't drive off any cliffs, not knowingly anyway." Tom smiled and went back to preparing Aaron's breakfast, hollering to Nina "Call me when you get there."

Nina took a good look around the living room, slung her bag and purse over her shoulder, and said, "Let's go...I'm ready for a little "me" time."

Perri grinned and replied, "You got it. Let's hit the highway, but we have to tank up on gas and more coffee first."

As the car exited the subdivision, Nina rolled down her window and leaned her head out the window, smiling. "You're like a happy dog out for a car ride," laughed Perri.

"Are you kidding? I haven't had a break like this for over a year and I'm sorely needing it." Nina closed her eyes and let the wind blow her hair, grinning.

"Well, girlfriend, you are going to start by getting bugs in your teeth if you keep it up. That or getting smacked in the face with something. Knees and elbows in the car please."

Nina laughed and pulled her head back in the window. She sighed a long, contented sigh. She turned to look at Perri and, suddenly serious, said, "You brought the wine, right?"

Perri raised her eyebrows and feigned a hurt look, "Seriously? When have I ever forgotten the wine? That was the first thing I packed. It wouldn't be a girl's weekend away without a nice glass of wine and yakking like a couple of magpies into the night."

"You got that right. Hey, where is the info on the B&B? I want to take a gander at the place."

Perri nodded her head toward the back seat, "It's in my satchel. In the front, outside pocket. It looks like an interesting place to stay..."

As Nina leaned between the seats, reaching for the satchel, she looked at the side of Perri's face and said, "What do you mean by interesting? Sometimes that doesn't mean what you want me to think it means. Is this one of those B&Bs you saw on a ghost hunting show on television?"

Perri released a quick puff of a sigh, and tartly replied, "No, it is *not*." She stared straight ahead for a few seconds while Nina pulled the paperwork out and returned to her seat, refastening her seat belt. "That one was full."

Nina chortled while reading the blurbs about the Crow's Rest B&B. "Where is this place? Is it near a town?"

"It is pretty rural, but it is near Mosley, which isn't much bigger than a crossroads. Mosley is where some of my ancestors lived when they first settled in Kentucky; that was at the tail end of the 1700s. It's closer to the Tennessee border than it is to Russellville, where I need to go to the courthouse, but it isn't that long a trip and we should only need to go to Russellville one day, provided I can get the documents that day. I did write them ahead of time to let them know which probate boxes I needed. The hotel should be in a quiet, relaxing country setting."

"Sweetie, when have we ever had a quiet, relaxing trip when we take one these adventures of yours?" Nina always spoke of the trips they took and the situations they sometimes found themselves in with a wry tone, but she enjoyed them as much as Perri. And Nina had as many adventures chalked up in her name as Perri did.

"We're saving up stories for the nursing home! We don't want to be bored in our old age, gotta pack it all in now."

The traditional opening of the trip completed, the car roared off down the highway.

Chapter 4

As Perri and Nina came within twenty-five miles of the Tennessee border, the Cooper left the dual lane highway to cut east through Kentucky on state roads. About an hour later, they had turned off old state road 102 and were following the curve of the country road with occasional overhanging trees. The catalpas had long, slender pods draped throughout their leafy green limbs. The terrain was gently rolling with alternating pastures, fields, and small remaining copses of trees or ponds. Leaning slightly over the top of the steering wheel, Perri quietly said, "I think that is the driveway just up ahead." She nodded toward a field stone wall that ran up to the shoulder of the road. There was a sign hanging from a wrought iron pole, but they couldn't read it yet at their current angle on the road.

As the car drew nearer to the driveway entrance, Perri and Nina could see the face of the sign. Bold calligraphy spelled out The Crow's Rest. An image of a glossy black crow was painted next to the name of the B&B. The sign rocked very slowly back and forth on its hinges in the barely perceptible hot breeze. The chat crunched satisfactorily as the car made its way up the long driveway. The

Crow's Rest wasn't a mansion or a show-stopper, but looked like just the place they liked. The two-story house was late nineteenth century, more than a farmhouse but not quite an estate. It was maintained, looked freshly painted, and had been landscaped with surprisingly well-chosen trees and plants.

The drive arced after leaving SR102 and approached from the southern end of the house, which faced west. It turned along the front until it again turned to connect back with itself, forming an oval of dark blue-green Kentucky Bluegrass with two willow trees gently billowing. There was a deep covered porch across the entire front which included a porch swing and numerous bent wood chairs and rockers. Lace curtains were visible in the windows of the main floor.

Perri pulled into a rectangular parking area just off the north curve of the driveway and chose a spot under a mimosa tree for the shade. Shutting off the ignition, she and Nina got out of the car and stretched legs stiff from sitting in the car for two and a half hours. "Let's go check in first, then come back for the bags," yawned Perri.

They walked up the old wooden steps and across the narrow-slat porch with a rag rug in front of the door. "I haven't seen one of these old wooden screen doors since I was a little girl at my Grandma's house," remarked Nina as she opened the door and the spring squeaked a little as it stretched out. She held the screen for Perri, opened the stained oak door, and walked inside.

The foyer was cool and smelled of the old kind of wood polish. Not too sweet and not antiseptic, just clean. There was a stairway directly in front of them, a room with bookcases, tables, and armchairs to the right, and a parlor to the left. They could hear footsteps coming toward them across the wooden floor. A middle-aged woman in light blue capris and a madras shirt with a dishtowel over her shoulder came toward them smiling. "Hi there! I'm Alice Wooldridge." Shaking their hands, she bubbled, "Welcome to the Crow's Rest. How was your trip here? Did you find it ok?"

"We didn't have any trouble finding it, thanks. I'm Perri, and this is Nina." Perri tipped her head toward Nina, who said, "Hi there, I was just telling Perri I hadn't seen a screen door like that for…a few years."

"That is original to the house." Her reddish hair was tinged with gray and wound into a knot on top of her head, dubiously secured by a scrunchie that had been around about as long as Perri and Nina. A few strands of hair had escaped and were curling around her face. "My husband, Danny, and I bought the place quite a while ago. A lot of people have moved away from this area, into the cities. As the older folks are dying off, places like this get put up for sale. Younger people don't often want to take on the burden of an aging house they aren't going to live in. It wasn't in very good condition, but we've been working at it for a long time. Danny likes to do woodwork and repairs, he's a carpenter, and I like to sew and I help refinish. We've had plenty to do." She turned toward the stair and put her foot on the wide and deep first step that flowed outward from its riser like a pool of glowing wood. "I know you already paid online, so that's all taken care of. I'll show you to your room and you can get settled in."

Alice led them up the staircase which had a massive newel and gleaming balusters. At the top, the hallway turned immediately to the left and again to the right. The upper two-thirds of the walls were lined with vintage photos over wallpaper with delicate flowers. As she unlocked the room's door, Alice glanced over her shoulder and noticed Perri stop to squint at a couple of them. "Those photographs are either our own old family photos or ones found in thrift shops, yard sales, or that people have given to us. I like those because many of them have a story to go with them. Are you here for the car show in Russellville this weekend?"

Perri replied, "No. I am doing some research and need to visit the clerk's office there. Nina and I try to take a girls' weekend away about once every couple of years, so we combined the two this trip." Alice nodded.

Alice stopped and swung the door open, saying, "Here is your room, the Hydrangea room." Perri nodded. "You have your own bath, right through that door over there. Your window looks out over the back garden, which you are free to use if you want. There's a pavilion out there with some chairs, very nice for sitting outside in the evening. There are some tiki torches scattered around that you can light if you sit out there, helps keep the bugs away. Matches are in the kitchen drawer by the refrigerator. I have breakfast ready every morning at 6:30, but if you want to sleep a little longer, it'll still be available until 8:00. I put out a little snack every evening before I go too. You can look for that in the library."

Nina asked, "Before you go? You don't live in the house?"

Alice waved a hand in the air, "Oh, we did, but we also have a smaller house that is on the back of the property, really only a cottage of sorts. We decided to move into the cottage and use the main house solely as the Inn. It is easier for us anyway, to downsize and keep ourselves to the smaller house." She moved toward the door, then turned to say, "Feel free to look around the house if you like later on; the rooms on the main floor are common use, but you'll be the only guests here tonight. There's coffee and tea in the kitchen cabinets, and some muffins in the bread box. There is regular butter and some flavored butter in the fridge too. Here is a key to the front door of the house, and another one for your room." She handed Perri a crow key ring with a couple of keys on it. "I'll be here until about 4 o'clock, but after that, call if you need anything at all. We're not far from the house. I hope you enjoy staying here."

"I'm sure we will." After a slight pause, "Why do you call it the Crow's Rest?" Perri asked before Alice started back down the corridor.

She considered for a moment, "I like the silly things, I guess. They are smart birds. They have that air of not taking any crap from anyone. I like that. You'll see them around. They are usually in the trees around the garden in the morning, you'll hear them, and sometimes again in the early evening." She turned, waving, and clomped off down the hallway.

They both walked around the room, peering into the bathroom, opening cabinets and drawers. Perri flopped down on the bed, "I like the room. It's comfy. This was built before they made closets; there's a wardrobe. And it has a writing desk. I'm glad of that. I'll have a place to look over my paperwork. I think the website said there was wi-fi too."

"Good," said Nina, "I have a couple of games on my tablet that I like to play and they need a connection. I have to keep up with my email too." She opened and closed the drawers of the writing desk. Indicating the lap drawer, she said, "Here's the wifi code."

"Well, let's go get the bags and think about heading into Russellville."

Chapter 5

After their bags were in the room, Perri flopped into a well-padded rocking chair and Nina was lying across the bed. Both were winded, not so much from hauling the bags upstairs, but from laughing.

Nina's oversized, wheeled duffle bag had rocked back and forth precariously as they came up the stairway, but because they were both carrying so much stuff, always trying to avoid a second trip, neither of them could reach out to stabilize it. Climbing behind, Perri watched Nina sway from side to side trying to keep her balance under the shifting weight of her overnight bag, her purse, and a small portable cooler she had brought. The suitcase swayed further in each direction, up on one wheel and then the other, with each step Nina took. Perri started to snicker halfway up the stairs and by the time they reached the landing, they were both laughing out loud. The unstable duffle finally performed a slow topple, twisting Nina around until she lost her balance, dropping the other bags, and sliding down the wall. Nina went down to the floor laugh-crying, "Oh! I have to pee. Don't make me laugh!"

Perri sighed and asked, "What on earth do you have in that thing?"

"Stuff I might need. You know how it is."

"Oh brother…yes, I do. I'm just as bad. Alice probably thinks we are gearing up for a party. Let's get these in the room before she thinks we're causing a ruckus and changes her mind about us staying here unsupervised."

After the laughter had died down and they had both visited the bathroom, they sat down to get their breath. "I better call Tom real quick, let him know we made it." Nina pulled her phone out and dialed. After a short pause, "Hey you, we made it!"

As Nina talked to Tom, Perri wandered down the hallway, looking at the old photos. She could hear Nina telling Tom about the B&B, but her voice faded away as Perri took in the framed moments of a time long ago. There were photos of young uniformed WWII soldiers proudly standing in front of their parents' homes, kids riding on horses and carts, formally posed portraits of dour couples, barber shop gatherings, general store interiors, people sitting on porches, and groups of people at picnics. Some were blurred or scarred by rough storage over time. There were studio photos in tones of sepia, gray, black and white that remained surprisingly crisp, capturing an instant of someone's life long ago, dressed in their finest.

Among these, high up on the wall, was a photo of a tavern called the Rogue's Harbor, as the hand-painted sign hung by the eave of the porch declared. There were at least fifteen men. There were young and old, handsome and those less so, most of them

28

smiling and obviously enjoying the photo taking; it wasn't something that happened very often for most people. Leaning forward and standing on tiptoes to see the photo better, Perri murmured to herself, "Boy, don't you all look like you could get up to some shenanigans?" There were a couple of horses tethered to posts. One man had a shotgun hanging from the saddle and was flanked by a grinning man who was pointing his own shotgun at another man who was standing near the door of the tavern. He was frowning at the pointing man, turned about thirty degrees from camera. Perri almost missed her, but there was a woman in an apron standing in the doorway to the tavern, somewhat in shadow, her hand on the door jamb, peering out with a serious look. The photo was intriguing. What would otherwise be a lighthearted group having their photo taken was made a little haunting by the woman. "I should ask Alice about this place."

Perri slung her satchel on her shoulder and walked back to the room. Nina was putting her phone into her purse. "Shall we head in to Russellville? I would like to have as much time as I can in case there turns out to be a lot of probate records. I won't have another day this trip to review them. I'd have to come back."

"I love your optimism, Perri!"

"Yeah, I know, I know. I'm hoping there will not only be a bunch of records, but this time the records I want weren't included in one of the two boxes that are missing, were lost in a fire in 1892, or, just two days ago were sent five states away to be scanned."

"You said you called ahead though, right? They would have told you if the records weren't here," Nina said encouragingly.

"And now I love *your* optimism."

Chapter 6

Perri steered the car through several miles of country roads past fields that were taking on a patchwork appearance as the tobacco harvesting began. Nina grinned, "I love it. This is Lickskillet Road!" Don't you wonder how places like this got their name?"

"I definitely do, and that's one I want to look up." The scattering of cotton ball clouds was brilliantly white against the cornflower blue sky. With the top down, sunshine flooded the interior and felt warm and golden on the top of Perri's head. The only oncoming traffic here was an occasional truck or a tractor pulling carts fully-laden with tobacco making their ponderous way to a curing barn somewhere. The yellowing, wilted leaves swayed back and forth on the sticks. The farmers waved as the convertible passed them. Perri and Nina lifted their arms and hooted a reply, enjoying the wind and sun. Perri stopped at the intersection of Highway 79, then turned right and headed northeast toward Russellville

As they drove into town, Nina had been studying the map of downtown Russellville that Perri had printed. She looked up and said, "We're only a few streets away. You're going to come to a light in a minute. You can go straight or turn left." They passed a few fast food places, a school, an automotive supply store, and a large cemetery. "Is that one we are going to?" asked Nina.

"No, of course not, silly. All the ones I need are out in the woods or on someone's land." A few turns later, Perri was pulling into the small parking lot of the County Clerk's office.

The building was a single story, low, rectangular stone building. It appeared to have been built by hand with white stones of roughly the same size, but of varying lengths and heights, the spaces between being filled with grayish mortar. "Wow," Perri exclaimed, "I didn't expect this. This has been here a long time." She parked the car in one of the few spaces in the small lot and walked around the corner of the building. Nina leaned on the fender of the Cooper, which was hot through her cotton shorts.

"Hey Perri! We gonna go in or examine the building?" Nina called out.

Perri reappeared around the corner. "Ok, geez."

"Well, time's a wastin' and I'm going to have to listen to you bellow about it all weekend if you run out of time."

Perri grabbed her satchel out of the back seat of the car. "I don't think we need to put the roof up." She opened one of the double doors beneath a canvas awning and walked in, Nina right behind her. There was no one at the counter, but before the door fully closed, a friendly faced lady who looked to be in her late 50's came around the corner of a partition. "Can I help you?"

"Yes, I'm Perri Seamore. I talked with Cora a couple of weeks ago on the phone about coming in to view some probate records. Records for a Berry Nichols?"

"Oh sure! I'm Cora. We pulled those records for you and have them here in the office. Come on over to our viewing room and I'll bring them to you." As they followed Cora, Perri glanced over her shoulder at Nina and made her what-do-you-know face.

Cora led them to a small room. Its contents included a table, a banker's style lamp, in addition to the overhead fluorescents, and a couple of chairs. The wall with the opening was glass; there was no door. There was nothing on the walls of the room and no other furnishings. "We can't allow any food or drinks, backpacks, large bags, or ink pens in here. You can leave your bag outside the door on this table and take what you need from it into the room. You can use a pencil to make notes; if you don't have one I can get you one. If you want copies of something, just let me know. You can use a digital camera or phone to take a photo, but you have to have the flash off. Sorry, but we have to protect the documents. You wouldn't believe what some people will do."

Perri nodded in agreement, "Oh, I totally understand. All I really need is my laptop, camera, and notepad. I'll use my camera for photos, but I probably also will ask for copies of any documents I need. I've learned the hard way not to totally rely on photos that aren't safely loaded to my computer, printed and backed up. I do have a pencil, thanks."

Cora smiled, "Cool beans. I'll go get the file." Cora headed off into the labyrinth of cubicles.

Nina took a seat and looked around. "Kind of like a police interview room, huh?"

"Well now, I wouldn't know that." Perri smiled and plugged in her laptop and turned her notepad to her notes about Berry Nichols. "And how is that you have come to be familiar with police interview rooms? Something you haven't told me?"

"TV. They always look like this, right? Even on those cold case shows that are real."

"Yeah, I guess they kind of do," Perri muttered from just outside the room as she shuffled through her satchel for a pencil.

Cora reentered the room with a folder about an inch thick. That brought a smile to Perri's face. "Here ya go. Just holler when you need copies or you're finished." She tapped the table once and left.

"Awesome. It isn't three sad little papers in a folder. Look at this! I'm hoping I find a document that specifies names. There has to have been a clerk who took the time to write down children's names somewhere instead of always referring to them as 'the Heirs of...'!"

"Well, dig in," replied Nina as she settled into her chair, "I'm going to catch up on my reading while you do that." She pulled her legs up onto the chair and flipped open her iPad.

Perri smiled to herself and opened the file to the top document. "Ok, what have you got for me?"

Chapter 7

A couple of hours later, Nina stood up and stretched. "I'm going to look for the bathroom. Need anything?"

"Not yet, I'm making a list of documents I want, but there's more to go. What time is it?"

"It's nearly 3 o'clock. They close at 4:30 right?"

"Crap. Yes. I'll hurry."

Nina stood outside the glass walled room and tentatively called out, "Cora?"

"Coming," came from across the room.

Cora directed Nina over to the courthouse where there was a public restroom. The courthouse was very close, down a short path and across a parking lot. When Nina returned, she stood for a moment inside the doorway and was deciding whether or not to announce her presence or just head back to the document room when she heard a jumble of voices talking with some urgency.

"What the heck?" "No way! What happened?" "Does anyone know anything?" said unfamiliar voices.

"No! They don't!" came an answer, from someone slightly out of breath. "Well...apparently..." the voice paused and Nina could hear the sound of someone sitting in an office chair and rolling it across a mat. The voice launched into a story, "William Parker, from the feed store, found her this afternoon. He told Emily, the dispatcher over at the Sheriff's office, that he went out to the graveyard to walk his dog." There was another pause and the listeners immediately cajoled the storyteller to continue.

"Ok, ok!. Had to catch my breath. I practically ran over here you know. I'm not used to runnin'. Ok, so anyway, Will said he was walking Brownie in the cemetery. He went in the south entrance, where the mausoleums are. When he was still a ways out from the big Clay mausoleum, he saw what he thought was a pile of clothes someone dumped in the lot" Quick responses of "Yes, yes" and "Go on!" rose up during any lapse of narrative.

"Will said he kept on walking past that and followed the road around the street side end of the cemetery. Before he got to the row of trees, he was kind of looking around where that pile of clothes was and figuring to himself that he'd mosey over there to pick them up on his way out and throw them away. He followed the road all the way around until he was coming back to where the road T's and he took the turn toward the old wall that goes around the mausoleum plots. As soon as he made that turn by all the big cedar trees, he could see a car all wrecked up against the stone wall just past the left-hand turn in the road. He sped up a little in case someone was hurt in it, but when he got there the car was empty. Now he was afraid that the pile of clothes wasn't just a pile of rags. He walked further down the road to go around the wall and headed over to the bundle. He said Brownie started straining on the leash. Brownie doesn't do that normally. He said he had a hard time holding on to the leash. It sure wasn't a pile of clothes when he got there..." The voice stopped for effect.

"What, what??" came the response, in unison.

"I'll be darned if it wasn't Amy Barrow, face down in the muddy grass and dead as a doornail! And Will says she sure didn't keel over of anything natural. That girl was just on about thirty and she wasn't sick. But that's all he'd say." Nina could hear gasps and whispering by at least a couple people besides Cora.

"Of course it wasn't natural, she was probably badly hurt in the wreck and died trying to find help! That's so awful. Poor Amy! Why didn't she call someone?" said one of the listeners.

"Will said it wasn't from the wreck."

There was some shuffling around and encouragement to continue by the eager listeners.

"So," continued the storyteller, still a little winded, "William high-tailed it out of there and reported it to the police. He said he practically ran home, best he could, he was afraid someone might still be hanging around the cemetery. There had to be another car; he said the damage wasn't from just hitting the wall because Amy's car was wrecked at both ends. He was afraid someone might still be hanging around. He wouldn't say any more, said they told him not to talk about it right now. He went home to have a pick-me-up beverage, I would imagine."

Silence as the information sank in.

Nina tiptoed back to the document room and then zipped in through the door. She bumped against the table just as Perri was standing up. Papers on the table scattered out of their neat stacks. "What's gotten in to you? They have an open bar over at the courthouse?"

Nina leaned toward her, took her elbow in hand, and whispered breathlessly. "Perri, you gotta hear this!"

"What?" Perri stopped gathering her belongings and looked at Nina, wondering what caused her dramatic entry.

"I heard them talking in the office just now. I mean, here, this office, Cora and a few others. One of them was telling about someone being murdered in a cemetery. Someone they know, it sounds like."

"What are you talking about? A murder? Here?"

"Yes! They were talking about how a guy from the feed store found the body in a cemetery this morning while he was walking Brownie. Brownie is his dog. William is the guy. The body was in a plot and her smashed up car was on the cemetery road. No other car was there. They don't know much else. But the guy who found the body was told not to say anything." Nina and Perri looked at each other.

"Well," Perri said, "that beats my probate record research. Let's go find out what we can."

Perri and Nina crowded through the door at the same time and turned left out of the viewing room, toward the rear of the office rather than back toward the desk. They could hear the sounds of several voices, kept at a low tone but gabbling all at once. Perri peeped around the corner of the cubicle and softly said, "Excuse me." Cora and two other women jumped up, startled. Cora rushed toward Perri, "Oh, my goodness, I'm so sorry, do you need something?"

"I'm sorry to interrupt. I know it's about time for you to close up." Three pairs of wide eyes stared at her. "I am finished with the Nichols file and wondered if I could get copies of the documents I need? I laid them out on the table in the viewing room." As Perri spoke, she gazed past Cora to the coworkers who had been discussing the exciting news a few moments ago. They both looked away and turned toward the desk, straightening papers and moving office supplies around.

"Sure, sure, you can, let me get right to that." Cora bustled down the corridor formed by the partitions. Perri and Nina followed her to the viewing room. Cora stopped at the table, flustered, and stared at the documents.

"I would like to get copies of these," Perri indicated a stack of papers.

"Ok," replied Cora, clearly distracted, as she swept them off the table and took them to the front desk, behind which the copy machine was located against the far wall.

Perri and Nina glanced at each other with raised eyebrows. "Um, everything alright?" Perri asked tentatively.

Cora kept copying, "Well yes, I…"

"We caught part of the, uh, conversation as we walked through the office. Someone has been found dead?

Cora spun around, "Yes! Oh, my goodness, I just don't know what to think. Susan works over in the court building. She came over to tell me and Jennifer, Jennifer works here with me, about Amy Barrow being found dead in the old cemetery. I guess they are saying she was killed, because the man who found her said it wasn't natural. I just don't know what to think. This is scary"

"Did you know her well?" asked Nina.

"Well enough to say hello and talk a bit when we saw each other. I know her mother better than I do Amy, but …" her voice trailed off, her brows knit tightly over her scrunched-up face. Then her face opened and her eyes grew large, "Margie is going to be upset! I should go by there. She shouldn't be alone. This is awful!"

"I'm so sorry. I can imagine it is a shock to hear about someone you know being killed nearby. What cemetery was she found in?" inquired Perri. She could see Nina's side-eyes.

"Oh, it was, um, shoot, we call it the Old Burial Ground, but its name is something like a bird, a bird name." She puckered her mouth as she concentrated. "Whippoorwill Cemetery. That's it. It's down the road a good piece. It's been there for a hundred and fifty years at least, probably longer. It isn't really used much anymore. They say there are people buried there who first came to Logan County, way back."

"Would Amy have gone there for some reason if it isn't used much now?

40

As she thought about it, Cora stared straight into Perri's eyes without seeing her. "Well, yes," she said quietly.

After a few moments' pause, Perri nudged, "Why do you think she might have gone there?"

Cora shook herself slightly and said, "She probably went to visit a grave. A friend of her *was* buried there recently." Seeing Perri's surprised look she said, "I know, the cemetery really isn't used much, but a friend of Amy's died last week, the burial was Monday of this week, and she…didn't have any family left here and didn't have a plot that anyone knew about."

"So they buried her in Whippoorwill Cemetery?"

"Yes." Cora turned and continued copying.

Nina ventured, "Is there an area of the cemetery for people without family or plots? I mean, there were plots available for someone who needed one?"

"Yes. To be truthful, plots there are available for people who can't afford one anywhere else. Like a pauper's section, I guess. That sounds really terrible. But, basically that's what it is."

Perri quietly asked, "Amy's friend didn't have money for a plot?"

"I guess not. No, I'm sure she didn't. Her name was Patricia. She and Amy went to high school together and were pretty close friends for a while. They had a falling out and didn't talk for several years. Patty didn't get along with most people. Her family either died or moved away, I guess. I just know she didn't have anyone here."

"You say they went to school together? How old were they, Amy and Patricia?" asked Perri.

"They would be in their early or mid-thirties now, I guess. Margie, Amy's mother, is my age. I really should go by there and see if she has someone with her or needs anything." Cora seemed lost in thought as she handed the copies to Perri and turned off the copy machine. "Oh, was that all you needed, or...?"

"No, no, this is all I need, but I need to pay you for them."

"Oh, darn it, yes. It's a dollar a copy and there were, oh gosh, ten copies."

"I think there might be more than...."

"No, I think it was ten. $10."

Perri got the money out of her purse and handed it to Cora, who tossed it in the drawer. Perri said, "Thank you very much for your help today. I don't want to keep you any longer. I'm really sorry for what's happened. I wish we could help somehow."

Cora looked at Perri with welling eyes and a reddening nose as she took the original documents and placed them in the Nichols folder. "Thanks. I don't know what anyone can do right now, we don't even know what happened yet."

"Yes, of course. We'll get going. Again, thank you so much for your help, Cora."

Cora nodded and disappeared into the maze of partitions.

Chapter 8

Nina and Perri got into the car and shut the doors. The sun was still very warm, but was dipping behind the old stone building. Nina asked, "Did you get what you wanted from the probate records?"

"I didn't get all the actual names I wanted, but I think I got something I can use anyway. It's a plat description of a land parcel passing from father to son, and it names the father clearly. I have a separate record of that same parcel being owned by the son, from twenty-two years later, including his name. That will probably be good enough for documentation of the relationship." She paused, "I wonder what this murder stuff is about?"

"I don't know," replied Nina, "it doesn't sound like anyone really knows yet.

"No. But I sure would like to know." Nina didn't respond, so Perri turned toward her, "Wouldn't you?"

"Ye-es. What are you saying?" Nina smiled. "I know that tone. Are we making a 'diversion' in our plans now?"

"Of course. I want to find out. I want to go to that cemetery. We came here to go to cemeteries, what's one more?"

"I don't think you'll be able to go poking around in there right now, sweetie. Crime scene and all that." Nina smiled a crooked smile with more than a little relief that they probably wouldn't be able to get in.

"No, that's true. But there are sure to be some people standing around, there always are with stuff like that. Maybe we can find out what happened." They sat in silence for a minute or two. "Better yet, we have to eat, right?

"I certainly hope we are going to eat. What are you thinking, Perri?"

"I think we need to eat and we are already here in town. We should find a small place, not a chain restaurant, but more like a diner or pizza place. Somewhere the local people go."

"I'm not going to argue about food, that's for sure. I'm hungry. We didn't eat lunch, did we? I didn't even think of that until now. Now I'm starving."

"It's just after 5 o'clock. The downtown businesses are letting out. Let's have a look around town and see if there is anywhere with a lot of cars."

Perri started the car and backed out of the parking spot. As she stopped at the street she glanced in her rear-view mirror and saw Cora exit the building and hastily jog over to a brown sedan, unlock it, and toss her purse into the passenger seat. Perri pulled out behind a plumber's van and followed it to a stop sign where the road circled around a small grassy park. A fountain was visible and what appeared to be flags and a plaque or historical marker. She pointed and said to Nina, "We need to go there tomorrow and have a look at that little park, see what it is."

Nina pointed and said, "I think there might be a café on the other side of this. See the building with the bright red awning?"

As the rounded the curve, they could see a sign hanging next to the entry way, The Arrogant Rogue. Perri exclaimed, "Hey, I like the sound of that! Let's try it. Think there are any handsome rogues loitering about the place, or do you think they are just all arrogant?"

Nina shook her head. "I'm sure if there is an arrogant rogue anywhere in this county you will find him."

"Rogue seems to be a popular term here. I've seen it twice today now. On the wall outside our room, there's a photo taken sometime in the 1800s of a bunch of naughty looking devils outside a tavern called Rogue's Harbor. They looked like they could get up to some shenanigans, for sure." As she pulled past the front of the tavern, Perri said, "This place seems popular enough. There aren't any parking spots in front of it. I'll go around again to find one."

They curved left again halfway through the adjoining block and found a spot at the next curve, almost back to the stop sign. Perri pulled in and raised the roof of the car, waiting to get out until it snapped into place. "I'm going to put my stuff in the trunk."

"You don't think someone wants to steal your copies of centuries old probate records, do you?" Nina laughed.

"NO...I just want them in the trunk, ok?" Feigning injured dignity, Perri popped open the trunk and nestled the satchel between the emergency road kit and the duffle bag with her cemetery kit. "Let's go, I could use a beer."

Chapter 9

The two friends walked along the sidewalk, rounding the curve in the opposite direction they had driven. Most of the buildings were occupied, which surprised Perri. So many times, these smaller towns had half-empty downtown areas. There were the expected attorney's offices, dentists, and optometrists. But there was also a barbershop, a men's clothing store, a breakfast café that closed at noon, and some scattered boutiques selling everything from clothing to handcrafts to vintage items. The area between the sidewalk and the street was planted with Bradford pear trees; a couple missing where previous storms had snapped them off.

The door to the Arrogant Rogue was an enormous wooden one with a pane of old glass that was wavy in places. The walk was ramped upward from the sidewalk to the door and covered with black and white tiles, only a few were missing. The name "Heath" was spelled out in the center in slightly larger black tiles and surrounded by a red diamond shape. There was a large window with a display area on both sides of the entry, going from the door to the edge of the building, like Perri had seen in photos of old general stores. No telling what had been displayed in those windows over the decades. There was still a transom over the doorway, but it was sealed shut. The heavy door stuck a bit before it opened, but swung easily once it started.

Out through the door and into Perri's nostrils wafted the aroma of food, good food, battered, hot, crispy fried food. She looked back over her shoulder to Nina, sighed, and said, "I love the smell of hot grease and salt."

"Hey there" came a greeting from a tall, slender girl in an apron approaching them from the back of the room and carrying a round tray as big as a table top that was laden with plates. "You can have a seat anywhere. Someone'll be with you in just a minute." The waitress put the tray down on a nearby table and distributed the food and a fistful of craft beers around the table of five people then whisked off to the kitchen.

Perri pulled out a chair at a table for four along the wall and hung her purse on the back of the chair next to her. The walls were exposed brick, with some of the plaster still clinging to the rough surfaces. The ceiling of pressed tin was mostly intact but had a few water damaged areas. The walls were covered with an assortment of framed posters and images and souvenirs of some of the best bad boys and girls. There were actors, sports stars, musicians, characters from movies and books, you name it. Craning her neck and twisting about in her chair, Perri took it all in. Filling in the spaces between the posters was a variety of items: holsters, a Zorro mask, a sword, handcuffs, sunglasses, a tricorn hat and eye patch, even a whip with a braided leather handle. "Looks like Indiana Jones has been here."

The tavern occupied two adjacent buildings on the street; a doorway had been put through halfway along the wall to the bar area. The other side appeared to be just as full of patrons as the side in which Perri and Nina were seated.

"This place is great, I like it" smiled Perri. She opened a menu and scanned through the appetizers, sandwiches, and daily specials. Nina did the same.

"Can I get you ladies something to drink?" the waitress arrived at their table. She was probably late 20s, long highlighted hair pulled back into a ponytail.

"I'll have whatever dark beer you have on tap," replied Perri.

"And I will have…do you have any wines that are sweet?" Nina asked.

"We do have a sweet red table wine. Is that ok?"

"That sounds perfect."

"You want a glass or a carafe?" Nina hesitated, the waitress said, "The carafe is a better deal."

"Ok, a carafe it is."

"I'll give you some time to look over the menu and take your food order when I come back with the drinks." The waitress hustled to the bar and said to the bartender, "A Dead Guy and jug of red table."

Nina was facing the bar, Perri had her back to it. Nina leaned slowly to the left of Perri and said, "Yummy. There's a tasty looking morsel."

"You aren't talking about food, are you?" Perri asked knowingly. She nonchalantly turned around to look, then back again. "The bartender? What are you doing, scoping him out? I'm telling Tom."

"Come on, I'm shopping for you. He's pretty choice, Perri dear. Tall, dark hair not too long, not too short, nicely shaped 5 o'clock shadow, a little peek of a tattoo at the neckline, looks lean, can't see below the waist but the top half is primo."

Perri risked a second look just as the bartender looked their way, "Crap. I have terrible timing. You sound like you are sizing up a buffet, but, yes, I agree."

"Call it what you will" she bobbed her head to the music. "I'm imagining him starkers behind that bar. I'd stay and drink all night." Nina thrummed her fingers on the table. "I don't know if I can drink a whole carafe."

"You'd stay and drink all night but you don't think you can drink a carafe of table wine? You goofball. I can help you if you can't manage it all," Perri offered. "We'll just have to eat a lot and walk around for a while. I don't want a DUI, that's for sure."

"No, that would not be good for either of us. You may be between contracts, but I'm staff and I don't think that would go over well and I have to be able to drive to get to work."

"I know. I wish you could go prn too. Did you and Tom get a chance to talk about that anymore?

"Yeah, a little. I think he's ok with it, but he has to get used to the idea, just like anything else. I have to approach him the right way, meaning in a way that he thinks it is his idea."

They both laughed as their drinks were deposited on the table. "Now, what can I get for you?"

Perri started, "Is the cole slaw creamy or sweet/sour?"

"It's creamy" replied the waitress.

"Alright then. I am going to have the fish and chips platter, with cole slaw and fries as the sides."

Nina took her turn, "I want the fried tenderloin with sweet potato chips and cole slaw."

"Got it. We're slammed right now, but I'll have your food out as soon as it's ready."

Perri and Nina replaced their menus behind the condiment tray and sat back to start on their drinks and take in the crowd. Joan Jett's 'Bad Reputation' was playing, loud enough to feel the rhythm, but not too loud to carry on a conversation, or try to overhear a little of the conversations around them.

Perri sipped her beer. It was ice cold and served in a frosted glass. She turned her chair a little sideways to get a better view of the room. A table of seven people was leaving, which cut down on the extra noise in the room. Nina poured herself a glass of the red wine and took a few small drinks. "Not bad for a tavern. Sometimes it is a little off, you know, vinegary."

Nina turned her chair as well, and they both ended up with their backs against the brick wall. After a period of no talking between them, Nina could discern that the group at the table behind her was talking about Amy Barrow. She made a very small nod of her head toward the table. Perri turned toward Nina and leaned forward to try to hear what was said. Evidently, one of the diners at the table was Emily, the dispatcher. Emily had an eager audience as she talked about her day.

"I have to tell you I have never been more shocked in my life when Will Parker called that in. I just about fell off my chair! Of course, I have to be professional and handle the calls calmly, but I sure had a hard time of that." Emily looked at her fellow diners and shook her head, lips pursed.

"Tell us again what Will sounded like when he called in." said a plump blond at the table. Her hair was relentlessly bleached, she wore a Clash t-shirt and a pink ring through the right side of her upper lip. The very thin young man in a camo shirt sitting next to her had his arm across the tops of her shoulders. The fifth member at the table was a curly headed man with what Perri usually described as spectacles. His suit coat was draped over the back of his chair and his tie was loosened, he wore suspenders in lieu of a belt. The man sitting next to Emily had his hand on the nape of her neck.

Emily took a healthy swig of the 'lite' type beer in a bottle in front of her, placed both palms face down on the table, drew in her breath and began, "It had been a pretty quiet day, you know, for a Friday anyway. I was glad it was the afternoon, most of the day over with and about time to go home. This call comes in and I answer it. I'm kind of relaxed and figured it'd be another call like I get most of the time, like Mrs. Balemann calling to say that someone walked through her yard or tossed out trash again, or another call about drag racing out on Hopkinsville Road. Real urgent stuff, you know?"

She polished off the beer with a final long, noisy gulp and the man to her right asked if she wanted another one. "You know baby, I think I do. I'm just all shook up over this still." Her companion waved the empty at the bartender who nodded, then turned back to his wife.

Emily had everyone's attention, and she knew it. Even the couple at the next table were leaning almost imperceptibly toward her table to listen. "No one will notice, or care I don't think, if we join in," observed Perri. She stood up and Nina stood up with her without thinking about it. Perri walked over and said, "I'm sorry, I didn't mean to eavesdrop, but we heard you say you took the call for the body found today. That's amazing. We were in the Clerk's office when the news came through, but we haven't talked to anyone who was personally part of what was happening. We're curious about it, do you mind if we listen to what you have to say?"

"Honey, I don't mind at all, you all just pull your chairs right over here." The group scooted around the table to make room for Perri and Nina, who took their drinks with them and joined the table, Perri between Emily and Clash girl and Nina between Camo and Suit. Emily started right back in on her tale, introductions could wait.

"So, as I was saying, I figured the call would be another one of the regulars, or maybe the Friday night stuff starting early. I hadn't even gotten 'Logan County Police Department' out of my mouth yet when Will starts in talking a mile a minute. I had to ask him to start over and slow down. He takes this big breath and blows it out right into the mouthpiece. Then he says, 'This is Will, Will Parker' and he is, like, panting, you know? It scared me because I thought he was having a heart attack or something, so I asked if he needed the ambulance. He said, 'No, no. I'm not calling for me, Em, I'm calling 'cause I found a body! I found a body, Em! In the old burial ground. Oh, dear God. It was Amy Barrow. I thought it was rags, or clothes that someone threw out there. You gotta get someone out there. She's layin' there in the grass. She…Emily she's been killed. And her car is there all wrecked up on the wall, wrecked on both ends of the car. Someone hit her and left. Somebody did something."

Emily looked around the table at the attentive group. Her brows lifted and she nodded slowly. "So, I told him to just hold on the line while I got someone. I radioed out for anyone out by the west end of town for a possible 187, that's a possible murder. Joe Harper responded, said he was out that way not too far off and would check it out. I told Will to just sit tight, that I might have to call him back. And I told him not to go shooting his mouth off about it just yet since we didn't know the situation. He sounded disappointed, but said he would."

Camo said, "It didn't take long for it to start getting around. He must have told someone pretty quick."

"Yeah, it wasn't but another 20 minutes before I had to call him back and tell him Joe said to keep zippered up about the details for right now. In the meantime, he probably told someone he found a body, but I don't think he let slip any of the detail information. I haven't heard it repeated anyway."

The man in the suit asked, "When do you think they'll make some kind of statement, or put it on the news?

"I don't know. I would imagine they're out there now. You know, the police and coroner and stuff. I guess we'll find out soon enough, they can't keep it secret."

"Why do you think someone might have wanted to kill her?" asked Perri. The group looked at her. "Oh, I'm Perri Seamore, by the way, and this is Nina Watkins. We are in town doing some research, genealogy research, and we were over in the Clerk's office when the news started to spread. We heard about it there."

"Oh, I see. I'm Emily Keeling, I work at the dispatch, and this is my husband, Ed." Emily then indicated each person at the table, "This is Lacy, she works over at the Country Village Market, Jack works at the highway department, and Peter is a paralegal at an office here downtown."

Perri and Nina smiled in turn to each as the introductions were made; Lacy and Jack nodded to her and Peter reached across the table to extend his hand to shake theirs.

Lacy narrowed her small eyes, "So why are you so interested in Amy Barrow? You haven't even been here before."

"I'm here to do some research..." Perri began

"What kind of research?" barked Lacy.

Perri glanced around the table. Emily grimaced at Lacy's sharp tone and Peter was fumbling with his coaster. "I've been working on my family tree. I want to file for membership in the DAR which requires documentation for every generation. I got to the point where I needed to try to find that documentation to fill in some blanks and for proof." Perri paused. "Two and three generations back, my father's family lived here. That's why I'm here. Nina came with me so we could make it into a fun weekend, get away from the daily grind. We both work as nurses back home. We're from Vailsburg, IN. And as for your first question, I'm interested in this because part of my research here is going to several cemeteries to find my family's headstones if I can. If someone is going around knocking off people in cemeteries, I would like to know."

Lacy sullenly mumbled, "Oh," and looked at Jack, who looked away. Lacy frowned even more, her lips extending out into a pout.

Perri asked again, "Does anyone have any idea why someone would want to kill Amy Barrow? Cora, over at the Clerk's office, told us that she may have been in that cemetery to visit the grave of a friend who died recently, someone named Patricia?"

Peter shook his head, "Oh yeah. Patricia Blackwell. She died a couple weeks ago and was buried out there. She doesn't have any family around here anymore and the city buried her in a plot in the old cemetery. Amy must have been out there to visit the grave; that's the field Will said he found the body in, isn't it?"

"Yes," answered Emily.

Nina asked, "What happened to Patricia that she died at such a young age, had she been ill?"

"Not as such, not lately. I mean…" Peter hesitated. "Patricia was ill off and on. She was an alcoholic who stayed sober for periods of time but would fall off the wagon and go on a weeks' long bender. Then she'd be sick and trying to recover for a long time, sometimes she had to be hospitalized. At first, she'd be okay in the hospital but as she got to feeling better, she'd start raising hell with the staff. She had a lot of issues."

Lacy added, "Yeah, you never knew with her whether she was going to be friendly and talk your arm off or turn on you like a mad dog. She pretty much ran through all her friends and she didn't have any family left around here. They all moved away a long time ago or died off. Her Mom died a few years ago. Patricia caused a big stink after her Mom's death because she thought she would be inheriting her Mom's house and everything in it, which wasn't much."

"That's how I came to know her, or know of her anyway," said Peter. "Apparently, she wasn't on good terms with her mother, hadn't been for years, and they didn't talk much. After her mother died and the burial was over, Patricia started moving in to her mother's house. I'm not clear on all the early details, but shortly after she moved in, she woke up to find a couple of auction house appraisers in the living room. She ran them off, called the police, but it turned out that the property had to be sold to pay unsettled debts that her mother had left. An auction sign went up in the yard and Patricia had to be forcibly removed."

"It got pretty ugly," said Emily. "I know I took at least a half a dozen calls from neighbors and the auction company people about her breaking in or raising hell when they were there."

"She just couldn't understand or accept that the sale of the house was the only way to settle the outstanding debts her mother left. She kept going on about how they'd all be sorry, that she was going to show them. They knew she had taken some stuff out of the house, and at first they tried to get it back. That's how I came to know about the situation, because they came to the lawyer that I work for to get the legal paperwork done to keep her out of the house. In the end, they realized she probably had only taken stuff they couldn't sell and no one would want anyway, so they dropped it, the house and everything in it sold. The new owner emptied it. After that, Patricia realized there was nothing she could do and that was the end of it."

"Amy was about the only person left who had anything to do with Patricia?" Nods all around. "And you say that Amy had been back on speaking terms with Patricia lately?"

"Yes. I saw them together about a month ago, at the library," added Peter.

"At the library?" asked Jack in a tone of disbelief.

"Yes, it seems out of character for Patricia, doesn't it? I'm not sure what it was about, but Amy did mention to me once…well, I had asked her if she wanted to go to dinner with me that night. It was almost 5 o'clock and she was here dropping off some paperwork, so I asked her. She told me she would have but she had agreed to help Patricia that night in some kind of search she was doing, something she had to look up at the library." In answer to the inquiring looks, Peter continued, "I was more focused on her turning me down and thinking about asking another time than I was on listening to the rest of the explanation and that's all I remember."

"That's interesting though. Two friends who hadn't talked for years, then something comes up that was important enough to Patricia for her to ask Amy for help." Perri thought for a moment, "Could it have been something concerning Patricia trying to get ownership of the house that had been her mother's, even though it had been sold several years before?"

Peter replied, "It could have been, Patricia didn't have a good grasp of things like that, but I doubt it. That water passed under the bridge a long time ago and she hadn't made a fuss about it since. I don't know why she would have started it up again."

No one spoke for a few moments, Nina piped up, "As far as the murder, or possible murder, goes, I take it this type of thing does not happen often around here."

"Not at all. There's the occasional shooting in a robbery or drug deal, but for someone to be murdered for some unknown reason, I don't remember that happening." offered Jack.

Perri ventured, "I wonder how long it will be before they release some information."

"I would think they'd have to make a statement tonight, or at least in the morning. Everyone already knows something happened" said Lacy, finishing off her drink.

Jack nodded, "They sure do. I saw all the emergency vehicles in the cemetery on my way back into town." He looked at Perri and Nina, "We've been repainting lines out on highway 68, going west. At quitting time today, I went by my house to clean up before coming back into town because I had paint all over me. On the way, I drove right past the cemetery and the place was taped off. I pulled over by where Joe Harper was putting up some horses in front of the entrance and asked him what was going on. Kind of hard for him to say 'nothing' and leave it at that I guess, so he said they didn't know what happened yet, couldn't talk about it. I could see a wrecked car from where I was parked and asked if somebody smashed their car up in there. He just said that yes there was a car accident, but that he had to go. And off he went. I didn't know until I got back into town that there was a body and that it was Amy Barrow."

"Did any of you here know Amy?" Perri asked.

Jack again, "I knew her a little, through work. She worked in the Planning Commission office and I usually was the one to go over there for permits and things. She was always nice to me, but I didn't know her outside of work."

"Me too, I knew her a little through work. The lawyer I work for sometimes prepared some legal documents for the office and she'd come over to get them or deliver them after they were signed."

60

"Hmm. It doesn't sound, so far, like anyone knows of any obvious reason someone would want to kill Amy Barrow. Any ideas? Did she have trouble with anybody lately, a stalker, or someone she had a disagreement with?" Perri asked.

The five people in the group looked at each other and all shook their heads, then down the table, lost in thought.

"I am very sorry about your loss, even if she was only an acquaintance and you didn't know her very well. I hope this mystery gets solved, especially for her family," said Nina.

Perri looked around, stood up, and said, "It looks like our food has arrived. Thanks for letting us sit in, nice to meet you all." Perri and Nina went back to their table after thank-you's and goodbyes were said.

As Perri returned her chair to their own table, she casually glanced up at the bartender, who smiled right at her. After returning a quick smile, she sat in her chair, back to the bar, "Wow, this looks great, I'm starving," she said as the plate of sizzling battered fish was set down in front of her. "Yours looks pretty good too. You gonna be able to fit your mouth around that tenderloin?"

Nina looked down at her plate. The tenderloin dwarfed the bread and made it look like a miniature bun sitting in the middle. "On my gosh! This looks awesome" she almost squealed as she slathered ketchup over the crispy plate-sized tenderloin.

"Been a while since you've been out to eat?" Perri snickered.

"Your darned right it has been! I haven't seen something like this in months" shot back Nina.

The next few minutes were punctuated only by the sounds of crunching and indecipherable noises of enjoyment. Once they had slowed down between bites, Perri said, "So tomorrow we should head over toward 68 to see what's going on at the cemetery. We may not get in, but I want to try."

"Ok. Surely they'll have the wreck removed before dark tonight, we probably won't be able to see anything" said Nina thoughtfully.

"No, probably not. But maybe if there are some people standing around, we can talk to them and find out more about it."

"Wurmp uh ty."

"Uh, what?" asked Perri.

Nina held up one forefinger, chewed, took a sip of her water, and swallowed. "Worth a try."

"Alright then. When we finish up here, we'll get back to the room and I'll locate the cemetery on the map. We'll plan on going there first. Let's get up and get going early. I can't wait. This is an interesting mystery, because I don't have enough mysteries to solve, right?"

"That's for sure, but at least this one is in the same century as us."

Chapter 10

Perri and Nina woke up to the insistent cawing of crows. It sounded like they were right outside the window. Perri sat up and stood up, misjudging the height of the bed, which was several inches higher than her own, and stumbled halfway to the doorway before she caught her balance. Nina stirred, "What's going on?"

"That's me trying to be quiet and not wake you up yet as I went to have a look out the window. You're welcome." Perri walked to the window and pulled back the heavy jacquard drapes, "Do you hear the crows?"

"Yeah, I hear them. It's kind of nice though."

Perri squinted in the morning light after the darkness of the room. "There are several of them in a tree in the garden. Looks like Alice is putting some food out for them. They must be wanting their breakfast." She watched for a few moments. "I've heard that if you keep chickens, having crows around will help keep the hawks away from your chickens."

Nina sat up, "Are you planning on getting some chickens to keep?"

"No. Just a handy-dandy piece of trivia for you in case you ever get too much time on your hands with that cute little handful of yours."

"Which one do you mean, Aaron or Tom?"

"Point taken."

Nina yawned and stretched, "After that supper last night I shouldn't want breakfast, but I'm ready for it."

"Me too. If you don't mind, since I already showered last night, I'll run in the bathroom and get dressed quickly, and get my stuff together while you get ready, if that's ok?"

"Sure, that works for me." I'm moving a bit slow this morning anyway.

Perri picked up her clothes that she'd laid out the night before along with her facial soap and bath poof and headed into the bathroom. She hung her robe on the iron hook shaped like a swan on the back of the door, got a towel off the rack, and prepared to wash her face.

The most outstanding feature in the bathroom, and the first thing she had noticed yesterday when they arrived, was the claw foot tub. She'd nearly needed a stool to get into the tub, just like the bed. The round sink bowl was in the center of a very wide oval porcelain pedestal with two formed soap dishes near the taps and plenty of room for other toiletries on each side. The taps were x-shaped white porcelain with Hot and Cold in black letters, and in the center was a short metal rod with a knob on the end that said Waste. Perri turned on the hot tap and let it run long enough to turn warm. While waiting, she turned and pushed the Waste knob, and the drain popped up and down. "Huh, I've never seen one of these." The water ran hot so she turned on the cold to get the right mix.

The porcelain toilet bowl and seat were separate from the tank, which was wooden and located up near the ceiling. There was a long chain to pull to flush it. "Fancy." The bowl had a raised leaf pattern around the base, next to the floor. "I could get used to this," she thought to herself.

Freshly scrubbed and dressed in jeans and a cotton t-shirt, her straight, shoulder length brown hair brushed, Perri went back into the bedroom, where Nina was just ending a call to Tom. "Everyone survive the night intact without you?"

"Barely. Aaron fell and conked his noggin on one of the drawer handles in the bedroom. That child can find more ways to smash his head, eyes, and nose against some unlikely targets. It takes talent. He inherited that from Tom." Nina hopped off the bed and headed into the bathroom, sauntering and waving one arm in the air. "I'll be out after my luxuriant bath, Seamore. See that my meal is prepared, I'll be going in soon."

Perri exaggeratedly rolled her eyes, "Yes Mi'lady. You've been binge-watching Downton Abbey, haven't you?" She could hear the shower begin as she opened Google Maps to locate Whippoorwill Cemetery. It was only a few miles west of town, right off Interstate 68. She opened an app on her phone to plug in the location, not to navigate there, but to add it to favorites. She liked to keep a record of where she'd been in case she needed to return, or found something interesting while she was there and wanted to reference it later.

Nina and Perri found their way to the dining room, between the front parlor and the kitchen. Alice came in from the kitchen in an apron with flour spattered across the front and dough stuck to her hands. "Morning all! How did you sleep?"

"Very well, thanks."

"Like a log."

"I've got the sideboard over there ready for you; there are plates at the far end. I've got scrambled eggs, bacon, and waffles in the warmers, just put them in there about 10 minutes ago, and there's fresh fruit in the bowl, and syrups, cheese, and preserves for the scones, which I just took out of the oven. Coffee and juice is on the table, help yourself. Be right back."

"Oh man, I can't wait. That smells good" said Perri.

"You're not wrong about that. Let's get started," Nina said, rubbing her hands together.

They each took a plate and were loading them up when Alice brought in the fresh, hot scones piled in a basket and covered with a tea towel. "This is a feast, Alice, thank you!" Perri and Nina each took a couple of scones and spooned on some of the strawberry preserves. They sat at the long wooden table. Made from rough-hewn planks, it was a bit uneven, but had been smoothed and polished until it glowed.

"We saw the crows in the garden this morning. Do you feed them every day?" asked Nina

"Did they wake you up? I'm sorry if they did." Alice quickly replied.

"No, no, they didn't. We wanted to get up early and get going, but I did want to see them."

"I usually give them some of what's left over from the day before; leftover bread or crackers, scraps of meat, even cooked beans. They hang around in the morning waiting for it."

"Smart birds!" said Nina.

"This is delicious, Alice. Just what we need before heading out today. Going to poke around in cemeteries looking for headstones." Perri glanced up to see Nina smiling.

"I'll let you eat and get going then. I'll come back and get the dishes when you leave. You have a good day and I hope you find what you're looking for."

Both tried to reply, but with their mouths full, they opted to wave.

Chapter 11

Perri steered the Cooper out of the driveway, again with the top down, and accelerated back toward highway 79. "We're going to Whippoorwill Cemetery first."

Nina nodded, "Yep."

"We'd better get some gas before I get involved in this and forget. I don't want to run out of gas out in the boondocks." Perri drove to the highway and stopped at Rooster's Filling Station. Perri jumped out of the car and opened the gas cover. As she turned to the pump, a man, roughly 35 years old, came towards her with both hands held up, "Whoa, whoa, little lady." He laughed deprecatingly. "I think you might be in a bit of a hurry. I pump the gas here."

"Oh, ok." Perri stepped back from the pump a couple of steps. "I didn't see a sign that this was full-service; I didn't know there were places left that were full-service."

"Um hmm. You want a full tank?" He asked.

"Yes, please." Perri leaned back into the car to get her billfold out of her purse. Nina made a questioning face at her. Perri shrugged and backed out of the car.

"You aren't from around here. Plate says Indiana. You got family here or something?" smirked the man pumping the gas. His grimy shirt had an oval with the name Rodney in satin stitch.

"No. I don't" Perri replied flatly.

"What are you doing here then?" asked Rodney gruffly.

"Well, uh Rodney, I'm here to do some research for my family tree."

"What kind of research?"

"Family tree research. Is this a private gas station or something, because I also didn't see a sign for that? This is on a public road. You seem to object to me being here."

"Why would I object to you getting gas here?"

"I don't have any idea, but you seem to be irritated."

"Just wonderin'. I have to wonder about two women down here from another state, driving around without a man?"

"I wasn't aware that I was required to have a man with me? Is there a law in Kentucky that I am not aware of?" snapped Perri.

Rodney let out an unfriendly laugh. "Women shouldn't travel alone."

"And why is that exactly?" Perri's eyes were blazing, but she was trying to keep from losing her cool

Rodney laughed again. "Come on. Travel can be dangerous, and it also takes having a sense of direction and ability to handle things that come up, like a man. Women can't think about two things at once, so it's dangerous."

Perri's mouth dropped open. "You're kidding, right?" She paused. "You are just kidding?"

Rodney stopped laughing and frowned, looking directly into Perri's eyes. "No ma'am, I'm not. Traveling is a man's job. If a man wants to take a woman along, that's for him to decide."

"You seem to be living back in the days of the cave man."

Rodney returned the gas pump to its cradle, screwed the gas cap back on, and shut the cover. "I don't care what you think. Women on their own are bad news. Look what happened to Amy Barrow."

Perri was astonished. "She was murdered while she was visiting the grave of a friend! Are you saying she should have obtained an escort to go to a grave?"

"She got killed, didn't she?"

Perri shook her head as though bringing herself out of a daze. "I'd like to pay now, and go." She held up her debit card with a questioning look.

"We'll have to go inside for that."

Perri glanced at Nina, who was scowling and looked ready to get out of the car. Perri made a tiny negative head motion, "Well, let's go in then and get this over with. Then our lady rear ends can get out of your superior male gas station."

Rodney's thick-featured face crunched up in disapproval. He pivoted his pudgy physique around on his heels and stumped across the cracked pavement to the office of the station. His hair was unruly, but not in a good way. The soiled shirt was partially untucked and the buttons strained across his belly. The knees of his pants were not only dirty, but nearly worn through. It didn't look like the kind of grime one would get from working on cars, such as grease or oil. It looked like dirt, as though he'd been digging around or his clothes had been on the ground.

While Rodney was running Perri's card, she looked around the station. It had been a full-service gas station probably back in the 1950s or 1960s. The angled fluorescent lights were still standing over the newer gas pumps. The now filthy office was crammed with old furniture; the chairs upholstered in cracked yellow plastic and a small Danish style end table with the finish nearly rubbed off and sporting scattered cigarette burns. There was an ashtray on the table that looked as though it had begun overflowing sometime in the '80s and had never been emptied, and it smelled like it too. The floor was tile, but Perri couldn't identify the original color through the scuffs and debris. The shelves behind the desk held dozens of old Chilton manuals for various models of vehicle, some that probably hadn't driven into this garage in a couple of decades. There was a glass door from the tiny office to the garage area which had probably been bustling with oil changes and repairs in its better days. It was nearly empty now and looked sad and neglected. Even the hydraulic lift had been removed from each bay, leaving only the metal framework standing next to the gaping pit in the floor.

The bell on the door rang again and Perri turned to see Nina cautiously entering the office. She widened her eyes at Nina and stood by the door. "Looks like you have a little help to finish; that's probably a good idea."

"What's that supposed to mean?" snapped Perri.

"Well, maybe you aren't used to doing these business transactions by yourself," and he snickered again.

"Sign here. Here is a pen. Sign on that line right there." Rodney slapped the receipt down on the counter and tapped the bottom, leaving a black thumbprint on the corner. Perri said nothing, just wanting to get out of the office, and signed. She held her hand out for her card and receipt. Rodney took his time and finally handed them back to her. When Perri took the card, Rodney held on to it, "Watch yourself out there."

"I can definitely do that, thank you." Rodney let go of the card and Perri's hand recoiled back toward her with the release of the pressure. She turned and quickly left the office.

"What was with that guy?" asked Nina once the door had closed behind them.

"He's a cretin, that's what. He's the kind of goon who likes to have a submissive little wife at home that he enjoys belittling."

Nina said, "You don't think that guy is married, do you?"

Perri replied, "I certainly hope not."

"So, is that guy 'Rooster'? Oh, my gosh, does he think he's some kind of catch? Got a harem of little hens pecking around his yard? Gag!"

Perri giggled, just a bit, "Yeah, he probably thinks he's a stud; a gallant ladies' man, taking care of the little brainless women."

"The little brainless women who can't think about more than one thing at a time, right?"

"I'm sorry," Perri said, with an exaggerated look of puzzlement on her face, "I can't follow your thought. I already have a thought, so your thought makes more than one thought, and that's too much at once." They both laughed loudly and peeked back over their shoulder as they reached the car. They could see Rodney skulking in the doorway. He was watching them, hands in his pockets.

"Let's get out of here." Nina hopped into the passenger seat.

Once they were belted back into the car, Perri said, "I feel like I need to wash my hands after being in that nasty office and using that greasy grunt's pen!"

Nina dug in her purse, "Here, hand sanitizer."

"Thank you! At the first cemetery, I'll rub my hands around in the grass and dirt, they'll be cleaner than that office."

"Ok. I'll go back to highway 79. There is a road that cuts through from 79 over to highway 68, and the cemetery is on that road which does roughly follow Whippoorwill Creek. The cemetery is between the road and the Creek."

"That explains the name."

Chapter 12

It didn't take long to find the turnoff toward the cemetery. The road had many sharp turns, left and right, back and forth, winding around, just like the creek. "This probably was a trail following the creek a long time ago," said Perri. As they came around a right-hand curve, they could see a stone wall stretching back away from the road. A police car was parked by the central entrance where there was yellow tape looped around two wooden horses blocking the lane. There was also yellow tape blocking off the north and south entrances. A policeman was slowly walking around in front of the car. There was a knot of about ten to twelve people in the gravel between the road and the surrounding stone wall, talking and looking into the cemetery.

As the Cooper approached, the group turned to look. Perri eased just past the cemetery and pulled into the lot at its north end, which was also gravel. "Plenty of company. That's a good sign for getting some gossip." Perri turned off the ignition, stepped out of the car, and tucked the keys in her jeans pocket. Nina came around the car and they both headed across the rocky parking lot with weeds pushing up all over it, toward the group of people.

"Good thing we women folk have some men here to guide us, keep us from wandering off." They both laughed.

Perri could see Jack, from the tavern the night before, included in the onlookers.

"Hello, Jack. We were on our way out to visit a few cemeteries and, since we're staying out this way, we thought we'd come by to see what there is to see."

Jack had a large styrofoam cup of coffee. "Me too." He took a sip. "The body's been taken in, of course, but they haven't moved Amy's car yet. They called in some special examiner or investigator from Bowling Green to have a look at it before it was moved. Joe was out here all night watching the place. Leonard over there took over early this morning." He nodded to the policeman who was now ambling through the ironwork arch over the main entrance to the cemetery. "A couple ladies brought him some coffee and long johns. Not sure how long he's going to be here."

Jack pointed across the cemetery, "You can't see too much of it with all the people in the way, but the wreck is right over there. If you watch, every now then they move and you can just make out the back end of the car. It's right up against that wall that you see running kind of down the middle. It's supposed to be smashed up pretty good, both ends. Somebody was in there and hit her, more than once. But she wasn't found in the car, so she had to have gotten out. No one knows why she was in the grass, but supposedly they will have information sometime today about what killed her."

Nina and Perri watched for the next half hour as the various investigators hovered around the wreck like bees around a hive. They could see a woman, who, according to Jack, was the local detective, in chinos and a short-sleeved shirt. She carried a phone and notebook, which she wrote it occasionally. She frequently spoke with a man in a Tyvek suit who was kneeling down to look under the car, leaning into the open passenger door, and climbing over the wall to view the wreck from the other side. He appeared to be taking samples and handing them off to an assistant. A flat bed wrecker waited in the gravel south of the cemetery, its driver evidently asleep with his chin cradled in his hand.

"As much as I'd like to stay here and watch them remove this car, it could take a long time and we'd better get going or I won't get my own research done. Darn it! I'm curious about this," Perri said. Nina agreed to the part about leaving.

"You said you are staying around here, where?" asked Jack.

"At the B&B on 102, the Crow's Rest."

"Oh, ok. I've seen that place. If you want to come back by the tavern tonight, some of us will be there again. We might know something by then."

"Hey, thanks Jack, we'll do just that! Can't wait to hear about it." Perri and Nina headed back toward the car.

Back in the car, Perri fired up the engine and put the a/c on full blast. "I'm not going to raise the roof, but I want a bit of coolness. It should be better once we get going. We are probably going to get hot enough today." Perri turned back the way they had come. They waved at the clutch of people as they drove past.

Chapter 13

"This is the last one," Perri said as she turned from the paved road onto one of mixed rough gravel and dirt. It snaked between corn fields. The corn was high and was all that was visible. "We should come to a bridge over a small creek. Once we do that, we can park on the side of the road. The farmer said the creek is always dry at this time of year. We can follow it back to the tree line rather than walk through the corn."

"Ok. How far of a hike is it back to the cemetery?" asked Nina.

"It looked like it was about a half mile after we reach the tree line, maybe a bit less, but we aren't going to be on flat ground. We have to go through some trees first. After the trees, there's a path that goes to some old outbuildings. It's just past that."

"It's the most secluded one we've been to. I wonder what shape it will be in. Even some of the ones right by the road are awfully overgrown and neglected. I hope we can even get to the stones."

"I do have some pruning shears in my duffle bag. If the overgrowth is too much for that, we're out of luck."

"I don't do sticker bushes. If it is covered with blackberries or those nettle things, you're on your own, unless you have some gasoline and a match."

"Yeah, Nina, I don't think the owner would appreciate us torching his property. Besides, it would damage the stones. Otherwise, it is a tempting idea."

"Now I know why you wear jeans to do this. I'm glad you mentioned it because my legs would be scratched up if I had worn shorts."

"Here's the bridge. It's more like a paving over a culvert than a bridge, but I think this is it," Nina said as she craned her neck to look over the side. "He's right, the owner I mean, there's just a small trickle of water down the center. It still might be a little tough, some of those rocks are pretty chunky."

Perri slowed almost to a stop and leaned forward to look for a place to park the car. "Where are we going to pull over? There is a shoulder, but it's narrow and mostly loose dirt and gravel."

Nina looked down over her door and said, "I think if you just get past the creek a couple dozen yards, you should be able to squeeze over enough to park and still leave room for a car to pass."

"Ok." Perri drove forward a short distance and slowly eased onto the shoulder. "How about here?"

"Looks good."

Perri put up the roof, and when they were both out, locked the car. She opened the trunk and took out the duffle bag with her cemetery kit, shutting the trunk lid. "Let's go!"

They walked back toward the creek and carefully walked down the bank onto the larger rocks lining the edges of the creek. The stony creek bed was fairly clear of weeds but they had to watch their footing to avoid wedging their feet between the rocks. The creek curved away to the left, and they followed it toward the tree line.

Several minutes later, the end of the rows of corn was visible. They were soon walking out into a grassy area under the trees. Perri had looked at the map so many times, she had it memorized. "We just need to angle to the right a little, through the trees and over the low ridge. Once we get to the top, we should be able to find the path. It should cut crossways from the direction we come out of the woods, since it goes from the house to the outbuildings.

There was a breeze here and it was cooler beneath the trees, but they were soon on top of the ridge and looking down on the other side. The trees gave way to a fallow field covered with some kind of sparse scrubby growth. To the left was more field. To the right, Perri could see a couple of ramshackle stone buildings. The path was just visible about twenty feet from the edge of the trees. "This is it. We go right. The cemetery is supposed to be just past those buildings."

Perri and Nina crossed the area of grass, plantain, dandelions, and a few stems of Queen Anne's lace to get to the path. As they started downhill, Nina asked, "You said one of the stones we are looking for here is for Perlina Evans?"

"Yes. She's from my Dad's side and is my namesake. I know Mom and Dad meant well naming me after her, but it does sound out of date today. I go by Perri. She married my 3x grandfather's brother when his wife died. He'd been married for a long time and had numerous children. Only a few years after she married Francis, many people got sick with 'winter fever' and started dying. All but a couple of Francis's children were grown and gone, but Perlina found herself with the responsibility to bury her husband and his oldest daughter who was still at home. And Perlina and Francis had two children of their own who were both under four years old at the time. Can you imagine? The only reason we know that is from the receipts she kept and stuck between the pages of the family Bible."

"I remember you telling me that, but it was years ago and I wasn't sure I remembered the story."

Perri and Nina passed the two outbuildings on their left. Both were stone, one much larger than the other. The larger building looked like a barn or storage building, having wide double doors in one end, which had a wooden plank set across it, resting in metal brackets. The smaller building was too small for anything other than a garden shed or, as Nina suggested, an outhouse. "You gotta go when you're working in the fields too, you know?"

Perri smiled, "Could be. Depending on how long we're here, we may want to check that out."

The path ended at the larger building. "The farmer said when we get to these buildings, to go past them and we should see the cemetery just up on the next hill. There had been a lot of rain in the two weeks prior to their visit, and while the ground wasn't sodden, it was still a little soft, being at the bottom of a small valley of sorts between the hills. Perri and Nina had to watch their step as they walked past the end of the barn with the doors. There were tracks going through the grassy area and into the barn, and large clumps of mud had been thrown from the tracks and were drying to a concrete consistency along the edges of the tracks.

Once past the tracks, they struck up the side of the hill. It wasn't particularly tall, but the sides were steep. Once at the top, they turned to look around. "It's beautiful countryside," said Perri. The white steeple on the copper roof of the courthouse was visible in the distance. As Perri started to turn back to the hilltop, she pointed to the area to the right of and further away from the two stone buildings, "Look. There is a semi-circle of flowers, not blooming now, but the greenery looks like irises or daffodils that bloom in spring. I wonder if there might have been a house there at one time and those were in the front yard."

Nina looked where Perri was pointing and said, "Yeah. That is what it looks like. I wonder if the farmer knows what was there. He might."

"Yes, he might."

Perri closed her eyes, took a deep breath, and felt the sunshine on her face for a few moments. "Let's get looking. I see a few stones, so let's look at them first. I'm sure the one I want won't be one of them, but you never know."

Chapter 14

It had been three hours. Perri and Nina were both tired and grubby from crawling around in the grass and soil. Perri had recognized the names on a couple of them. She used her graph paper to plot the locations of the standing stones in the cemetery, and included some of the surrounding features. There was an enormous locust tree at the southeastern corner and a fallen tree across a broken stone in the opposite corner.

"I think I will try to find the top portion of that broken stone over there," Perri indicated the narrow stump of a stone near the fallen tree. The top section, the part that contained the name and birth date had broken off and wasn't visible. Perri wanted to see if it was just below ground level. The stone was no more than twelve inches wide and shouldn't be too much of a job to dig it out if it was there. "We don't know exactly when Perlina died, but the stones that are next to this one are from the same era. The probate records that I got last year confirmed she was buried in this cemetery. Fingers crossed."

Perri walked over to the duffle bag/cemetery kit and pulled out the slender divining rods she'd been given by Joyce and returned to the grave site. They were L-shaped, the short section was four inches long and the long section twenty-four inches long. They were no larger than the diameter of a wire coat hanger, but were steel and very strong; they reminded Perri of a very thin barbecue spit. Joyce had included a couple of five-inch-long sections of PVC pipe. She said they were to rest the short ends of the rods in so they would turn freely making it less likely that the hands holding them would either inhibit them or turn them purposefully. "I have never used these rods to locate, and I don't really need to do that now anyway, but I think I'll use them like a probe and see if I meet any resistance in the area around the stone. Maybe the top half is still here, just buried. It looks like the broken edge angles down from back to front with a crushed area just below the break. I'll check in front first."

"Good idea," replied Nina. She sat down on a patch of grass to watch. "I want to try locating with those sometime. It would be pretty awesome if it works."

Perri slowly pushed one of the rods down through the earth about two inches in front of the stone. It went all the way in the ground, right up to her fingers. She pulled it out again and tried several more times a couple inches away from the previous try, moving away from the stone. On the fifth try, the rod stopped suddenly. "You got something, Perri?"

"I think so." Perri tried again an inch away with the same result. "I think we should carefully dig here. I hope it is the missing part of the stone. It doesn't sound like a tree root. Can you bring the duffle bag over here?"

Nina got up and retrieved the bag. She set it down next to where Perri was kneeling, unzipped it, took out the hand spade and trowel, and handed them to Perri.

Perri dug quickly for the first few inches, then slowly as she neared the object. The tip of the hand spade hit something solid. Perri used the trowel to dig around the edges until she could see what was in the ground. It was definitely a stone. "I think this is it. Oh, I hope so." They both dug around the edges to make enough room to pull out the stone. "The ground is pretty wet. I think we'd better use a rope underneath before we try to lift it; I don't want to break it. We'll have to dig out a little further from all sides of the stone to have room for our hands to slip the rope under it and pull it across.

Nina asked, "Why are we going to use a rope? What will that do?"

Perri answered, "It will break the suction between the stone and wet earth. If we don't, we could break it further trying to pull it out."

They continued to dig to expose the full length of the buried stone which turned out to be fifteen inches long. They cleared the loose dirt from the sides of the stone until there was room for the rope to be slipped beneath the fragment. Perri pulled a length of nylon rope from the duffle bag and handed one end to Nina. "Let's start at the jagged end, the one nearest the standing stone and gently push the rope under the edge." After getting the rope under the stone, Nina said, "Now, gently pull the rope toward the bottom. We can slide it back and forth if we need to or move one side at a time if it gets too hard to move."

It was difficult to make progress at first, and it seemed the rope wasn't going to move at all. "Maybe it's stuck on something, something under the stone" said Nina, just as the rope moved forward a bit. They moved the rope back and forth and side to side until it cleared the smooth, rounded end. "Let's move it back just a bit, about a third of the way, and you lift gently up on the rope while I lift the broken end."

Nina slid the rope back a few inches while Perri dug her fingers in the muddy soil under the stone. It moved slightly and stopped. "Let's run the rope up and down once more, then lift right after the last pass. I think it sucked back onto the mud."

"Ok." They slid the rope back to the top, then down again. When the rope was about two-thirds down the length of the stone, Perri said, "Ok lift." There was some resistance, then a sucking noise, and the stone fragment came free. "Yes!"

The stone had fallen face down when it was broken. It had gradually sunk into the earth, further with each passing decade. Perri and Nina very carefully turned the stone over and laid it on the grass. Perri reached in to her duffle bag and got a bottle of water. Perri poured a little water on the stone and used a soft brush to remove the water and mud. The branches of a willow tree, billowing in the wind, could be seen carved at the top. She continued pouring water, a little at a time, and brushing it away. What had hidden the stone from view for countless years also protected it. The writing was much easier to read on this part of the stone.

Perri took a deep breath and sighed, lightly touching the edge of the stone. "It's her! Oh, thank goodness. I'm glad to have found her resting place." She read through the epitaph. "She died in 1862, only four years after Francis and his daughter. Life wasn't easy then, was it?"

Nina slowly shook her head, "No, it was not. Do you know what happened to her children? They would still have been very young."

"I do. Women needed to be married back then, especially if they had children. If their husband died, they usually remarried as quickly as possible. Same with the men really, because the men needed someone to keep house and take care of the children while he worked or farmed, or whatever he did. Today it would raise eyebrows to remarry so fast, but not back then. She married again within a year. When she died, the children she had with Francis stayed with her husband and his children by his former wife. Perlina had been married once before she married Francis too. He was quite a bit older than her and he died not long after they married. Not an unusual story.

Perri and Nina set the top portion of Perlina's stone in front of the lower half. "I'm going to take photos and mark it on the map, then I think we can..." Perri's sentence was interrupted by a click and a man's voice, "What do you think you're doing there?" Perri and Nina whirled around like a couple of tops to find a man pointing a shotgun at them.

"Hey, hold on," Perri said as she dropped her clipboard, slowly stood, and raised both hands, palms out. "We have permission to be here, to look at the stones. Who are you?" Nina stood still and stared at the man. He looked to be in his mid-sixties and had unkempt graying hair that probably would not recognize a comb. His clothes were a bit ragged, old jeans with the hem so worn it looked like fringe and a yellowed t-shirt with darker yellow stains under the arms.

The man motioned with his shotgun back toward the path, "You all just get out of here now."

Perri persisted, "We have permission to be here, from Mr. Freighley. He owns this land and I have written permission from him to be in this cemetery."

"That so? I don't care what you have in writin' lady, I lease the pasture from old Freighley and I say you go."

"We aren't *in* the pasture. We are in the cemetery. Do you lease the cemetery?"

"Listen, I ain't havin' none of your lip. You get out of here. I don't want you next to my property, and this is my property over here." He swung his head in an arc indicating the land behind him.

Perri tried to talk sensibly, "I understand that, and we appreciate that. But this cemetery isn't your land. We aren't going to come onto your land. We are only going to be here a little while longer and then we are going."

"You're going *now!*" The man raised the shotgun and fired a shot into the air.

"Holy shit, Perri, let's go. He's crazy," cried Nina in alarm. "I'm not down for getting shot."

"No, me either." Perri eyed the man, "Let us gather our stuff first, that alright with you?"

"Make it snappy." The shotgun was trained back on Perri and Nina. Perri turned around and bent to pick up her clipboard. Nina was placing items back in the duffle bag. Perri picked up the camera, turned it on, and took a photo of the stone.

"What are you doing?" shouted the man. "I told you to get out of here."

"Alright, alright." They picked up their belongings and Perri took another look around the cemetery. "I think we have everything. You have a nice day."

"It'll be a nice day when you are gone," hooted the man.

Perri and Nina headed back down the hill toward the path. As they passed the outbuildings, Perri said, "I'm calling the police, that whacko fired his gun! I'm going to let Mr. Freighley know what his tenant is doing too."

"I think I'm shaking a little bit. I've never been shot at!" said Nina as she held her hand out.

"At first I thought maybe the gun was empty and he was just trying to scare us away with it. Nope. No, that guy is a nutjob. What on earth is he doing on his property that he's this worried about us being here? He draws more attention to himself by waving a gun around and threatening people."

"I know," agreed Nina. "We would never have given a second thought to it."

Perri smiled, "I wouldn't want him to have gone to all that trouble for nothing. I feel compelled to justify his paranoia, don't you?"

"Mmm, I like the sound of that. I agree. His efforts were admirable and they should not go unrecognized or unrewarded."

"I concur." They laughed as they picked their way over the clods and dried ridges of mud by the stone barn. They still threw the occasional glance over their shoulder though, just to be sure.

The duffle stowed back in the trunk, Perri and Nina settled into the Cooper with relief. Perri leaned her head back on the headrest and exhaled loudly, "Well, that was a lot of fun until Pa Kettle showed up with this gun."

"Who?"

Perri chuckled, "Never mind, old show. Used to watch it with my Dad. Truthfully, that comparison isn't fair to Pa Kettle."

"Oh, ok. You going to call the police?"

"I think I'll stop by the police station and report it in person. We didn't have lunch and I figured we'd be going back to the Arrogant Rogue. The police station is practically next door."

"Sounds like a plan."

Perri carefully eased the Cooper off the rocky soft shoulder, which appeared prone to crumble into the ditch, maneuvered the car around to face the way they had come, and drove away.

Chapter 15

Perri parked in a spot on the far side of the police station. Inside, there was a counter running most of the width of the narrow building. The front was paneled in the light grayish paneling popular in the sixties and the top was covered with beige and white Formica. There was a handful of chairs, square chrome legs and black vinyl, lined up against the plate glass window. An officer appeared around the corner of the narrow doorway that led to the rear of the building. "What can I help you ladies with?" he smiled and slapped his hand onto the counter, sliding onto a stool.

"I'd like to report someone who fired a gun."

The officer's smile vanished. "Fired a gun? Alright, let's get the whole story here. Why don't you start…"

"At the beginning," Perri finished the sentence. "Yes, no problem." Officer Wilcox, as the nametag indicated, listened and made notes about the incident as Perri told her story. She began with an explanation of the purpose of their visit and their presence on Mr. Freighley's land, and ended with their departure from the cemetery.

Officer Wilcox heaved a voluminous sigh and thrust his hand through his thinning hair, "That's Milton Sauer, the guy with the

92

shotgun. Not the first time we've crossed paths with Milton, or the rest of his family for that matter."

"Not a new thing, huh?" asked Nina.

"Yes and no. Not new that a Sauer is causing trouble, but yes, it is new because Milton has never fired a gun at someone before. You say he shot up into the air?"

"Yes, yes, he definitely pointed it up, at about a 90-degree angle, and fired. But the threat felt pretty real."

Nina asked, "You say you've had trouble with the Sauers before, how many of them are there?"

"Not as many as there were, used to be a dozen of them. Now it's down to Milton and his two sons, Howard and Rodney. Not Howard anymore though, because he moved away."

"Rodney?" asked Perri and Nina in unison.

Perri continued, "Is that the guy who works at the filling station?"

Officer Wilcox laughed, "So you've met Rodney."

"They should rename that place 'Cuckoo's Filling Station.' He's a pig."

"Ma'am, I have heard your opinion expressed before, I'll say that." He tore the piece of paper off the pad, pulled out a form, and said, "If you don't mind having a seat over there for a few minutes, I'll write this report up and have you sign it. We'll go out and talk to Milton, see what's stuck in his craw this week."

"Thank you." As they turned to have a seat, the door opened and the detective they had seen in the cemetery walked through.

"Hey there, George."

"How you doing, Sarah? Finished out at the cemetery?"

"Yes, the car is being brought in now. I called ahead and let Martin know it was coming."

"Sounds good."

"Getting to wear your Detective hat today? How's it feel?" asked George.

Sarah chuckled, "It's a nice change of scenery, George. Thankfully, I don't have too much opportunity to switch gears."

"Gotcha."

Sarah ran her eyes over the waiting area, "Everything ok here?"

"Yeah, yeah. Just a complaint about Milton Sauer." George nodded at Perri and Nina, "These two were up at Freighley's old cemetery looking at stones, had his permission, Milton decided to threaten them and fired his gun to run 'em off."

"Really. He fired a gun? What kind?"

"Shotgun, that old thing he's been pointing at people for years."

Sarah stepped over to Perri and Nina and briskly shook their hands, "Hi, I'm Detective Sarah Vines. I'm concerned about Mr. Sauer's behavior. He's been a bit of a loose cannon, so to speak, over the years but he's never gone as far as shooting. You both alright?"

"Oh yeah, we're fine, we were just a bit shaken. I haven't been nearly shot at before," replied Perri. "We, uh, stopped by

Whippoorwill Cemetery on our way out this morning and saw you looking over the wrecked car."

Sarah nodded, "Yes. This will be a puzzle, I'm afraid. Well, I'm glad you are ok. If you have any further trouble while you are here," Sarah transferred her gaze to Officer Wilcox, "I'd like to know."

"Will do, Sarah," answered George.

Sarah passed the counter and then turned around, "If they were in the cemetery, they weren't even on Milton's property. What's his problem?"

Officer Wilcox waved the report and said, "That's what we're going to find out."

Chapter 16

Sarah Vines walked past the reception area of the station and down the hallway to the kitchen. She poured herself a mug of coffee, added sugar and creamer, and took it with her to the combination interview room/conference room. She flopped the file folder with her accumulated case information down on the table and slumped into the folding chair with a grunt.

"Crap." She stared down at the coffee in her cup and knew it would be awful. If the creamer doesn't lighten the coffee much at all when it is stirred in, the coffee's old as dirt. And this coffee was a grayish brown, not a light brown. She sipped it. Yep. Awful. It wasn't really better than nothing, but it was more than nothing and she didn't want to make more.

Sarah could hear the sound of the station door opening and closing followed by a familiar voice greeting Officer Wilcox. Sarah was pleased and displeased at the same time. Daniel Bales had been the station's detective, when needed, prior to Sarah. The Russellville police department didn't need a full-time detective, but there was always at least one officer with the title who was in charge of investigations when they came up. A little over twelve months ago, after several years in Russellville, Daniel had been offered a choice, full-time detective position in Nashville and had moved on. Sarah had been promoted to Daniel's position at that time. They kept in touch, although less regularly as the months went by.

She could hear Daniel's footsteps approaching. She straightened her back and quickly opened the folder, rapidly spreading what paperwork there was across the table. Daniel entered the room to find Sarah intently studying her notes. Daniel breezed into the room, his suit coat over his shoulder and his tie loosened, his black hair windblown.

"Sarah! S'up?" he laughed his easy laugh. "Heard you got a murder case going?"

"Hi, Daniel. How are you doing?" Sarah turned in her chair as Daniel plopped down into the remaining chair.

"I'm good, real good. What about you?"

"I'm doing just fine. What drew you away from the big city to our patch of ground?"

"I've been in Frankfort for a few days to give testimony in the trial of the Russellville local we arrested in Nashville a few months ago, the one who was peddling methamphetamine."

"That guy. Turned out he was manufacturing in Logan County, had a pretty big operation, going back and forth?"

"That's the one."

He sighed, "Glad that's over. I was driving back and since I was practically going right by here, I decided to make a small detour and see how things were going. And to see you. I love my new job, but I miss everyone here too." Daniel glanced furtively into Sarah eyes and scooted the chair closer to the table. "Can you tell me about what's going on?"

Sarah grinned, "I'm glad you came by. I miss your harebrained humor. I'm starting to feel like a dour-faced matron with no sense of humor."

Daniel threw his head back and guffawed, "You? A matron? Oh, come on…you serious? What's going on, Sarah?"

"This is a weird one. I just got back from Whippoorwill Cemetery, which is where the body was found…" Daniel's expression became serious.

Sarah ran through the story from the moment William Parker had called the station. She ended by saying, "What we're looking for is a car painted tan or beige which should have significant front-end damage. Here are photos of the tire tracks from the verge. They are the only discernible ones; the deep ruts, weeds, and mixed tracks in the road made it pretty much impossible to single out any tracks well enough. I have finished interviews, at least preliminary, with Amy's mother, her employer and a couple of coworkers, her neighbors, and I have two more interviews to complete today."

Daniel was scrutinizing the photos. Sarah continued, "And…she was shot with an AR-15. No brass recovered from the scene, so the person responsible took them with him or her. There were at least two shots; the first one missed its target and was found in the mud five yards from Amy's body; the second round was recovered inside her skull. We haven't yet found a car that is consistent with the paint and damage on Amy's Focus, we haven't found the gun, or anyone who knows why someone would have killed Amy. It doesn't make sense; I'm a little baffled. But, there could be something from the car and I still have a couple more interviews to do. By then the search of Amy's apartment should be finished. I hope something comes up there."

Daniel looked steadily into Sarah's eyes. Neither said anything.

Sarah broke eye contact first, "I really better get going or it will get a bit late to ask for interviews.

Daniel sat back and smiled a little wistfully, "Right, I'm sorry I didn't call, I know you're busy." He stood and picked up his suit coat, "I should get back, I'm supposed to show my face in the office sometime today."

Sarah rose from her chair as she gathered her paperwork, "It really was great to see you, Daniel." She turned to him, "I'd be glad to see you whenever you are up this way, I'm sorry I'm swamped right now." Sarah's face and ears warmed under Daniel's brown-eyed gaze. "I'll walk out with you."

Daniel and Sarah walked single file down the narrow hallway, past the counter and the now empty reception area. The two women filing a report had gone. Daniel leaned across to shake George's hand, "Good to see you again, George."

"You too, Detective Bales."

"I'm going out for a couple of more interviews, George. Not sure when I'll be back."

"Alright, I'll call you if anything comes in."

Daniel opened his car door and, with one foot on the frame, spoke to Sarah as she walked past the front of his car, "Don't worry, Sarah, you'll do fine. Everyone feels some frustration and confusion with cases like this. And I know it feels awkward; you haven't had enough cases to feel comfortable in the new responsibilities yet. I have a lot of faith in you." Sarah gave a half smile and nodded. Daniel said, "I'll call you soon. See how the case is going."

"Ok, I'd like that. Be careful, and talk to you soon." Sarah gave an awkward wave and walked toward her own car. She looked back as she sat in the front seat to see Daniel waiting for her to look at him. He waved at her through the passenger window, backed his car out of the space, and drove away.

Sarah fastened her seat belt and stared unseeingly at the dashboard for at least a minute. She tossed her hair back from her face, "Ok, Sarah, get moving. Onward." She pulled away from the police station and drove in the opposite direction from Daniel.

***

Sarah felt the dread in every bone in her body as she knocked on Margie Barrow's front door. She stood, waiting, focusing on the three narrow, horizontal windows in the faded 1950s wooden door. The pale blue and yellow ruffled curtain covering the living room window fluttered a few moments before Margie opened the door.

"Margie, I'm sorry to intrude right now, I really am. Can I come in and talk to you for a few minutes?" Sarah asked.

Margie's eyes and nose were red and swollen from crying; even her lips were red-rimmed and raw. "I know you have to, Sarah. Come on in." She opened the door and stepped back for Sarah to enter then closed it behind her. She stood still, leaving her hand on the knob, just staring at it.

"Margie, let's sit down, ok?"

"Yeah." Margie went into the living room and sunk onto the sofa. The living room was a little crowded, but was clean and homey. The coffee table sat on a braided rug of blue and brown, with a tan recliner at one end and a light blue one across from it, near the window. In the far corner was the television. Numerous small end tables with knickknacks and bookshelves lined the remaining wall space. Photos of the family were arranged on the wall next to the doorway to the kitchen.

Sarah sat perched on the edge of the recliner opposite the couch. "I can't even describe how sorry I am about Amy; there really is no way to do that. What I can say is that I want you to be certain that I will do whatever I can to find...to figure this out."

"I know you will." Margie sucked in short gasps of air as the emotion threatened to overwhelm her again, even though she obviously was struggling not to cry in front of 'company.'

"I need to ask you questions that I'm sure you've been asked, and I apologize for that, but it will help me to talk to you." Margie nodded and blotted her tender nose with a man's white cotton handkerchief, the embroidered monogram 'JDB' in one corner. "Thank you, Margie. Is there anyone, anyone at all, with whom Amy had an argument, a problem, or any kind of issue in the last six months?"

"No. There really wasn't. I know people always say the person had no enemies, but Amy really didn't. Not that I know of anyway. She would have said, I'm sure of it."

"I know she had a cell phone, but had there been any calls for her here at the house, or any people visiting her here that you didn't know?"

"No. If Amy was going to meet someone it was usually somewhere else anyway, not here. I mean, like going for supper or to a movie."

"Alright." Sarah was sliding back on the slick vinyl of the recliner; she shifted forward and continued. "I know that Amy had been helping Patricia with some research she was doing. Do you know anything about that?"

Margie lifted her bleary eyes to Sarah's face and made an effort to concentrate on the question. "Well, I guess. She said Amy wanted to do some checking on her family tree, or something like that. They had been friends in school, well, you know that. Patricia knew Amy was used to doing research. She did research for her job too, you know?"

"Yes, that's right. Did Amy tell you anything about what she was looking for or perhaps what they may have been finding?"

Margie gave an exhausted sigh. "I don't know." She turned the handkerchief around and around, then said, "Amy did talk about it while we ate supper sometimes, but I'm sorry to admit I didn't always...listen as closely as I might have."

"Tell me what you do remember, that will be enough."

The skin between Margie's eyebrows creased deeply as she thought, "Any was telling me that when Patricia first asked Amy to help her, she was kind of mad about it, or about something. Later, after it had been going on for a while, after they'd gotten together at the library several times, Amy said Patricia wasn't mad anymore but was happy. Maybe not happy, I can't think of a word for it. More like determined or satisfied, you know what I mean?"

"I think I do, yes. So...you think, from what Amy told you, that Patricia had found what she was looking for?"

"I know Amy said Patricia found some relatives of hers that she didn't know she had. They didn't live here. I never thought of Patricia as someone who was interested in family ties, but people change."

"You feel that Patricia had changed and wanted to get to know these other family members she had found?"

"What Amy said was more like Patricia was going to contact them. She was going to call one of them. I can't remember what she said it was for, but I don't remember her saying anything about wanting to visit with them. I'm sorry, it seems like I can't tell you what it was for, but I can tell you what it wasn't for. Darn it! Why didn't I listen closer?"

"It's ok, Margie, really, don't let it upset you because you've thought of quite a bit already."

Margie stared intently at the rug, "We were eating supper: meat loaf, lima beans, and mashed potatoes, when Amy was telling me about that. It seems to me I remember thinking 'Oh, that'll come to no good.' I just can't remember what it was Amy said."

"Ok. As we go along, that may make more sense than you think it does. Anything else you remember?"

Margie drew in another large breath and looked to the ceiling as she exhaled. "No, that's all I remember."

"That's perfectly ok. Margie, you did a great job, I'm sure your information will help me." Sarah rose from the recliner, "When is Amy's showing and funeral? I want to be there."

"Monday afternoon, it's at Watson's." Margie's chin and lower lip quivered.

"I'll be there. Thank you for talking to me." Sarah moved to the door. "Please let me know if there is anything any of us can do for you, Margie. And call me at any time if you think of something else, no matter how small it might seem."

"I will, Sarah. Let me know what you find out."

"I definitely will, you can count on that." Sarah stepped out onto the porch and heard the door softly shut behind her as she descended the three steps to the walk.

Chapter 17

The police report completed and signed, Perri and Nina were ensconced in a booth at the Arrogant Rogue with iced tea and an appetizer plate of Buffalo Wings.

"I'm probably going to need a bib. Why can I not eat these without getting it all over me?" Nina said in exasperation, looking down at her smeared shirt.

"It's part of it, makes it taste better if you rub it on your clothes." Perri watched Nina dab at the stain with her napkin dipped in water. "Don't worry, I got something really messy for the entrée and I promise I'll drop some on myself."

"You'd better." Nina made an exaggerated frown at Perri.

They enjoyed their food and the music and reviewed their day. "I'm interested to know if the police find out anything from Mr. Crabby Appleton," said Perri.

"Me too." Nina drummed her fingers on the table in time to Motley Crue. "I hope you don't need to go back to that cemetery though. I think I'm good on that one."

"Well, I won't be going any time soon. I got a photo and I can remember its location well enough to add it to the map I made."

Perri leaned side to side, stretching her back. "I know we were going to look for Jack and the others, but I don't see them right now. And honestly, if you are done, I'm ready to get a hot bath and put my feet up with a glass of wine or three."

"Oh, my gosh, that sounds good. Let's get going."

As they neared the door, it flung open and Rodney Sauer barged through, knocking over the 'Please Seat Yourself' sign. "YOU bitches!" he shouted, fists balled up at his sides.

A hush rapidly swept over the entire room, extinguishing all conversation, everyone turned toward the front of the tavern. "I told you! You women are trouble. You bitches sent the cops to my house." As he lunged forward, Perri and Nina stumbled backward into the edge of a table, lifting one side which thumped back down, spilling the drinks. The customers seated at the table leapt up and backed away.

Rodney stopped a yard away, raised his fist, squeezed so tight his fingers were white, and said, "That's right you bitches, you'd better cower. You ought to be at my feet. I think you better kneel down…"

As Rodney reached out as though to grab Perri's hair, the bartender they had seen the night before darted around the end of the bar and approached Rodney, menacing a short bat in his hand. "Rodney, get the hell out of here and don't come back." Rodney stood still. "Right NOW!"

"Shut your mouth, Nick! These two floosies have been poking around our property, snooping around like women do." He lowered his arm but kept the fist and turned back to Nina and Perri, "What the hell are you looking for, huh? What you doing up there?"

"Floosies?" gasped out Perri. "You pea-brained, sexist primate…" Nina put her hand on Perri's arm and shook her head. Perri took a deep breath. "As I told your father, we were in the cemetery to look at the old headstones, looking for a particular one. It isn't on your property anyway, and we never set foot on your property."

"That isn't for you to decide."

Nina piped up, "What are you talking about? It's a property line. It sure isn't for you to decide!"

Rodney narrowed his eyes and glared at Nina, "You need to be slapped around."

Nick stepped forward a few paces, raising the bat ominously. "Rodney, get out of here, pronto! If you'd prefer to spend the night in the jail, we've already called the police."

Rodney turned and kicked the seating sign into the hostess stand, then pushed the stand over. It crashed onto a wooden bench just inside the door and they both tipped over and clamored to the floor. People from the other side of the tavern were craning their necks to look through the doorway. Rodney turned back, looked around the room full of people, and pointed at Nina and Perri. "You'd both better go back home. Now! Or I'm telling you, I'll teach you the lesson you should've learnt by now!" He wrenched the door open, hinges protesting, and stormed out.

A middle-aged couple paid their bill and left. As the waitress was taking their payment, a man at a table near the back of the tavern was standing by his table and impatiently gesturing for her to bring his bill. As she tore it from her order pad, he snatched it and rapidly shoved it back in her hand along with some cash then rushed out the door. Once the door had whooshed shut a second time, general silence blanketed the room. "Well, I didn't expect that," said Perri a little shakily as they sat back down at the table they had just vacated.

Nick came to their table, leaned down to eye level, and asked, "Are you guys ok?" He returned his gaze to Perri.

"Uh, yeah, just surprised, I guess. Not surprised that he's a goon, just that he came in here. We had the misfortune to him at his gas station this morning."

"Sorry to hear that. I'm Nicholas Silver, Nick." He extended his hand to Perri.

Shaking Nick's hand, Perri answered, "I'm Perri Seamore, and...this is my friend Nina Watkins." Nick turned to shake Nina's hand.

"I'm glad to meet you. You were here last night."

"Yes, we were. We enjoyed it so much, we came back." Perri grinned.

"I'm glad." As Nick spoke, an officer entered the tavern. Nick gave a crooked smile as he turned to the policeman. The officer noted the toppled furniture, spilled drinks, and general disruption. Nick said to the office, "It was Rodney Sauer, threatening customers and causing a disruption." He jerked his thumb at the door, "He just took off, mad as a hornet."

The officer used a radio to ask for assistance in locating Rodney while he took a report at the tavern. All eyes were on Perri and Nina. Perri felt her face and ears burning and was sure they were bright red, but not entirely from the incident with Rodney.

The policeman looked around the room, "Ok folks, what happened here?" This was Officer Harper, who had been at the cemetery the night before.

All the patrons turned to look at Perri and Nina. "Apparently…Rodney is upset that my friend, Nina, and I made a report this afternoon that his father threatened us with a shotgun while we were in an old cemetery. He fired the gun, up in the air, but he fired it." Amid gasps and whispers, Officer Harper asked Nick, Perri, and Nina to give him a rundown of what had happened. Nick righted the bench, hostess stand, and sign as they gathered in a knot to tell their story.

"Alright, Nick, ladies, thank you. We'll invite Rodney to spend the night in the jail again if we find him."

Nick excused himself, "I need to get back behind the bar." He turned to Perri, "I'll probably see you around again?"

"Probably so," Perri answered.

Joe Harper went on to explain to Perri and Nina that when the police had visited the Sauer house, Milton had admitted he fired his gun but didn't have a good reason. He said he just didn't like people close to the property. He was given a citation and told he would need to make a court appearance, the gun was confiscated, and he'll appear in court. Joe also told them they had talked with Mr. Freighley about it. He said he had no idea why Milton would be upset that someone was in the cemetery. He said he hadn't been down there since at least the year before, so he didn't know if Milton had something going on in the woods by the property line or not. Officer Harper left the tavern.

"Well that's twice in one day we've had to make a police report and I've never had to make one before. This is going well." Perri turned a worried face to Nina, "I'm sorry, I hope this isn't ruining the trip for you. I sure didn't think some sourpuss old geezer with a shotgun and his caveman son would be popping up like Whack-a-Mole all weekend."

"Are you kidding girlfriend? This is the most excitement I've had for a long time." She nudged Perri in the ribs with her elbow. "Let's go have that wine!"

Chapter 18

Sunday morning dawned with a graying sky, fast moving clouds, and high humidity. The gabbling of the crows again greeted Perri as she woke. She dressed and sat down to organize her notes while Nina got ready for the day.

After another excellent breakfast, provided by the incomparable Alice, Perri and Nina were relaxing in the gazebo next to the pond, drinking some coffee and enjoying the outdoors before it got too hot. Nina was curled into a wicker chair reading a book on her iPad and Perri was typing away, making notes on her laptop. The border around the gazebo was planted with chives, mint, and other herbs. There was a steady buzzing of bees from the blooms. The koi in the pond frequently came to the surface and made bubbles, then swished their tail, slapping the water as they retreated to the bottom.

"If I had some crumbs, I'd feed the koi," said Perri lazily. She stared at the pond for several minutes. Her face showed an expression of concentration. "Hey."

Nina looked up from her book. "Hey what?"

"I was making notes and writing down everything that happened yesterday. Something doesn't make sense."

"Ok, what doesn't make sense?" Nina unfolded her legs and stretched.

"Remember when Officer Harper was telling us that they talked to Mr. Freighley?"

"Yes."

"And Mr. Freighley said he didn't know what had gotten into Milton?"

"Ye-es." Nina leaned forward in her chair.

"Well. Mr. Freighley also commented, apparently, that he didn't know if Milton had 'something going on' by the property line or not because he hadn't been there since last summer. He hasn't been well since winter. He hasn't been out on his property."

"Yes, I remember that, but I'm not sure why that matters?"

"Because...if Mr. Freighley hasn't been down that path since last year, then he couldn't have made the tire tracks going in to the stone barn. Those were deep and fresh. So, who did? We assumed it was from farm equipment or a vehicle belonging to the farm. But it can't have been."

"You're right, I didn't even think about that. The tracks were made at least in the last couple of weeks when the ground was sodden from all the rain."

"The Sauer's lease out the pasture, but the pasture is clear on the other side of the farm. They'd have no reason to be running a tractor or anything."

Perri closed her eyes and tipped her head back for a moment, thinking. She raised her head and opened her eyes to see Alice hurrying across the yard to the gazebo.

Alice seemed uncomfortable. "Sorry to bother you, but Sarah Vines is here." Alice paused and said, awkwardly, "She's from the police. Is there a problem?"

Perri sighed. "Oh. Not really, I mean, not here or with us exactly." Alice's forehead wrinkled in dismay. Perri told Alice, briefly, what had happened the previous day as they shut off their electronics and followed her back to the house. Alice tsked and tutted, "Those Sauers have been a thorn in everyone's side for a hundred years! Even my grandmother had a low opinion of that bunch. They are always causing trouble. If there's a big stink around town, there's usually a Sauer involved. Now they're shooting at people?"

"He didn't shoot *at* us, just into the air."

"That's bad enough. Because what's next then?"

They reached the kitchen door and Perri and Nina went through to the parlor. Sarah Vines was standing by the large front window, looking out over the hills across the road. She turned when she heard their footsteps approaching.

"Hi, I'm Sarah Vines, we met yesterday at the police station when you were there to make a report about Milton Sauer."

"Sure, I remember. What can we help you with?"

Sarah said, "I'm sorry to bother you with this, but I just have to make sure." Perri and Nina nodded. "You told me yesterday you had come here to do some family research, including visiting several cemeteries in the area. You also mentioned you had been to Whippoorwill, while we were inspecting the scene."

"Yes," Perri and Nina both looked at Sarah with worried faces. Nina felt her palms starting to sweat.

"No, don't worry, there isn't anything wrong with that. I just wanted to ask you a couple of questions. Since you have been in other cemeteries this weekend, some of which are not visited often, I wanted to know if you saw anything in any of them that was unusual."

"Unusual. Not really, no. I mean, most of the cemeteries we went to were fairly untended with few visitors. We mostly saw bugs, tall grass, and lots of brambles."

Sarah nodded and made a note. "My other question concerns Whippoorwill Cemetery. Had you been to the cemetery prior to yesterday morning, when you told me you went by?"

"No. It wasn't on my list to visit, and I hadn't even heard of it before Friday evening, when the story about Amy Barrow was being told." Sarah looked at her. "We heard about it when we were out for supper in town, at the Arrogant Rogue Tavern. Well, the first we heard of it was in the Clerk's office that afternoon. We were curious, so we did drive by it before we started on the cemeteries on our list."

"Ah, ok." She bobbed her head up and down as she made more notes.

"Can I mention something to you?" asked Perri.

"Absolutely."

Perri and Nina looked at each other and nodded. "You asked if we saw anything unusual, and we haven't, but I heard something that seemed unusual. After Rodney Sauer came into the tavern last night and made a big ruckus, Nina and I, and Nick the bartender, were telling Officer Harper what happened. After we finished telling him about the incident that had just happened, he brought Nina and I up to date on their interview with Milton Sauer as well as Mr. Freighley.

Sarah was listening intently, "Go on."

"Officer Harper said that Mr. Freighley stated that he had not been down to that part of his property since last year. When we were there yesterday, there were deep tracks coming from the area of the road, across the path we were on, and into the stone barn that is just below the hill where the cemetery is located. The tracks were pretty fresh, and they were deep because of the recent rain. We had to pick our way over them so we didn't sink in the mud or trip on the clods thrown up around them."

"I see. That is something unusual if Mr. Freighley truly hasn't been down there, and hasn't hired someone to do the work he can't do right now. He may have though, since he's been sick or ailing for several months. I'll check that out with him. Thank you."

Nina asked, "Have you any idea who killed Amy Barrow?"

"We haven't made an arrest."

Nina smiled, "I understand, you can't say anything."

Sarah hesitated. "I can't give you any information about what we may or may not have found out, but I can ask for any information that might concern a motive for this crime." She looked from Perri to Nina and back.

"Since we don't live here, we didn't know Amy and have no inkling why someone wanted to kill her. We definitely will pass on any information we might come across."

Sarah pressed her lips together, nodding. She started to rise from her chair, but sat back down. She sat quietly, thinking, and appeared to make a decision. "One other thing."

Nina and Perri looked at each other and back at Sarah, "Of course, what else would you like to ask?" said Perri.

"We have talked to everyone who knew Amy, even only casually. We've gone through her apartment, including all her paperwork." Sarah hesitated, looking uncomfortable.

"I'm sure you have been very thorough," offered Nina.

"Right. Let me back up a little bit. I take it that you were aware that Amy was visiting the grave of a school friend of hers when she was killed?"

"Yes, we did hear that."

"Patricia died almost two weeks ago, and it isn't far-fetched that Amy would visit her grave. What's niggling at me about this is that, while Amy and Patricia hadn't associated much, if at all, for the last few years, over the last six months or so, Amy appears to have been helping Patricia with some sort of document search."

"Document search? What sort of documents do you mean?" asked Perri.

"Old documents, documents that are from the late 1800s, as well as a few from the early and mid-1900s. "

"Oh, do you know what Amy was trying to find out?"

"See, that's the thing, I don't know. It could be she suddenly became interested in family history; some of the documents are about her family, back several generations. But some of the documents don't seem to have any relation to anyone in Amy's family. I just can't see a connection."

"What kind of documents are they, the ones that seem unrelated?" Perri asked.

"Aside from the papers that related to her family, birth certificates, marriage records and such, there were stock market reports, partial printouts of what looked like a website about the history of the western expansion, that kind of stuff.

"Maybe they are unrelated and just got mixed together," suggested Nina.

"Maybe, but they were together in a snapped folder in a desk drawer with rubber bands around the folder. And whatever Patricia was working on, it was important enough to her to ask Amy for help." Sarah sighed and raised her left hand palm up. "I had heard you were here doing just this type of research; Emily from dispatch told us when we interviewed her, since she was the one who took the call in from Will Parker. I don't know what your immediate agenda is, and I can't bring you in on all the details of this case, but I am wondering if you would be able to review the documents we found and see if you can see a pattern. We'll supply you with a list of Amy's known relatives and their whereabouts to help find any connections."

"I'd be more than happy to help you with that. I only hope I can glean something from Patricia's paperwork."

"Thank you. We will make any other documents you need available to you and get you set up over at the Clerk's office, if that's alright?"

"Absolutely, not a problem. Will it be ok if Nina is with me, she can help read through documents? Two sets of eyes are better than one."

Nina spoke softly, agreeing, "Definitely, I'd love to help."

"Yes, yes, that will be fine."

"Perfect. I'll let you get back to your morning. I'll work on getting this set up. Can you come to the Clerk's office tomorrow morning at 9 o'clock?"

"Yes, I'll be there."

Sarah gave one firm nod, "Here's my card, call me if you have any questions. Otherwise, I'll see you both tomorrow morning."

Sarah let herself out, the screen door banging back into place.

"That's exciting!" squealed Nina.

"It is. And it is definitely a twist to our trip. Are you going to be able to stay another day? Tom expects you home tonight. I kind of volunteered you, but you said you aren't scheduled to work again until Thursday, right?"

"Are you kidding, like I'd miss this? I'll call Tom and explain. If he wants help with Aaron, he can call my sister."

"Ok, but only if it doesn't cause any problems, I don't want to cause a rift over you staying away longer than expected. I wouldn't want any future trips to be a problem either."

"He'll be fine. He's made lots of business trips to exotic, fabulous places over the last couple of years – he owes me."

"Akron, Ohio is exotic?"

"It is when you don't get to go anywhere at all."

"Alright then, as long as you are sure. See what Tom says. If he objects, I can take you home and come back here."

"I'll tell him, but you'll see, he'll be ok with it," said Nina assuredly. "Tom's pretty good about that sort of thing and I haven't done anything but work at work and work at home for two years and more."

"I hope so." They sat quietly, each thinking their own thoughts for a few minutes when Perri spoke up, "Ooh, we'd better check with Alice to make sure we can stay another night, or two, if needed." Perri looked sideways at Nina.

"Let's do that now, before I call Tom." They got up from their comfy chairs. "I wonder if they'll go check out the barn," said Nina.

"I bet they do, if they aren't already there.

Chapter 19

Detective Sarah Vines made a phone call to the station as soon as she was in her car in the little parking area in front of the Crow's Rest. "Russellville police, Officer Petrea."

"Hey Norman, this is Sarah."

"How you doin' Sarah? What's up?"

"I don't know for sure. Has anyone been sent to interview Mr. Freighley yet?"

"Yeah, I sent Brett Maddux out there about twenty minutes ago."

"Norman, call Brett and ask him to stay put. I'm heading out there."

"Sure, Sarah, you think you got something?" asked Officer Petrea.

"I don't know, but we need to check on it. I'll be out there in less than half an hour." Sarah ended the call and started her car.

***

Sarah pulled the Subaru off the gravel road and stopped on the shoulder at the entrance to the seldom used grass and weed choked lane that led to the outbuildings on Alexander Freighley's property. It was covered with growth, but she could see that the taller grass was mashed down in each rut like it would be if a vehicle had driven down the lane recently. The seeding plantain and grasses were tall and unbent in the middle and each side of the subtle tracks, and the foot-tall dandelion stems in the center were bare, the seeds having either dispersed or been knocked off. She could see Officer Maddux's patrol car parked in the driveway of the farmhouse a little further up the road.

Sarah got out and locked her car. She walked along the incline of the road to the house. The edge of the road was a loose mixture of large gravel, mud, and bits of trash that had been faded and torn by the wind. She climbed the stairs to the porch and knocked on the door, which was opened almost immediately by Officer Brett Maddux.

"Hi Sarah, come on it. Norman said you had something to follow up on?"

"Yes, I need to speak with Mr. Freighley."

"In here youngin," called a voice from the kitchen. Sarah poked her head through the doorway. The farmer was sitting in a rocking chair in the large kitchen. Wearing faded denim overalls over a flannel shirt despite the heat; he looked frail. Sarah's family had known the Freighleys for as long as she could remember; she'd grown up playing with their grandchildren when they came to visit.

"Mr. Freighley, how are you doing?" Sarah smiled warmly as the elderly man took her hands in his and patted them.

"I'm doin' alright, Sarah girl. Had a hard winter with a cold but I'm on the mend. How's that mother of yours?"

Sarah replied, "She's doing really well, Mr. Freighley, I'll tell her you asked about her."

"Yeah, Brett here told me about the trouble with old Sauer yesterday. Shootin' at people, was he?" he shook his head.

"He shot into the air. No one was hurt, but he crossed the line this time. He was very agitated that there were people in the cemetery on your ground."

"I heard that. I told that young lady it was fine with me if she went in there and looked around."

"That's what she told us. There is something I wanted to ask you about."

"Surely, you go right ahead." He continued to rock as contentedly as if Sarah were there for Sunday lunch.

Sarah pulled one of the teal colored chairs from the dinette over near the rocking chair. "Now, as you said, you were ill over the winter, and I'm glad you are feeling better, but you said you hadn't been down to your outbuildings since last summer. Is that right?"

"Yep. Haven't ventured down there. I could have, I s'pose, but I don't really have any reason to right now. I haven't used them regular for years, not since I quit farming."

"Yes, that's what I understood. There would be no reason for someone to be driving a car or other vehicle into your barn recently?"

The old man puckered his lips then said, "Well, no. There shouldn't be anyone going in there."

"Have you heard anything, seen anything, that was out of the ordinary? Any indication someone might be messing around down there?"

"No, but then I don't sit around listening for it either." He smiled.

"The reason I'm asking is that someone reported some pretty deep, and newly made, tracks from the lane going into the barn, most likely made during the rain we had recently. You know anything about what that could be?"

"No, I sure don't. You want to have a look, is that what you want Sarah?"

"I'd appreciate it Mr. Freighley. We don't know why Milton got edgy when there were people in the cemetery. I'd like to just have a look at both buildings, if you don't mind, especially since they are relatively close to Milton's property and definitely not visible from your house."

"You go right ahead."

"Can I get the keys from you?" Brett stepped forward.

"Don't need keys. Ain't locked. Just has a board over the door to keep it from swingin' open. I didn't think there was any reason to keep it locked."

"Okay, we'll head down there now. I'll come back before I leave," Sarah said as she placed the chair back in its place at the table.

"I'll be here." The farmer continued rocking as the two left through the rear kitchen door.

***

Sarah and Brett followed a path of paving stones that started at the back door, went past an old concrete fish pond about the size of a bathtub which was dry and empty except for some leaves. The path wound around trees and fences, down the hill, toward the barn.

As they walked, Brett commented, "Haven't seen much of you around lately, Sarah."

"I know, Brett. I've been busy playing catch up with training requirements: diversity and comprehensive communication training, as they call it. If I get even a little bit behind, it snowballs. How are you?"

"I'm good, I'm good. Let me know if you want to go have a drink or something, sometime when you aren't tied up with a case or those requirements," Brett grinned.

"I'll do that." Sarah took a deep breath and slowly let it out.

The top of the barn was visible through the trees as they descended the hill behind the house and the path soon emerged into the sunshine at the back corner of the barn. Sarah and Brett walked around to the far side, where the large double doors were located. The barn was built on an angle to the cemetery, the doors facing roughly halfway between the cemetery and the lane leading to the barn from the road.

"No lock on the doors like he said, but as he said, he doesn't have anything in here he feels he has to lock up." Brett slid the wooden beam out of the brackets and flipped open the latch. "You grab that door and I'll get this one," he indicated to Sarah. They tugged on the doors and swung them open.

They each drew their revolvers and moved to peer into the wide door opening. There was no sound, no movement detected other than a few stray stalks of long ago harvested straw stirred up by the doors opening. They looked through the gloom at the interior. There was a row of stalls on either side of the barn, probably for livestock, with the center portion open. Right in that central area sat an old beige Chrysler. It was parked with the rear of the car inward. The tire tracks stopped short of the car, about ten to fifteen feet away. "This wasn't driven here. No tracks from the car; it was brought with a wrecker." Brett pointed, "You can see where the wrecker stopped to unload the car. That's why the tracks are deep, combined weight of the wrecker itself and this car."

They moved slowly, weapons drawn, one on each side of the car, checking inside before advancing. They reached the back of the car together. Sarah looked around once more. There had once been a loft, but the floor had either fallen through or been removed. "No one here. There's damage to the front end. It looks like the radiator emptied out on the floor, there's a darker spot in the dirt around the front," noted Sarah.

As Sarah continued around the other side of the car, back toward the front, Brett donned gloves and opened the passenger door. "Nothing in the front seat that I can see."

"This color paint is very similar to the color left on Amy Barrow's car, and right here..." Sarah pointed at several areas around the headlights, taking care not to touch the surface, "there's blue paint. Amy's car was blue. I'll call for someone to get down here to go over the car, then we'll have it taken in for a better inspection. Maybe we are starting to get somewhere."

They had both returned to the rear of the car. Sarah commented, "The plate is from Arkansas. We need to find out who this car is registered to and who brought it here, but I'd pay money that this plate doesn't belong to this car. Let's have a look into that small building too."

Brett followed Sarah to the small stone building. Weapons still drawn, and one on each side of the door, Brett flung the door open. Nothing. Brett peered around the doorway and relaxed. Sarah stepped up to look through the door. "Nothing here," said Brett, "just some old paint cans and rusty tools."

Sarah pulled her phone from the pocket of her twill slacks. With eyebrows raised, she said to Brett, "We won't know for sure if this is the right car until the lab guys are done testing, but either way, we will need to get over to the Sauer's to have another talk. If they've been patrolling the edges of their property, they may have seen something. It could be an explanation for Milton's increasingly odd behavior." Brett nodded and walked back toward the barn.

Sarah called the station, "Hey Norman, this is Sarah. Get the crime scene guy, whoever is on today, and send him to the outbuildings at the bottom of Mr. Freighley's farm. Found a car in the barn that could be the one that hit Amy Barrow's car in Whippoorwill Cemetery. It's a '70s model Chrysler Cordoba. Have them go over the car, and then over the small outbuilding next to the barn. Also, check on the plate, Arkansas 549 MBH, expires in February 2016. I doubt it belongs on the Chrysler, let's find out where it came from, I want to talk to the owner if you find one." She paused while Officer Petrea replied, "Good deal. Get back with me on that as soon as you do. Nothing obvious in the car. We need to make sure we don't miss anything, get prints, he knows the drill. Also tell the towing guys to be ready to remove this vehicle." Another pause, "Yeah, one of the tanks. Thanks."

Sarah started to disconnect, but swiftly said in the phone, "Norman, hold on! You there?"

"Did anyone catch up to Rodney Sauer since last night? He was last seen at the Arrogant Rogue after causing a commotion."

"He hasn't been brought in, but let me check." Sarah could hear the phone being set down on the counter and muffled voices in the background. Norman returned, "No, Sarah, they didn't find him. His car is at the gas station but his tow truck is gone."

"Ok. Have everyone keep an eye out for him. I want to talk to him." Sarah hung up.

"Ok, Brett, let's head over to the Sauer house, and let's take your car," said Sarah as she headed back up the path.

Chapter 20

Milton Sauer came out of his house and stood on his sagging porch with a pinched expression and his fists on his hips. Officer Maddux parked the police cruiser in the stony, weedy area that served as a driveway and he and Sarah exited the car. Milton shouted, "What do you want here? You aren't welcome."

"Just cool your jets, Mr. Sauer," drawled Brett, "we want to ask you a couple of questions, that's all."

"It's Sunday, boy. Why you here on a Sunday, don't you respect that? I already talked to you people yesterday anyway. You told me I have to go to court in a couple weeks. Why are you back?"

"I do respect your time, Mr. Sauer, but there are times when we can't do that." Sarah replied as she and Brett stopped a few yards short of the porch steps. "You aren't going to pull a gun on me now, are you Milton?"

Milton frowned, "You got my gun! And I didn't shoot nobody. I got a right to protect my land."

Sarah answered, "Yes, you do, Mr. Sauer, but no one was on your land."

"They darned near were, and I didn't know what kind of nosy business they were up to. I'm protecting Alexander's land, too, from prowling around and stuff."

"Milton, you could see they were looking at stones in the cemetery, and Mr. Freighley gave them permission to be there. They weren't trying to come on to your property. What's your problem, what's going on?"

"I don't like Nosy Parkers snufflin' around my property." Milton frowned and stared.

"Can we come up on the porch and talk to you?" asked Brett.

Milton Sauer shuffled his feet and jammed his hands into his pockets. "Alright, but only for a few minutes. My boy'll be home soon and we got stuff to do."

"We'll try to take up as little of your time as possible."

Sarah and Brett stepped up onto the porch. It was littered with an assortment of appliance and car parts, yard ornaments, and disintegrating lawn furniture pushed up against the face of the house. Milton stood squarely in front of the door. "Now, what do you want?"

"Milton, you said Rodney would be home soon, do you know where he is right now?"

"He's out doin' his own business. I don't pry, but he'll be back real soon and he won't like you being here anymore than I do."

Brett returned to the previous topic, "Mr. Sauer, you have always felt, um, very strongly about protecting your property, and that's fine, but when you start firing your shotgun, something's different. You've never done that before. What's going on?"

Milton Sauer glared at the weathered boards of the porch as though he was trying to drill a hole through them, but he didn't answer.

In a soft voice, Sarah said, "Mr. Sauer, please. We don't want to drag this out any longer than we have to, but we know there has to be a reason for the way you acted yesterday. It's better to tell us now than wait. If you don't tell us, there are going to be more people out here, pressing you for answers, maybe even getting a warrant to search your house and property..."

"Nothing doin'! You aren't doin' that." Milton protested vehemently, his face reddening.

"Mr. Sauer, believe me, I do not want to do that, no one does." Sarah paused, "So come on. Don't make us have to go ask for a warrant, we have other things to do too."

Milton considered, looked around and behind him. "Oh, hell's bells."

"What is it, Milton? You got trouble?" asked Brett.

"No. Yes. I don't, but my boy might."

"What do you mean?"

Milton obviously was struggling to give an answer. "Alright, alright." Sarah and Brett nodded reassuringly. "Rodney went out Friday, kind of early for him, especially since he didn't come home until the wee hours the night before. He was drunk as a skunk too when he got home Friday night, just after supper time. Ain't all that unusual, but he had some stuff with him that he didn't have before."

"Such as what," asked Sarah.

"He had one of them laptops and a fancy new phone, the kind I see on tv all the time. We don't even have computer service at the house, so I asked him why he had a laptop. He got all mad and told me to shut the hell up and mind my own business. He had a couple of bags with him too that he took in his room, but I didn't see what was in them."

"Can you get the bags and show us?"

"I'd rather not."

Sarah realized his refusal was probably just as much not wanting to know himself what Rodney had brought home as it was protecting his privacy.

"Ok. Depending on what else you tell us, and what comes of this, we may have to see what Rodney brought in," encouraged Brett, "but for now, please go on."

"He came out to the kitchen Saturday morning with a new radio, one of those real expensive ones, I can't remember. They're little things but make a big noise."

"Boze?" asked Sarah.

"Yeah, yeah that's it. I said to Rodney, 'Ok, you gotta tell me where you got this stuff. You stealin?'" Milton looked defiantly at both Sarah and Brett. "We aren't the best people, I know that, but I don't like stealin' and I won't have it." Milton pressed his lips together in a straight line, shifted his weight back and forth, and continued, "He got all het up again, said he'd hit me if I didn't shut up. That ain't like him, I mean, he doesn't say stuff like that to me." Milton hung his head a bit.

"I can imagine that was very upsetting to you, Mr. Sauer. What happened then?" asked Sarah.

"I asked him if he didn't steal the stuff, where'd he get it. He said he paid for it. I asked him what with, because that gas station don't make enough for him to buy all that stuff at one time. He started laughing and said he earned it, that he was a real businessman now, he was branching out."

"Branching out?" Sarah and Brett spoke at the same time.

"I asked him that, ok? He took a long time but he finally told me some guy had come into the gas station and asked if Rodney knew someone who could do a job for him. Rodney said depending on what it was, he might could do it." Milton hesitated.

"Yes?" Sarah stepped a pace closer.

"He said he had a car that he didn't want anymore, and since he had a new car, he couldn't take the old one with him. He needed someone to get rid of the car."

Sarah slowly drew in her breath, "What kind of car?"

"Well…he said it was an old car that didn't run well, was starting to leak and needed more work than it was worth, and he didn't have time to handle it, you know, sell it or take it to a junk yard, whatever. That part was ok, but it bothered me when he said the guy made it real clear that the car had to be gotten rid of somewhere private, not sold or left out somewhere. What he said, he meant he wanted it quiet. That's what Rodney told me."

"Rodney took the job and that's where he got the money. How much?"

"That's the thing, this guy paid him $1,000 to do it. That's a lot."

Sarah felt her pulse quicken, "Yes, yes it is, quite a lot. Mr. Sauer, did Rodney tell you where he got rid of the car."

Milton twisted his features around and wouldn't look directly at either Sarah or Brett. "Mr. Sauer, you haven't done anything wrong, other than fire your shotgun of course, but this is very important. I'm not sure you realize yet how important it is and your help with this will go a long way in resolving your own issue. Please tell us where Rodney took this car he was hired to dispose of." Sarah asked as gently as her rising excitement would allow.

Milton blew out a big sigh, "He put the stupid thing in Freighley's damned barn! Old Alex ain't never down there, no one is. But Lordy, Rodney acts like he don't have a brain in his head. He can't leave it there, and I told him so. I told him it was only going to cause trouble. He said he knew that, but wanted to get it out of sight and then think about where to take it on his own time. Stupid kid."

"This is why you reacted the way you did when you saw a couple of people in the cemetery? You had just found out about the car being there and you were scared they would find it. You figured that then Rodney and you both would be in trouble, is that right?" inquired Sarah.

"Yep. I knew it was a mistake to do that, only drew everybody's attention, but I was frettin' over it pretty bad."

"I can understand that."

Brett had been quietly ruminating over what Milton said. "Did Rodney drive the car to the barn?" asked Brett.

"No. Rodney said the guy told him it didn't run, radiator was spitting or something. He put it on his flatbed, you know his tow truck?"

"Yes, he keeps one at the gas station for towing service. I've seen it," said Sarah

Brett continued, "If the car didn't run, the man who hired Rodney couldn't have driven it to the gas station, so where did Rodney pick up the car?"

"It was way out, north of here, on one of the old mining roads. He drove up there Friday night to get it, had to wait until dark he said.

Sarah asked, "If the car was several miles north, how did the man get to the gas station?"

"I don't know exactly, Rodney said he came in a black car, expensive looking. He had to know the guy had money.

"Mr. Sauer, thank you very much for your cooperation. This has been more help to us than you realize. We are going to have to talk to Rodney, though." Sarah attempted to relay the information without upsetting Milton further.

"I know, I know. But he ain't here now and...I honestly don't know where he is or when he'll be back. He took off Saturday night like a bat out of hell when he found out you people were here about the gunshot. He hasn't come back yet."

Sarah smiled and said, "Ok, Mr. Sauer. Would you please let us know when he does return, or if you find out where he is?"

"Yeah, I suppose. But I won't do it where Rodney will know."

"I understand." Sarah reached out to shake Milton's hand. Milton looked at her hand uncomfortably and finally shook it with a little softening of his features.

"You won't hurt my boy, will you? I mean, you are just going to talk to him, right?" Milton asked tentatively.

"At this point, that is all we need to do." Milton turned away and went into the house and shut the door.

As Brett started the car, Sarah said, "We have got to locate Rodney Sauer. It sounds like he may have taken payment from the person who murdered Amy Barrow to get rid of the car that was used. We have to find out what he knows." Brett eased the police car to a stop next to where Sarah's car was parked on the verge. Sarah pondered for a moment, then said, "I wonder why the guy went to the trouble, and the exposure, of hiring someone to get rid of the Chrysler? It gives me a little hope that maybe we can trace the car, that somehow there will be something leading to the killer. Otherwise, why risk it?"

"You're right, there has to be some reason for it." Brett nodded, thinking.

Sarah opened her door, "I have to make some arrangements for a document search at the Clerk's office tomorrow morning. Can you get started asking around, try to find out if anyone has seen Rodney since Saturday night?"

"I'm on it." Once Sarah had started her car, Brett headed back to town.

Chapter 21

Sarah woke at 6:00 a.m. Monday morning, thirty minutes before her alarm would beckon her with its nerve-grating beep. She turned over to go back to sleep but couldn't. She knew it was futile to try. Once the thoughts and plans started swirling through every sleepy corner of her brain, she couldn't shut them off. They started by poking their noses through the gray fog of sleep, like seeds sprouting. If she wasn't able to force them back down right away, they grew faster and faster, like vines spreading and covering everything until they filled her mind and demanded she pay attention.

She threw back the sheet and sat on the side of the bed, the daylight trying to pry back the edges of her blackout curtains to stretch their greedy beams into the room. "Oh gawd," Sarah exhaled. She felt like she had dreamt all night long, and she knew Daniel figured in at least some of them. "I don't have time for this," and she marched into the bathroom to get her shower and start her very busy day.

***

When Sarah arrived at the Clerk's office at 7:30, Cora and Jennifer were already there and had the document room opened and lit, with a legal pad, pencils, and a lighted magnifying glass in the middle of the table. Jennifer was making coffee in the small kitchen and had set out several mismatched coffee cups on a tea towel. Cora's voice came from the rear where the file storage was located. "Be with you in a minute."

"It's just me...Sarah. Take your time. And thanks for coming in early to get this set up, I appreciate it."

"Nooo problem. I'm pulling the files you asked for, just about done," came the muffled reply.

Sarah had felt guilty about having Cora and Jennifer come in early, but as she looked around at the preparations, she realized that for them this was an event, something exciting and out of the ordinary routine of the office. She greeted Jennifer as she walked into the kitchen. "That coffee smells great, Jennifer, mind if I get a cup?"

"You go right ahead, that's what it's for." Jennifer finished washing her hands and wiped them on a dishtowel. "Holler if you need anything, I'll be at my desk."

"Thanks, Jennifer."

Sarah took a seat at the table outside the boxlike document room and sat drinking her coffee, going over what she did know. She pulled her phone out to make some calls while she waited. "Morning Joe, this is Sarah, can you check on the license plate from that Chrysler we located yesterday?"

"Sure thing, hang on." The sound of the stool scraping against the wooden floor was audible as Joe left the counter. He returned a couple minutes later, "Sarah, the plate was stolen from a Cutlass Ciera in Fayetteville, Arkansas on August 16."

Sarah was irritated and replied briskly, "I was supposed to get a call about this as soon as they got something."

"I know, and they were going to call you this morning but were trying to get hold of the owner first. Do you want to contact the owner?" asked Joe.

"I do, but I need to get things moving here at the Clerk's office now. Can you put the information on my desk? As soon as I'm finished here, I'll come back to the station and contact the owner. Thanks."

Her second call was to Ted in the small lab at the station to see if he'd discovered anything in the Chrysler found in the barn. "Ted Baker," came the response when the call was answered.

"Hi Ted, this is Sarah. I'm wondering if you found anything on the Chrysler?"

"A lot, I just don't know how much of it will be pertinent."

"Go on."

"The car is a 1975 Cordoba. It's like examining a forty-year-old vacuum cleaner that hasn't been emptied. There were more than a dozen different samples of hair, fingerprints on nearly every surface, body fluid traces, some of which were blood but it was so old it was oxidized and useless. I got a large bin full of trash, most of which was fast food wrappers. If you are in the market for some vintage Farmer's Daughter and Burger Chef bags, I'm your man."

"Thanks Ted, but no thanks. What about the prints?"

"I am running several sets of them, nothing so far, which is what I expected. Most of the prints from the steering wheel and handle were smudged and older. Whoever was driving wore gloves which smeared the prints in the most common hand positions on the wheel, but not otherwise, which means the person driving didn't wipe the steering wheel. I suspect the prints are all old. I say that because it doesn't look like the car was driven for quite some time, for years. It appears to have been made road worthy perhaps just long enough to fulfill its use."

Sarah asked, "What makes you think that?"

Ted replied, "Several reasons. It was extremely dirty, inside and out, coated with a thick layer of greasy dust, like it had been parked near trees that release sap which combined with dust from roads or fields. This layer of grime on the back-seat area and passenger sides wasn't even disturbed. Of the trash inside the car and trunk, none of it could be dated later than 2003, and I am taking that date from a rolled-up newspaper from Elkton that had never been taken out of the rubber band. The rubber band was broken and had adhered to the newspaper."

There was a pause and Sarah could hear Ted take a drink and swallow, then continue, "And...under the hood were the remains of what was obviously a pretty massive rat's nest."

"Did you say rats? A rat's nest?"

"Yep. It had been cleared away, but there were bits and pieces of straw, fabric scraps, fiberglass left stuck to oily surfaces and in crevices as well as plenty of rat droppings throughout the engine compartment. There were some new parts: some of the wiring which had either corroded or been chewed away by the rats was replaced, a battery, oil and air filters, some hoses, which indicates someone replaced enough parts to get it running."

"In the trunk, there was an old wool blanket that was dry rotted, a jack and tire iron, more trash.

"Thanks Ted. Let me know if you get any hits. Bye."

Sarah dropped the phone back into her purse. She was startled from her thoughts by the sound of several pairs of footsteps coming toward the room. She jumped up, sloshing a little of the remaining coffee on her blouse. "Oh for…" she stepped out and put the cup on the table.

Cora had a couple of manila folders in her hands and was escorting Perri and Nina through the labyrinth of partitions. As they came into view, Sarah greeted them, "Good morning, ladies, thank you for coming."

"You're welcome." "We're happy to help out," from both of them.

"Come on in and have a seat. Cora has a couple of files I wanted you to start with." Cora set the files on the table and exited the room. "I have some information for you regarding Patricia's family as well. Hopefully, between the two, you can find something, any indication of a connection."

Perri and Nina put their purses on the table outside the room and went in. "We'll give it our best shot." Perri and Nina seated themselves at the viewing table. Perri sat with only her toes on the floor, joggling her legs up and down in anticipation. "You're jiggling the table, sweetie," pointed out Nina.

"Sorry," Perri gave a sheepish smile and sat still.

Sarah pulled a third chair into the room and sat down on the opposite side of the table. "As I mentioned to you yesterday, Amy had been helping, or working with, Patricia in a document search of some sort. Cora has pulled the files that Patricia asked for on all her previous visits. Requests are logged into the system when they are made and include the name of the person requesting it. It was possible to do a query on Patricia's name to find what she had asked for. One folder, this one," she held one up and placed it in front of Perri, "has the birth and death certificates she requested to view and for which she requested copies. She did not ask for copies of all documents she requested. The other folder contains other types of legal documents: court records, payment slips, and guardianship documents. Most of these people are Patricia's relatives, or rather, she is descended directly from them. They lived in this area and this is where she was born. It wasn't hard to see the relationship of these people to Patricia herself, but the significance of those relationships escapes me right now. That's what I'm hoping you can help me see."

Perri asked, "I'm still wondering if it could be a red herring and not related to Amy's murder? Was Patricia maybe just putting together her family tree and needed some help from Amy because Amy was accustomed to looking at these types of old documents?"

"That could be, but we don't know that and we don't have anything else." She paused, "As they say, I don't enjoy speaking negatively about someone who has passed on, but truthfully, this is not something I would ever have expected Patricia to spend her time on. She just wasn't the studious type." Sarah slid her own file folder across the table. "These are Patricia's notes, found at her apartment. There is a lot more information about her immediate family members because she knew them all, and you will see that she started with herself and worked backward. According to this, her line seems to have died out with her. We don't know if she was possibly trying to find out if there were more family members that she didn't know about, or if she had another purpose. After the death of her mother, she didn't have anyone. Maybe it prompted her to look for an unknown relative."

Perri pulled the folders toward her and Nina. Sarah continued, "Besides her notes and a few copies of documents she got here, there are some photos, most of them stapled to notebook paper with a short description of the picture. Some of the photos are older, thirty to forty years old and some look like she printed them on an ink jet printer. Maybe from the internet. I guess someone could have emailed photos to her if she made contact with them. The lab guys have her computer." Sarah looked at Perri and Nina, and back to Perri. "Go ahead and have a look through everything. Make notes, ask for whatever you need. I'll be back later to check in with you, or if you need me sooner, have Cora give me a call or call my cell phone."

"We'll do the best we can." Perri was already removing the certificates from the folder. Nina had started a heading on the legal pad and was sorting through Patricia's notes.

***

As soon as Sarah sat down at her desk, she picked up the police report from Fayetteville which was made on the Arkansas plate that had been on the Chrysler. The license plate had been taken from a 1994 Oldsmobile Cutlass Ciera. The report stated the owners, Mr. and Mrs. Bradley Monroe, had been at church at the time and their car had been in the church's parking lot. Sarah picked up the desk phone and dialed the number.

"Hello," came the voice of an elderly man.

"Hello, this is Sarah Vines, I'm a detective in the Russellville Police Department, in Kentucky. Is this Mr. Monroe?"

"Yes, it is. What can I do for you?"

"I wanted to go over with you the incident of your vehicle plate being stolen, if you don't mind."

"I don't mind. Did it turn up?" asked Mr. Monroe.

"It did. Had you noticed anyone around your vehicle or notice anything out of place?"

"No, no I didn't see anyone. My wife and I were in church, it was Sunday you know, and I parked right about where I always do in the lot after I let Diane out at the door. After church we came out, got in the car, and left to go to a restaurant like we always do. Some

144

of us go out to eat after church every week. We look forward to that."

"Did you notice at that time that the plate was missing?"

"No, we were talking with other people from the congregation and didn't look at it. We just got in and left."

"When did you notice it missing?" asked Sarah.

"Why, when the policeman pulled me over!" exclaimed Mr. Monroe.

"Ok, can you tell me about that?"

"I was driving down the main drag, so I pulled onto another street and stopped. The policeman asked me for my license and registration, like they do. I gave them to him and he asked me why I didn't have a plate on the car. First I heard of it and I told him so. He said hold on a minute while he went back to his car. He said he checked and it showed I had paid for my tags. He wanted to take a report. Said I had to get some more plates. That upset Diane and me both, I'm telling you. I didn't appreciate having to pay for another plate, you know? That's not cheap."

"No, sir, I'm certain that it wasn't, I'm sorry you had to do that. You didn't see anyone hanging around the parking lot, maybe as you arrived at church or were walking in to the building?" Sarah asked hopefully.

"No. Wish I had though."

Sarah's mind was working through the details. Amy Barrow had been killed by someone in the Chrysler with that plate on August 27, at least a full eleven days after it was stolen. Since the plate had been reported in Arkansas on Sunday, August 16, Sarah had been wondering if the person who stole the plate put it on the Chrysler and drove through several states managing to avoid being pulled over for a stolen plate for that length of time, or if they had simply taken the plate and brought it with them in another vehicle until they arrived at their destination, and then switched plates.

Mr. Monroe expanded further on his displeasure in having to purchase a new license plate. "I don't like spending more money on something I already bought. We didn't like being late to our lunch either. Everybody made a big to-do over me and Diane getting pulled over by the police right in front of everybody. I had to tell about it a couple of times."

"Yes, sir, I…"

He was picking up steam on his complaint, "I'm glad you got that plate back, but that doesn't do me much good now, does it? I already shelled out the money for a new one." He paused, and before Sarah could speak again, said, "You get the lousy thief who took it?"

"Not yet, but I believe we will, Mr. Monroe."

"Good! Now listen to me, you get $74.61 out of that guy when you do, and send it to me, you hear me?

"Mr. Monroe, I…" but he had hung up already.

"Ok then." Sarah put the report aside.

Chapter 22

Perri ran her fingers through her hair and stretched, her shoulders were pinched and aching from hunching over the table. Nina's stomach growled and she said, "My breakfast has run out. I'm hungry, aren't you?"

"Yeah, but I hate to stop. Maybe we can get something sent over and eat it out in the lobby or in the car and then get back to work. It will take a couple more hours to get through the court records. It isn't that there are so many of them, but they are time-consuming to read. I know paper was at a premium, but this is like the clerk was having to pay for paper himself," she chuckled. "I've not seen many examples of handwriting as tiny and crabbed as these. I'm just glad the clerk didn't decide to start writing along the margins when he reached the bottom of the page or turn it upside down and write the opposite way between the lines."

"Me too." Nina stood up, bent, and touched her toes, there was a popping noise. "I'm falling apart. You hear that pop? My hip. Working on my feet all the time is going to kill me. I'm going to go find someplace to order some food, just some sandwiches maybe. Bathroom break too. I'll be back."

"I'd better take a break too. I will go ahead and ask Cora to look for these other items to see if they are here and I'll get online to search for census records. As Nina went outside to order take out, Perri spoke with Cora at the desk and handed her a piece of paper with a few items scrawled on it. Cora disappeared into the back. After the short trip to the court house and back, Perri returned to the table, bending her head to peer through the magnifying glass at the flowery, swirling script that covered most of the page.

***

Perri deposited a folder on top of the stack. "That's the last document. What time is it?" They had rapidly eaten a couple of greasy burgers while sitting in Perri's car before starting in again.

"Two thirty." Nina yawned.

"I have to stand up. Let's review some of this while I walk around a little." Perri walked to the opposite end of the room. "We have each generation in Patricia's line, starting with her, going back to her great-great-grandfather, Jonathon Blackwell. He was born in 1856, married Susannah Martin in 1882 in Russellville. They moved to a farm just south of Russellville very shortly after they married. They had two children; Seth was born in 1883 and Naomi in 1885."

"Right. Both Jonathon Blackwell and Susannah Martin appear on the 1880 census, two years before they married, living with their respective families," Nina read from her notes.

"And there is no 1890 census for this area, not even a surviving fragment, which is exactly the one I'd like to have a look at."

Nina asked, "I meant to ask you, why is there no census at all from 1890?"

"It was a comedy of errors, at best. The 1890 census was the only one since census taking began in 1790 that did not require all parts of the schedules to first be filed in the local county clerks' offices before being sent to Washington. The original census is said to have escaped damage in a fire in 1896 that did destroy the special schedules. It was a close call, and one you think would have given the people responsible for the census a heads up. By 1921, the original and only existing copy of the 1890 census was stored on shelves in the basement in the Commerce Building."

"And then what happened?"

"Another fire started – makes you wonder, doesn't it - and this time the census records did receive fire damage, but not in its entirety by any means. The most significant damage was caused by the water used to put out the fire. Some of it was even under water. In 1933, there had been years of requests from historians, genealogists, and anyone interested in restoring the documents to obtain the remaining records for salvage. They wanted a dedicated storage facility to be built for the safekeeping of unique and irreplaceable records. Unbelievably, the 1890 census was quietly destroyed anyway by the Department of Commerce, no explanation given. Ironically, Congress authorized their destruction only one day after President Hoover laid the cornerstone for the National Archives, where they would have been destined for salvage, copying, and storage. It makes me angry and sick all over again to think about it." Perri pursed her lips and shook her head, hands on hips.

"So back then, Congress had no more interest in the people's wishes than they do now," stated Nina.

"Pretty much."

Cora stopped in the doorway, "Sorry girls, there's no death certificate for Jonathon Blackwell. There is one for his wife, Susanna, but she had married again and her name was Susanna Groves. She died in 1926. Patricia never requested it, but Amy did, just about six weeks ago, so I pulled it."

"Thank you, Cora. Can you make a copy of that for us?" Perri gestured at the certificate in Cora's hand. "We are going to call Sarah Vines and let her know we are finished. Is it ok to use this room to go over this with her?"

"You bet."

***

Sarah sat down eagerly to hear what Perri and Nina had to say. "What do you think?"

Perri took a deep breath, "Well, there isn't anything that really jumps out at me as a motive for murder. Most families do have a few quick marriages and dubious relationships, but…"

"Yes," Sarah leaned forward.

"I don't know if this has any significance at all."

"Doesn't matter, I want to hear it. You never know what might matter or lead us to something else."

"Ok." Perri arranged Nina's and Patricia's notes next each other and tried to summarize as much as possible. "We know from Patricia's notes, the documents she had requested here, and that Amy requested just six weeks ago, that Patricia was doing research on her family tree. The Clerk's office requires a form to be completed by each person for each document they want to see or get a copy of, which means there's a paper trail of what she requested. Doing genealogy in itself is not at all out of the ordinary, but she seemed to be very heavily focused on her father's line only, with no mention whatsoever of her maternal side." Sarah nodded.

"Patricia had attached photos of various family member's funerals and gravesites to her notes about them. It isn't unusual for families to keep photos like these. Most of them are contemporary with the time of the funeral or burial, showing the actual casket or flowers piled onto the gravesite."

"I see," said Sarah. "You say most of the photos were contemporary, and the ones that aren't? Was she out in cemeteries taking photos?"

"The contemporary photos were from the 1960s and 1970s; the colors are yellowing, the way prints from that time tend to do. Other than those, it looks like she downloaded and printed a couple of photos from Graves Online." Seeing Sarah's expression, Perri said, "There's a notation on the back of those printouts citing the person who originally took them and a Memorial number. I checked each of the memorials, and they do match. Those were of more recent graves; her mother being the most recent and an Uncle in 2006."

"Graves Online?" Sarah still looked perplexed.

"It's a website that features online memorials for the deceased. Usually the memorial is created by a family member, but there are always those numbers people out there, or "Collectors" as they are called, who create memorials daily for everyone in the obituaries or all the stones in a cemetery that don't have one yet."

"Why?"

Perri shrugged, "I guess they find satisfaction in their high number counts. Don't get me wrong, most people do a lot of work for no reason other than to help, but not everyone does. The numbers people tend to prize how many memorials they manage, how many photos they have uploaded, the amount of requests they get for transfer. Some of those people tend to be resistant to transfer memorials to actual family members of the deceased who would like to manage the memorial themselves; it affects their numbers. Just like anything, the majority of people are doing this for the sake of memorializing their loved ones and/or to provide publicly available documentation for people doing genealogy who don't live in the area where an ancestor was buried and wouldn't otherwise have access to a photo. Unfortunately, there are some who use it as a personal ego trip. At any rate, the site has developed into a wealth of information for genealogists; although everyone should use it as a guide, still do their own research, and not take everything posted as fact. There are plenty of mistakes made in the information."

"Ok, Patricia had been on this site looking up these memorials for her family and printing the photos?"

"Yes, it appears so," answered Perri. "In going through her notes and comparing them to the certificates she requested, she may have been trying to validate the birth/death of each generation back through her father's line. Photos of gravestones are widely considered solid documentation for dates." Perri turned the list of family members toward Sarah. "As you can see here, Patricia started with herself, at the top, and worked her way backward. There are no notes for relatives earlier than Isaiah Blackwell, her Great-Great-Great Grandfather, that's normally referred to as 3x grandfather. She stopped there for one of any number of reasons: she may not have been able to find any record of Isaiah's father and was still looking, she died before she got that far, or she wasn't interested beyond Isaiah."

"Ok." Sarah waited for more.

"Well, "Perri paused and thumbed through the certificates, "Sorry, I feel like I'm conjecturing too much if I…"

"No, please do. That's what I need. You have done this type of research before and have much better insights into what someone might be looking for in these documents than I would."

Perri continued, "Even though Patricia made notes about Isaiah Blackwell, born in 1832 in Todd County, KY, her focus seemed to be centered more on his son, Jonathon Blackwell, who was her Great-Great Grandfather, or 2x grandfather. He was born in 1856, also in Todd County. He married Susannah Martin in 1882, they had two children: Seth Blackwell in 1883, who was Patricia's Great Grandfather, and Naomi Blackwell, born in 1885."

Sarah said, "Ok. We know who they were, and I take it she had birth and death certificates for those people?"

Perri continued, "There was no reliable form of standardized birth certificate in 1832 and not for some time after that. There could have been a document, but most likely it would have been a birth register rather than a certificate as we know them. However, if there was one, she hadn't found it. Many times, birth dates or years are found in family Bibles or in other records and are written by family members, nothing official. The earliest birth certificate Patricia had a copy of was from 1914, when her grandfather, Nathan Blackwell was born."

"She did request a death certificate for Jonathon Blackwell, but none was found. Cora checked again today and there isn't one here. The same day, Patricia requested a Will or Estate documents, for Jonathan and there were none of those either. That's reflected in her notes. She commented that she couldn't find anything with a death date or any information at all after 1885, which is when she found a birth registry for his daughter Naomi and he was named as the father. Of course, the 1890 census would have been a great help, if we had it, it would be crucial since censuses are only done every ten years and there is a gap of twenty years from 1880 to 1900."

"Let's get the census if it isn't here. Where can we get it?" asked Sarah

After Perri had explained the lack of an 1890 census to Sarah, she continued with the notes that Patricia had made. "She made a lot of notes about her 2x Grandmother, Susannah. Evidently Susannah remarried in 1891, here in Logan County, to Albert Groves. She was then twenty-nine years old and the children were six and eight. It would seem that Jonathon either died or they divorced, although there is no divorce record or documentation of one. They must not have just separated because Susannah was able to marry again."

Perri put down Patricia's notes and picked up those Nina had made. "We went on the internet to look at census records, just to get some idea of who was where in 1880. The Groves family was a neighbor of the Martins, Susannah's parents. The 1870 and 1880 census show Susannah in the household of her parents, she was 9 and 19 on those census records. Albert Groves was seven years older than Susannah, born in 1854, he was also still in his parents' household in 1870 but in his own home in 1880, age 26 and married with three children. We didn't look for documentation for it, unless you want us to, but Albert's wife probably died sometime after 1880, leaving him with the three children. Susannah's husband either died or they divorced between 1885 and 1890, leaving her with two children. Susannah and Albert married and stayed married until they both died. There is a death certificate for each of them: Susannah in 1926 at age 65 and Albert in 1918 at age 64."

Sarah looked at Perri and Nina distractedly, "So…what do you think this…could this mean anything?"

Perri said, "Well, I think it means something, I just don't know if it has any bearing on Amy's death. At any rate, although Patricia documented births, deaths, marriages of her more recent family, which is easier to do of course, she really seemed to have spent more time and effort on Jonathan and Susannah." Perri was thoughtful for a moment, then said, "I really do have the impression Patricia was targeting Jonathan; she was looking for something, something specific."

Sarah asked, "But you don't think she found it?"

"I can't tell that from her notes, her notes don't indicate that she did, but if she did find what she was looking for, she may have stopped writing things down. And about the notes...the only handwriting in her notes that differs from what is apparently her own, may have belonged to Amy. The additions clearly appear to be added at a later time; they are in a different hand, different ink, are a bit crammed between other lines with arrows pointing to Patricia's notes."

Perri stood up and leaned over the table, "For instance, here," and she pointed to a notation made in black ink in the right margin next to Patricia's notes, which were in blue ink." "Right here, Patricia made a note that she couldn't find a death record, or anything else, on Jonathon Blackwell, at least not in Logan County. The added notation, presumably from Amy, says, 'Search other counties for death record, new marriage record, Equity case.' It sounds like Amy was giving Patricia ideas on how to find out more about Jonathon."

"I wonder why she was intent on getting information about a distant ancestor. It was such a long time ago." Sarah said, mostly to herself.

"It could be simply an interest in her family history; a lot of people do enjoy learning about their family. And since he seems to have disappeared, she may have been intrigued with the story."

"It could be, Sarah said, thoughtfully, "but somehow that doesn't fit with her personality. Not that someone can't change or have interests no one suspects, she could have. But my inclination is to look for another reason."

"I will say, that inclination is supported by the fact that she seems to focus more on Jonathan than on his father, Isaiah. If she were trying to go back through the family line, I think she would have been more actively searching for Isaiah. She did have some information on his wife, Judith Blackwell."

Sarah pointed at the stack of remaining documents on the table, "Was there anything in the court records that might point us in the right direction?"

Reading from Nina's notations, Perri said, "There was a claim filed by Albert Groves for a guardianship allowance on February 18, 1887, in Logan County. There are also Guardianship documents, from February 27, 1887, making Albert Groves the Guardian of two Wards: Seth Blackwell, age 4 and Naomi Blackwell, age 2."

"What does that mean?"

"Well, it indicates that Jonathan Blackwell is definitely no longer in the picture. The courts didn't assign a guardian unless the father was absent, for whatever reason. It looks like whatever that reason was, he wasn't expected to come back. Susannah's children were made Wards of Albert Groves. Albert was awarded $7.50 per month toward the children's care, $4.00 for Seth and $3.50 for Naomi. Albert and Susannah married about a year and a half later, on September 22, 1888."

"But the documents assigning Albert Groves as the Guardian came after the claim for funds? Why is that?"

Perri replied, "Albert was probably already sheltering and providing for the children, and maybe even Susannah. Since he and Susannah weren't married at that time, Albert filed the claim to obtain funds to provide for the children. Once he appeared in court and gave his account, the court awarded him the funds and followed up with legal guardianship nine days later. Once they were married, the guardianship allowance would have stopped."

"I see." Sarah sat without speaking. She looked up at Perri and asked, "What's next? Do you think you can find out more about Jonathan Blackwell?"

Perri responded, "I can try, but we do already know there are no further records on him in this Clerk's office. Cora checked for any type of document and there was nothing."

"Ok, if this was your research, what would you do next?"

Perri considered, "I probably would check to make sure there were no further records for Susannah, either under the surname

Blackwell or Groves, which might contain information about Jonathan. Also, I'd check the records in neighboring Todd County. Patricia's notes indicate Isaiah and Jonathan were both born in Todd County. Maybe Jonathan went back there for some reason."

"Are you willing to spend the time to do that?" asked Sarah hopefully.

"Sure, I'd be glad to. I'm feeling pretty invested in this project now too. I want to find out what was going on, if anything," answered Perri.

Nina added, "Me too. I'm good here for another couple of days, but then I'll have to rescue my husband and go back to work."

"Thank you both. You are probably getting headaches from squinting at these records all day."

"I'm up for checking on any more records for Susannah today in this office. We're already here and we've already found some records up to her death in 1926. There probably won't be many more, if any."

"Ok, then. I need to get back out there. We haven't located Rodney Sauer yet; no one has seen him since his display at the tavern Saturday night." Sarah stood up and got her car keys out of the zippered pocket of her purse. "Which reminds me, I do have to ask you both where you were Saturday evening and night."

Nina volunteered, "We ate at the Arrogant Rogue and then went back to the Crow's Rest. We didn't leave again. Alice may have noticed us come back, but she wasn't in the house."

"Thanks. I'll check with her. Talk with you later, call if you find anything," Sarah said as she left.

Perri and Nina looked at each other. "Coffee break then back to the grindstone?" asked Nina. "You got it," answered Perri.

***

Sarah slid into the bucket seat, buckled up, and turned the air to high. Back at the police station, George Wilcox dialed Sarah's cell phone number with a shaky hand. "Sarah Vines," came the abrupt answer.

"Sarah," George was a little out of breath. "You need to get out to the Point at Lake Inola, now."

"George? You alright? What is it?"

"They found Rodney."

Chapter 23

Sarah slapped the mobile light on Subaru's roof, and mashed the accelerator to the floor with mostly urgency but part exasperation. "Damn, damn!" In her head, she ran through George's directions to the little-used road that dead-ended at Lake Inola. "A dead-end road off a dead-end road. Frickin' perfect!" She realized, though, that she was glad it wasn't one of the main roads around the lake or they would have a lot of onlookers in the way, trampling over tracks and any evidence remaining in the area.

"This is not helping!" Sarah yelled at the universe. She slammed the flat of her hand on the steering wheel, hitting a nerve and making part of her thumb and next two fingers go numb. "Crap." She flexed her hand, "Ok, calm down," she coached herself as she sped up the highway.

***

After making a too-fast turn off the highway, Sarah followed, as swiftly as she could, the narrow, paved road to the narrow gravel road to the even narrower dirt road. She practically skidded to a stop behind Brett's patrol car, clouds of loose dust rising in the still,

161

humid air. As she clambered out of her car, another patrol car pulled in behind her and two officers got out.

"Brett, what the hell?" she hurried toward him.

Brett held one hand up to slow her progress. "Hang on. Just a word of warning…"

"Come on, Brett, I'm not a cream-filled puffball I won't deflate or collapse. What's going on?" Sarah demanded impatiently. "You found Rodney?"

"Yes, well, some hikers did. They're over there, by the first car. They are staying in a camper on some relatives' ground, other side of the lake, for a week of vacation. They decided to putt around the lake in a little pontoon boat. They wanted to pull into the bay that runs parallel to this road and as they passed the tip, there's a break in the trees where this road ends, just where the truck is parked, and they saw…it from there."

"It? Saw what?"

"Come on, I'll just show you." Brett spun on his heel and headed away from Sarah, hurrying down the road.

As they swiftly paced down the road, Sarah could see the side of a tow truck. The truck was parked almost exactly crossways in the road, as though in the midst of turning around. As she got closer, Sarah could see the lettering on the door, 'Rooster's Towing – You Crow We Tow." She winced. Rodney's truck. The low-hanging tree limbs on the left side of the road, where the winch was located, hid the end of the truck from Sarah's side, but it would have been visible from the water. Brett looked back at her over his shoulder and pointed toward the rear of the vehicle. "Over here."

Sarah ducked under the foliage and raised her gaze, she stopped. "Oh, God."

"Yeah."

The boom was elevated from its horizontal position. The metal winch cable, used to pull disabled cars onto the flatbed, encircled Rodney's neck at least three times, serving as a noose. The cable continued down and was wrapped around his arms, pulling them so tightly behind his back that his elbows were touching."

Sarah stood at the edge of the bumper and looked up. The position of the cable behind Rodney's head tilted his head forward slightly. The neck was elongated, his normally ruddy complexion was pale just around the lips, which were tinged blue, and the rest of his face was florid. His jaws seemed puffed out slightly, his eyes were milky. There was a fog of flies buzzing around the entire back half of the wrecker; one crawled across a dry, hazy cornea.

Sarah walked to the side of the wrecker facing the lake and looked behind the body. The fists were dusky. "We need to get him down from there. Where is that photographer? And where is the Coroner?" Sarah asked the few officers standing near the wrecker. They all shook their heads. "Get them here now."

"I'm sure they are on the way, Sarah." Brett shifted uncomfortably. "Mike said he'd grab the camera and ride out with Joe. The Coroner was at his home but said he'd be here in twenty minutes. Would you like me to call them again?"

"I'm sorry, no, I'm sure they are on the way." Sarah motioned for Brett to follow her a few yards away from the truck. "Anyone have a look through the cab yet?"

"No. We waited for you...and we didn't want to touch the door or handle, or anything, even with gloves, until Ted had a chance to go over it. Don't want to smear any prints that might be there. It's pretty high off the ground; if we have to grab hold of the handle to get to the cab, so did the person who did this, if that person got in the cab at all."

Sarah nodded thoughtfully, "Of course." She looked into the distance and saw clouds of dust rising in a line toward their location. "Looks like the troops are arriving. I want to talk to the people who found him."

Brett led Sarah back toward the line of police cars. On the opposite side of the first car was a group of five people, two adults, a teenage boy who looked about 14 or 15, and two younger children, somewhere around 8 and 10. As Sarah approached, the adults turned their distressed faces in her direction with relief. "Hello, I'm Detective Sarah Vines. I would like to ask you a few questions and then we'll let you get out of here."

"Please do," rushed the response from the woman, "we need to get the kids away from this. I just can't believe..." she swallowed hard and looked at the man, who extended his hand and spoke.

"I'm Andrew Miller and this is my wife, Rosy."

Sarah shook his hand, nodded at his wife. "Officer Maddux says you are vacationing here and found the body while out on the lake?"

"Yes. We, my family and I, are staying at my brother-in-law's place across the lake. We come down here every other summer for a week's vacation and to visit my wife's family. We live in Colorado."

"You just happened to see the body as you were cruising by in a pontoon boat? Is that right?"

"Well, yes, in a way. I mean, we were just about past the point when we decided to go up the bay we had just passed. We had to turn back a little and as we faced the shore, it was directly in front of us. We weren't that far from shore. It was in plain view. I called the police on my cell phone immediately. They asked us to pull up to shore, away from the area, and wait for them, which we did."

"Did you see anyone moving around the truck or in the woods near it?"

"No," Andrew looked at each of his family members, who all shook their heads.

"Did you hear anything? Anything at all?" They shook their heads again, Sarah pressed, "Nothing? No sounds of another vehicle engine, tires on the road? See any dust rising?"

"No, nothing." Andrew looked pained, "Can we please go?"

"Will you be here until the end of this week?" asked Sarah.

"Yes, until Saturday, when my wife's brother will drive us back to Nashville to catch our flight back to Colorado. I gave our address here and cell phone numbers to one of the officers."

"Ok, thank you very much. If you don't mind, I'd also like you to give this officer your address in Colorado. I'm sorry to prolong this for you."

Sarah crossed the road and walked back to the wrecker. An officer was busy taking photos of the body and the Coroner was unpacking his kit in preparation for on-site examination before transport. The late afternoon sun was slanting across the lake, the water sparkling like gems. Cicadas sang their raspy tunes from the trees surrounding the road. A mosquito made a high-pitched whine in Sarah's ear and she swatted it away.

***

"Brett, why don't you ride back to town with me? Officer Carmichael can take your car."

"Ok, sure." Brett tossed his keys to the other officer and followed Sarah to her Subaru. He slid into the passenger seat.

"I would like you to go with me to make the notification to Milton Sauer."

"I thought you might. That's fine. I dread this though. It's a bad enough job, but with Milton, it could be hairy."

"Exactly. I do feel for him though. No matter what a child is like, it is still losing a child."

"Right." Brett watched the fields pass by as they wound through the roads back to the highway. "Do you have any idea what is happening here?"

Sarah measured her words, "Well, the pieces of this mess are starting to at least seem to have some relationship to each other, I just don't know why."

"What do you mean?"

Sarah stopped at the stop sign then pulled out on the highway. During the fifteen-minute drive back to town, she explained to Brett what she had learned that morning from Perri and Nina.

"Did you ask those two where they were Saturday night? I know they had a couple of altercations with Rodney."

"I did. They were at their hotel. We'll verify it, but I don't think they did this." She reasoned, "It seems likely that the person who killed Amy also killed Rodney. Rodney was killed to ensure silence, not sure about Amy yet, but it appears to be for something that she knew."

Brett smirked, "I am sure the man who hired Rodney to quietly dispose of the car had no idea what he was getting into, because Rodney was probably the last choice for discretionary work."

Sarah frowned and wanted to rebuke Brett for making the joke, but couldn't help smiling. "I know. Good grief." After a couple of minutes of quiet contemplation, Sarah adjusted the a/c directly to her face and said, "What is starting to bother me, and I don't want to make this into a bigger problem than it is, is the fact that Patricia died not long before Amy." Brett turned in the seat to face Sarah, his face shadowed with the dawning realization of what she was saying. "So...if Amy was killed for finding out something by helping Patricia, and Rodney was killed because he disposed of the car used when Amy was killed..." she trailed off.

"Oh, say it isn't so." Brett puffed out a breath and let his head fall back on the headrest.

Chapter 24

"That's it. There is nothing else to find here that I can tell," said Perri as she stacked the last file folder at the end of the table. "I'm beat. Let's call it a night."

Nina stood and stretched, "Tomorrow we go to Todd County? Where do we have to go to look for records there?"

"Elkton," responded Perri with a tired sigh.

"How far is that? Will it take us long to get there?" asked Nina in a weary tone.

"No, not at all. Our hotel is a little bit closer to Elkton than it is to Russellville."

"That's handy."

"That's one reason I picked the Crow's Rest though, because it was kind of in the middle. The second cemetery we went to on Saturday was in Todd County."

Perri and Nina left the files in place and gathered their belongings from the table outside the door of the document room. Cora was at her desk near the front door as they walked toward the exit. "We're done here, Cora. We left the files on the table," Perri hooked her thumb back toward the document room, "and we are headed out."

"Alright-y. You going over to Todd's clerk's office tomorrow? I heard Sarah talking to you about it."

Perri nodded, "We'll go see what we can find there, if anything."

"Well, you girls be careful, ok? I hope you find something. I'll be glad when all this business is over." Cora shook her head slowly back and forth.

"Thank you, we will." Perri and Nina each pushed open one of the doors and stepped out into the warm evening.

The parking lot was in shade and the lowering sun reached its beams along the top and edges of the building. Perri said, "What do you say we pick up something, a pizza maybe, and take it back to eat in the room. I'm done for the day."

"Me too. I don't want to read anything more complicated than a menu the rest of the night. Pizza it is."

Perri realized how hungry she was and looked forward to a pizza, or two. "There's a pizza place on 68; we'll stop there."

They had just gotten back into the Cooper, Nina balancing two hot pizzas straight out of the oven on her purse in her lap, when Perri's phone buzzed. "Hello?"

"Hi Perri, this is Sarah Vines. I'm sorry to bother you, I know it's been a long day."

"Yes, it has. I didn't find anything else in the files today. Sorry, I was going to call you later. Nina and I just picked up a pizza and are headed back to the hotel. We're toast."

"Oh, don't worry about that, no problem at all. Trust me, I would be worn out if I had to look through as many documents as you have today," reassured Sarah. "I wanted to touch base with you about going over to Todd County tomorrow, that still ok with you both?"

"Yes, we were planning on it. That's one reason we wanted to make an earlier night of it tonight, get some rest and head over there in the morning. What time do you want us to be there?"

"I'll call them first thing, around 8 o'clock and ask them to go ahead and start pulling files with the Blackwell's names, in any category. If you can be there at 9 o'clock, I hope that isn't too early, that should give you time to search through the records."

"Do you want us to copy everything?" asked Perri.

"If possible. If there turns out to be a glut of information on Isaiah, give me a call. I'm more interested in Jonathan. We may be able to pick and choose if there are a lot of documents on Isaiah."

"Ok, thanks. That will help. Most of the time I would feel I was being overly ambitious if I was afraid of too many documents, but this would be the one time there might be a cartload." Perri breathed a sigh of relief.

Sarah laughed, "I understand." She paused, "And Perri, there's something else."

"Ok, what?"

"I wanted you to be aware that Rodney Sauer's body was found this afternoon. I know there was an incident where he threatened you following your encounter with his father."

"Oh, my gosh! I see." Perri's face blanched a little bit. She turned to look at Nina with wide eyes and a startled expression.

"What? What is it?" asked Nina. Perri held up one forefinger.

Nina whispered, "What?" and Perri shook her head.

Sarah continued, "I wanted to let you know because he didn't die in an accident. He was killed, um, murdered, and we are concerned that his death is connected to Amy's." She paused and heard only silence. "I can't give details, but I want you to know we feel strongly the deaths are related and if you don't want to continue with the document search, I will understand completely. I don't want you to do anything you aren't comfortable doing."

"Uh, yeah, I thank you for that. I can only speak for myself, but I definitely want to continue. I feel vested in solving this mystery, at least the historical part of it, if I can. But, I can only speak for myself. Can I call you back after I talk to Nina? Just a few minutes?"

Nina plucked at Perri's sleeve again, "What, what?"

"Certainly. I'll wait to hear from you."

Perri ended the call. "That was Detective Vines. She said that Rodney Sauer was found dead today...murdered." Nina let her mouth fall open, said nothing, "...and that they feel pretty sure his and Amy's death are related. She said we don't have to continue the research if we feel uncomfortable. Well, you heard the rest."

"Yeah. Yeah, ok. I don't know. I mean, do you think it's dangerous for us?"

"I have no idea. I want to continue, but Nina, if you don't, I get that. You have a family."

"Uhhhh. I want to, but, you're right. But I don't want to miss out." Nina thought, then said, "Look, tomorrow is my last day to stay here. We're going to another county and will be in a government building all day, right?" Perri nodded affirmatively. "I want to go tomorrow but no more cemeteries or weird abandoned places, ok?"

"No, definitely not! We'll only go the Clerk's office and back here, and we'll get drive through for food rather than go in somewhere, or even ask someone to get it for us, ok? After that, unless there is something else I can do, we'll both be going home Wednesday morning and leaving this behind. Deal?"

Nina nodded, "Deal."

"Alright, I'll call Sarah back and let her know we'll be there."

Chapter 25

Sarah was trying to quietly finish brushing her teeth while she listened to the Coroner's post-mortem examination of Rodney Sauer. When the Coroner was finished, she thanked him and hung up. Based on significant engorgement of the head, it was determined Rodney would have been alive but unconscious when he was hung by the winch cable, his knees bent and the dorsal surface of the feet in contact with the bed of the wrecker. He had first received a strike to the back of the head with a heavy, blunt weapon, the swing progressing from lower to higher, crushing the occipital bone, rendering him unconscious and resulting in a subdural hematoma. The ligature, in this case the winch cable, had been placed high on the neck restricting the flow of blood away from the head while still allowing flow of blood into the head from the deeper placed arteries. The body was no longer in rigor and rigidity had completely subsided; time of death was placed between ten o'clock p.m. Saturday night and two o'clock a.m. Sunday morning. He certainly never regained consciousness, which was a small mercy. It explained how the murderer had been able to wrap Rodney's hands and neck with the cable without resistance, although it wouldn't have been an easy job even with the help of the electric winch. Rodney wasn't a slender guy, which indicated strongly for a male assailant.

***

Perri and Nina were settled at a conference style table behind filing cabinets in the Todd County Clerk's Office. There were two short stacks of files on the table in front of them.

"This isn't too bad. You ready to get started?" Perri asked Nina.

"Bring it on!"

***

They worked through the records in three hours. While many of these documents were quite early, they were not as closely written, making reading easier and quicker.

Nina slumped down in her chair and stretched her legs and arms out in front of her, rotating her ankles and wrists. "Should we call Sarah and see what she wants us to do now?"

"Yes. I think we made some progress." Perri pulled out her cell phone and hit redial from Sarah's call the night before.

"Sarah Vines," came the clipped answer.

"Hi Sarah, this is Perri Seamore. We have finished going through the records here. I'm just wondering where you'd like to meet, and when, to go over the findings."

"Ok, great. You found something?"

"We found a couple of items that shed more light on Jonathan Blackwell, although I think it might bring up more questions," replied Perri.

"Did you get copies of those documents?"

"Yes, we did."

"Ok, fantastic. Can you meet me in Russellville at the police station, at, say, 2 o'clock?"

"Will do. See you then." Perri disconnected. "What do you say we drive through somewhere and eat lunch in the car on the way back to Russellville?"

"Sounds good to me, I'm starving." Nina gathered her purse and notebook.

Perri put the copies in her satchel and her purse on her shoulder. "Let's hit the road."

***

George Wilcox was manning the desk when Perri and Nina entered the police station. "Hello, ladies. You're here for Sarah, aren't you?"

"We are, yes," answered Perri.

"Come right on back." George got up from the stool behind the counter and motioned for Perri and Nina to follow him. Perri walked down the narrow hallway behind George. He was just slightly taller than Perri, a little paunchy, and was doing a halfway decent job of dealing with his thinning hair without making it into a comb over. His belt and holster made a leathery squelching noise as he walked, keys jangled at his waist. "Right in here, have a seat. I'm sure Sarah will be in shortly." George pointed into a room with a table, a few chairs, a sink, small countertop, and a couple of cabinets. "I'll tell Sarah you're here as soon as she gets here." George returned to his post at the front desk.

Perri retrieved the copies from her satchel and put them on the table, as did Nina the notebook with their notes. Perri began sorting through the few documents, putting them in the order she wanted to present to Sarah. George's booming voice greeting Sarah as she arrived was plainly audible.

Sarah entered the room with a smile and grabbed a chair at the end of the table depositing her purse and a briefcase on the floor next to the wall as she sat down. "Sorry I'm a few minutes late."

"No problem."

"Alright!" She scooted the chair closely to the table and leaned on both elbows, "Let's see what you've got." She tucked her dark auburn hair behind her ears and waited expectantly.

"We found some information on Isaiah Blackwell, who appears to have been born in Todd County; his father was Josiah Blackwell, who is noted on the tax records for 1830. My best estimate is that Isaiah was born there because, according to later census records, he was born around 1832. And if so, his father was already in Todd County before he was born. Isaiah stayed in the county throughout his life, passing away 9 June 1888. I have his death date from the Kentucky Death Records listing for 1888. It indicates he died of consumption, which was a term frequently used at the time for tuberculosis of the lungs."

"Of the lungs? It's always of the lungs, isn't it?" asked Sarah.

"No, TB of the lungs is the type we hear about most; it is very contagious. But TB can appear in other organs or body systems like the kidneys, heart, lymphatic system."

"Oh, I didn't know that. But Isaiah had the lung kind, the kind books always describe as coughing up blood?"

"Yes, he had pulmonary tuberculosis. Since there was a death record, I looked for and found, a Will, as well as related documents, like an Estate Inventory and Appraisement. I'd like to show you a couple of other things first and then come back to the Will, if I can."

Sarah nodded in understanding, "Sure."

Perri continued, "Since Isaiah Blackwell lived in Todd County most of his life, he wasn't too hard to keep track of, through census records, tax lists, etc. Something that jumped out at me was a claim included in Isaiah's probate records by a Susannah Martin. There was a copy of a notice in the Elkton Gleaner on July 23, 1888, for all persons with claims to the estate of Isaiah Blackwell to present their claims to the county court prior to the commencement of probate business, which was scheduled for November 12, 1888. One of the claims submitted was filed by a Susannah Martin for a settlement due 'the heirs of Isaiah Blackwell for financial support for their care and well-being,' and it states those heirs as being Isaiah's grandchildren, Seth and Naomi Blackwell; Jonathan's children.

"Really! Ok, what does that mean?" asked Sarah

"Several things. The first thing I would like to do, maybe while we are going through the other stuff is…can we ask Cora, or someone at the Clerk's office here, to look for a record of any kind

178

in the name of Susannah Martin from 1885 through 1888, and let us know if there is one? We know Jonathan was still around at least in early 1885, and Susannah married Albert Groves in 1888. Those are the years we want to check. On Monday, we were looking for records in the name of Blackwell, but if she was using her maiden name, Martin, we would have missed it."

"Definitely, let me call over there." Sarah called the clerk's office and, after a brief discussion, set her phone back on the table and said, "She will look right now, and if she finds something, she'll just run it over to us."

"Great, thanks." Perri picked up the next document. "Isaiah's wife, Judith Parr Blackwell, survived Isaiah. She died in December of 1901 at age 71. When Isaiah died back in 1888, his estate was inventoried and sold to pay all outstanding debts, and his widow was given an allowance of the remainder. The amount of the allowance, $523.02, as well as chattels, that's personal property, that the widow, that's Judith, was allowed to take with her, are itemized and valued. It wasn't a huge fortune, but it wasn't a pittance either. She purchased a small house in Elkton and lived there the rest of her life."

"Ok, does that mean anything?"

"That in itself doesn't, but when I looked through the Bill of Appraisement for Judith's estate done in 1902…"

Sarah interrupted, "Do you mean an Appraisal, like when people have an appraisal done of their house before they sell it?"

"An Appraisement does include appraisal of a house and property, but it also includes all the deceased assets, like money in the bank, carriages, farm equipment, livestock, household furnishings, things that a general property appraisal doesn't include."

"I see, go on."

"When I looked through Judith's Bill of Appraisement, she had a lot of assets and a lot of personal property that she didn't have right after Isaiah died."

Sarah asked, "Why is that unusual; she bought the stuff after Isaiah died."

Perri nodded, "Yes, she did, but the reason it seems strange to me is that even with the allowance Judith was given; after the purchase of her house, and taking in to consideration her living expenses for the next thirteen years, there wouldn't have been enough money for her to purchase these things as well. That is, not on the income she appears to have from the Will and the following years' tax records."

"Ok, I get that, but I don't know how that relates to any of this stuff, the murders…" Sarah frowned.

"I know it doesn't seem to, yet. And I'm not saying I have definitive proof of anything, but something isn't right. There is something about this that is scratching at the back of my mind. I feel like I should recognize it, that it makes sense, but I haven't fit the pieces together completely."

Perri picked up another piece of paper. "This is the Will of Isaiah Blackwell. It was written on October 16, 1887, most likely

Isaiah realized he wasn't going to survive much longer and started getting his affairs in order. He also appointed an Administrator for his estate, his son James Blackwell. James was Jonathan's younger brother, again an indication that Jonathan wasn't around. However, one of the bequests in the Will was "I give to my son, Jonathan Blackwell: Seventy-five dollars, one fine saddle, one double barrel shotgun, one double barrel pistle (pistol), and two horsewaggons."

Sarah asked, "That seems normal to do, to leave something to his son."

"Yes, it does, but the reason I think it is significant is that we know Jonathan seems to have disappeared after 1885. This was written in 1887, so even if Jonathan wasn't in Logan County, he wasn't dead or missing. Isaiah wouldn't have mentioned him in the will if he was, and he died in 1888 without changing it."

Sarah gave a confused sigh. Perri leaned forward and pointed to the items on the copy of the Will. "These items listed as bequeathed to Jonathan were not included on Isaiah's Bill of Appraisement, which they would have been if they were still in the estate when the probate was conducted in November of 1888."

"What does that mean?" asked Sarah.

"I think it means that the items left to Jonathan were given to Jonathan as stated in the Will. It's possible that he was nowhere to be found and the items were distributed somewhere else, but the Executor would have been required to itemize that action, and he didn't." To Sarah's still-puzzled expression, Perri said, "That means Jonathan was somewhere in late 1888, even if it wasn't here.

Someone knew where he was and that he got the items his father left him. And because Susannah filed a claim for support in 1888 and was using her maiden name then, they were no longer together. Susannah's claim was granted, which indicates she had good reason to request it. Maybe Jonathan left the area, abandoned Susannah and the children and never came back. That happened then just like it does now, and it was even easier to do it then."

"Oh. Yes, I can see that. You think that Jonathan was not dead, but was living somewhere, and that someone here was keeping in contact with him?"

"Yes, I do."

As Perri answered, George showed Cora into the room and said, "Hey Sarah, Cora here has something for you."

"Come in, Cora, what do you have?" Sarah stood and made room for Cora at the small table.

"You were right about that, Perri, there was a document under Susannah Martin." She laid a two-page copy on the table.

Perri picked it up, "It's a divorce decree!"

"Read it," "Let's hear it," from Sarah and Nina.

"It's dated August 10, 1887, just under two months before Isaiah wrote his Will. Perri read, "This day, this cause...blah blah...the reading of the Bill and the Deposition filed...blah blah...satisfaction of the court that the proofs have been duly executed and the court now being fully advised in the decrees and orders that the said Susannah Martin Blackwell is hereby divorced from her said husband, Jonathan Blackwell.""

"It continues on to explain the proofs, as it calls them. There is some wording that refers to 'proof' that was submitted that Jonathan was alive and had returned briefly to Logan County at some point, but it doesn't say what the proof was. It says that while he was here, he 'made no contact with his wife and offered no relief to his wife or children' and then evidently disappeared again. It gives their date of marriage, April 8, 1882 and states where they were married and where they were living." Perri scanned the document, "Here, it says, '…states that they lived together as man and wife and a little over six months' time ago, in January 1887, said Jonathan Blackwell voluntarily left his home and their bed with the intention of abandonment, and up to this time he continues and gives no cause for such abandonment.' It also says, 'Said Sarah Martin Blackwell sets forth that said Jonathan willfully abandoned and ceased providing for her or their children. She is asking for a divorce.'

"The divorce was granted based on abandonment," said Sarah.

"Yes. The run down would be that Susannah and Jonathan married in 1882, had their first child, Seth, in 1883 and their second, Naomi, in 1885. Jonathan up and leaves in January of 1887, doesn't come back to Logan County except for at least one time that was discovered, and doesn't provide for his family. It seems to be that at least Isaiah and Judith, and probably James, knew where Jonathan was, but there is no mention of it."

"That must have infuriated Susannah," said Nina, shaking her head.

All three sat quietly, until Sarah said, "So where does that leave us?"

"The last thing I have." Perri pulled out the last copy.

"What is it?" asked Sarah, wearily.

"I know this is dry, but this last document won't make sense unless you know the backstory."

"Ok, I'm sorry, I'm not implying you are boring or anything, I just…"

"The information can be pretty tedious when presented like this. But maybe this will help."

"Ok, what is it," Sarah yawned as she set her chin in her hand with her elbow on the table.

"Jonathan's mother, Judith, died December 1, 1901. Her probate was conducted in March of 1902. Sometimes it took a while to hold probate because they had to make an announcement for creditors, that kind of thing. Among the settlements made, per her Will, was her property, including her house and furnishings, her two horses and carriage, jewelry, as well as a nice bank account. These things, the Will states, were to be divided between her two sons, the youngest being James Blackwell of Russellville, Kentucky, and her eldest son, Jonathan Blackwell, of Guthrie, Oklahoma."

"Oklahoma?" Sarah perked up, "He went to Oklahoma?"

Perri speculated, "Yes, and I think that over the last ten years or more of her life, Judith may have been funded, at least in part, by her loving son. That could be how she was able to afford the luxuries she had when she died. He appeared to have money from something, enough to send a significant amount to his mother, yet he discarded his wife and children."

"Could Patricia have found this out too? Do you think this is what she was trying to research?" Sarah wondered.

"It could be. Maybe she was curious to see if there was still any money in the family, but I can't see how she imagined it would include her. I don't know much about her immediate family, but it sounds like she wasn't close with the few relatives she had."

"No, as far as we know, she wasn't." Sarah confirmed.

"She wasn't close to any living relatives, yet she had been creating some memorials on Graves Online."

Sarah looked up at Perri, "She was? "

"Yes. I checked for memorials for Patricia's family and the one for her father, mother, and grandparents were created by her." Perri drew a stack of papers out of her satchel, "In the cases where she had them, she was scanning and using these old photos of graves to put on the memorial." She tapped the one on top, "Like this one, it's the grave of her grandfather, Nathan Blackwell. He died in 1976. The photo was taken at that time, as you can see by the discoloration and the clothing the people around the grave are wearing."

Sarah looked across at the photo and started to ask another question but stopped and yanked the paper with the photo stapled to it across the table. She stared, disbelieving, at the photo.

"What is it?" asked Nina, who looked at Perri questioningly.

"Oh, my god! This car," she spun the paper around to face Perri and Nina. "This car, right here, parked on the road in the background." Sarah stabbed at the picture with her forefinger.

"Yes, I see it," said Perri, and then looked back at Sarah, perplexed.

"It isn't with the cars on the grave side of the photo. There is a man leaning against the door staring toward the grave. *This* car is the one we recovered from Mr. Fraleigh's property, the one that was used to wreck Amy's car, used by the person who killed her." Perri and Nina stared open-mouthed at Sarah. "This car was at the cemetery when Patricia's grandfather was buried!"

"It was 1976, could it just be a car that looks like the one you recovered?" asked Perri.

"Of course, it *could* be" Sarah spat out vehemently, "I know I don't have proof of this, but the paint job is the same and the car is in the cemetery where Patricia's grandfather had just been buried, here in Logan County. It could be a different one, but it seems unlikely. I have to find out who this man is leaning against the door. Look at him. He's watching the people around the grave."

"He is, that's true. Could he just be waiting for someone, or maybe was at the grave and returned to his car?"

"That could be it, of course, but he isn't parked near any of the other cars. That doesn't mean much in itself, but he seems out of place. Everyone else who appears in the photo is dressed for a funeral. They are wearing their better clothes: dresses and hats with heels, suits and ties. This guy is wearing jeans and what looks like a short-sleeved knit shirt. Also, his stance, arms crossed, deep frown, it doesn't fit to me." Sarah continued to stare at the photo. "I'm going to take this to Ted, see if he can identify anything specific about this car and the one we have. Kind of a long shot though, the entire car isn't in the picture."

Sarah put the photo and the paper it was attached to in a separate section of her briefcase. "I realize you are leaving in the morning," to which Perri nodded. "Could you do some checking online this afternoon just to see if you can find out if there is any record of Jonathan Blackwell in Oklahoma and if so, what kind of business he might have been in? I'm not asking you to stay here to do it, you could do so wherever is most comfortable for you."

"Sure, I can do that." Perri looked at Nina and said, "I think we'll go back to the hotel now. I can check from there and call you if I find anything."

"Works for me." Sarah stood and said, "Now I need to get in touch with the lab and see if we have any new information."

"I hope you do."

Sarah walked out with Perri and Nina. "I really do appreciate your help with this. It was fortunate for me that you are here right now. I could have looked up the records, but I really didn't have time for that and I'm not familiar with the online resources. Thank you both again." To Nina she directed, "And thank you for staying a couple of extra days, I realize you had to make arrangements for that."

Nina grinned and replied, "I was happy to do it. I've enjoyed the work as well as the comfort I feel in knowing my husband got to experience two more days of household chores and close bonding with our son. It was a real opportunity for him."

"Gotcha. Thanks to your husband too!" Sarah hit the remote to unlock her car and waved as she got in.

Chapter 26

"Well, looks like we are done in town. Let's head back to the hotel and enjoy some of the garden and country peace, shall we?" suggested Perri.

"That sounds good to me."

As they walked to the Cooper, a voice said, "Hey there, are you guys leaving town now?" Nick, from the Arrogant Rogue, was striding up the sidewalk.

"Oh, hi there, Nick. We were headed back to the hotel. We're planning on leaving in the morning." Perri said softly.

Nina looked at Perri, noticed the blush, and smiled. "Hi Nick, how are you?" asked Nina.

"I'm good, just heading over to the bar to start my shift. Why don't you ladies come in for a drink?"

Perri looked at Nina and stammered a few uncertain syllables. Nina responded, "Well, that sounds like a good idea. I was getting pretty dry after all the talking, aren't you Perri?"

"Yes, definitely, a drink would be great." Perri put her keys back in the zippered pocket of her purse and returned to the sidewalk. The trio walked past the door to the police station toward the entrance to the tavern. Nick held the door open and waved them in with a flourish, "After you, gentle ladies."

"You just need a costume; you would make a wonderful pirate or medieval gentleman," laughed Nina.

Nick's grin made Perri smile. She was consciously trying not to be what she thought was too obvious. She didn't want to be one of those women. She chalked up her response to having not had more than a couple of dates since her divorce and, even then, it had been more than six months. She told herself it was more nervousness over being out of practice in how to act rather than to the person talking to her. Then she realized she was thinking about dates, and all Nick had done was ask them to come to the tavern for drinks. She felt a little foolish when she realized that she was hopeful about Nick.

"Grab a stool at the bar," Nick said as he walked toward the employee area of the bar, "I'll be right back, just have to clock in."

Perri avoided looking at Nina since she could feel her stare boring into her. She hung her purse on the hanger along the underside of the bar, settled on the stool, and after reading the same line on the draft menu several times, she finally turned to Nina and said, "What?"

"Not a thing Sweetie, just glad to see you react, at least a little, to a very handsome guy. 'Bout time." Nina smiled widely.

"I don't want to 'react,' I feel stupid."

"You aren't stupid. I will call you stupid though if you don't react or you say no."

"Say no to what exactly, he hasn't asked me anything."

"Not yet, good grief, give it time. You don't expect him to run you down in the parking lot after meeting you a couple of times and ask you on a hot date, do you? You'd be the first one to recoil from that." Nina laughed and Perri looked sheepish. "Come on, he asked us to come here and I doubt it was just to sell a couple of beers."

"Yeah, ok. I know. Just don't embarrass me…"

"Why would I embarrass you? I'm hurt," said Nina with mock offense.

"Come on. We aren't sixteen anymore so let's try to behave like…"

"Bwa ha ha, you are too funny. Don't worry, I won't intentionally embarrass you," Nina assured her as Nick came back behind the bar.

"What can I get for you? I'm buying." A dimple appeared on the left side of Nick's mouth when he smiled.

"I'll have a glass of red wine," said Nina.

Nicked nodded and looked at Perri, "And what can I get for you?"

Perri answered, "I think I should have a Dead Guy." Nina shot a questioning look at Perri.

When Nina turned, she said, "Simmer down, it's a kind of beer remember? I figure since this is the Arrogant Rogue, I should have a Rogue's Dead Guy."

"Excellent choice, Perri. Comin' up." Nick took a wine glass from the rack above the bar and filled it with wine that glowed red with the low bar lights. He pulled a bottle of beer from a chiller at the other end of the bar and popped the cap, then set both down on the counter.

"You're going back to the land of the Hoosiers tomorrow morning, huh?" He leaned on the heel of his hands, far apart on the bar, looking at Perri.

"Yes. We had initially planned to go home Sunday, but we were asked to help Detective Vines out with some research so we stayed a couple of extra days."

"Well, I'm glad you did. It sounds like things are getting a little weird, what with Rodney Sauer turning up dead too. First Amy and then Rodney." Nick put a few empty bottles in the recycling bin and wiped the counter, "You haven't had any trouble, have you?" Nick asked.

Perri responded, "None other than with two of the Sauers."

"I heard about Milton running you off his neighbor's property. That guy isn't right."

"I'm sorry Rodney was murdered, but he was thoroughly unpleasant and I don't find it difficult to believe that he got himself whacked."

"Perri…my goodness," exclaimed Nina, staring at Perri with meaningful eyes.

"No, I agree," chuckled Nick, "he was headed for an abrupt end with his attitude and all the things he got into."

"Did he have a lot of familiarity with local law enforcement?" asked Nina.

"Oh yeah! Always something with him. His brother, Howard, used to be like that, but he finally grew up a little bit. As soon as he got some sense about himself, he moved away. Somewhere in Florida I think. Haven't seen him for years."

"What happened to Mrs. Sauer?" Perri wanted to know.

"I think she left a long time ago. I don't remember exactly when but I kind of remember there being a Mrs. Sauer when I was a kid."

There was an awkward silence until three construction workers came in and sat down along the far end of the bar. "Be back in a bit," said Nick.

"Oh, that's fine, you're at work, we understand," Perri quickly took a swig of her beer and nearly choked.

Nina turned in concern, "You ok?" as she handed her a napkin.

"Yes," Perri sputtered as quietly as she could. "I inhaled and drank at the same time. Man, I hate when I do that."

"Look on the bright side, you didn't spit it out all over the bar. That would be bad. And you were worried about me embarrassing you." They both laughed.

After Nick served the three construction guys, a couple more groups of people came in, meandered around, and finally settled at tables. They ordered drinks which kept Nick busy for about fifteen minutes, but his furtive glances back to Perri did not go unnoticed, mostly by Nina who occasionally remarked, "You see that? Mmm hmm." Nina and Perri were both finished with their drinks when he came back, at the same time as more people filtered into the bar.

Nick watched them enter but leaned over the counter, across from Perri. "Now, you guys are heading back up north tomorrow, right?"

"Yes, we are done here. I came to get some research done for myself and to have our annual Girls' Trip, although we didn't do much of the relaxing we were going to do." Perri cast an apologetic look over at Nina, who waved it away. "Then I ended up doing some research for Sarah Vines."

"I heard about that, impressive." Nick nodded, looking Perri in the eye.

"Not really, just looking up records in the Clerk's office. Sarah didn't have time to do it."

"Well, she asked you to do it. That's something that doesn't happen often."

"Really? She seemed very organized and personable enough."

"Yeah, she is, but she hasn't had that position for very long and, you know how it is when you're trying to prove yourself, not wanting to ask for help. There were a couple of other officers who felt they should have gotten the position when Daniel Bales left to take a job in Nashville."

"Oh, I see. I don't know if what we found will help her or not, but I hope so."

"What did she have you doing, if I can ask?"

"She never said not to tell, so I guess I can." Perri told Nick about trying to find some indication of what Patricia may have been looking for in the research she had asked Amy to help her with, as well as the contents of the documents they had found.

Nick whistled lowly. "My, my, Patricia was looking into some serious stuff." He thought for a few moments, "Sarah Vines is thinking that Amy was killed because she was helping Patricia?"

"I believe she does think that, yes. As to the details of why someone would kill her, that I don't know for sure. I traced Jonathan Blackwell to Oklahoma and Sarah asked me to look into anything I can find out about him and his life in Oklahoma tonight and let her know, but that should be the end of it for me."

"Hey Nicky!" came a call from across the room. Nick grimaced and straightened up. The source pointed at an empty glass and bottle, asked, "Another?"

"Ok, Kevin, just a sec. You two want another drink?"

Perri answered, "I do, but I think I'd better pass. I have to drive and I don't want to have to head back to the police station," Perri grinned. "Nina, if you want…"

"No, I'd better not or I'll be snoring like a buzz saw in the car on the way back."

"We'd better go. It looks like your shift is about to get pretty busy."

Nick agreed, "It's that time, I guess."

Perri and Nina stood and slung their purses on their arms. Perri could feel the warmth of Nina's scrutiny, like someone shining a sun lamp on the side of her face. She said to Nick, "Thanks very much for the drink, Nick, I enjoyed talking to you."

"It was all my pleasure, Perri." Nick hesitated, then said, "You know, it's too bad you have to go back now. There's a festival this weekend, nothing much, just a kind of harvest thing, but it's a lot of fun. Can't I tempt you? Plenty of food, drink, and good company, and there's usually a bonfire once it gets dark."

"That sounds great, I'd really like that, but…" Perri stammered.

Nina came to Perri's rescue, "She means 'but I have to take my friend Nina home in the morning so she can get back to her family and to work on Thursday.'"

"Ah, I see, well I will choose to take that as an acceptance of my offer which is only prevented by the interference of a prior commitment." Nick leaned forward a bit, "How's that?"

"That's exactly correct," Perri said with a smile that reached her eyes.

Nick waved in response to another signal from the same table before saying, "Uh, if you don't mind, can I call you?"

"Sure, that'd be fine." Perri stood staring at Nick.

"Can I get your number?" he asked.

"Yes, I'll write it down for you."

Nick slid a paperboard coaster across the bar, turned it over, and pointed to it, "Write it on there, if you don't mind, and I'll be sure not to lose it."

Perri wrote her cell phone number on the coaster and smiled, "Well, goodbye. Thanks again."

"Bye ladies. Please drive carefully and have a safe trip home." Nick smiled, the dimple returning on the left side of his mouth. He waved again as he walked backward toward the opposite end of the bar.

Perri and Nina walked through the big oak door of the tavern. As they started down the tiled ramp another customer, a blond, curly-haired man pushed roughly past them as he came out of the door behind them. Shuffling forward a few steps, Perri exclaimed, "Excuse US." The man hustled away from them without looking back.

"Well, really!" Nina blurted loudly as the man disappeared around the corner.

She and Nina walked into the humid night, the sidewalk still radiating the heat of the day. The crickets had started their evening program and the air was dead still.

When they were a block from the tavern, Nina turned to Perri and said, "'Sure, that'd be fine?' Are you kidding me?"

"What? What should I have said?" came Perri's defensive response.

Nina started to laugh, "It sounded like an answer to someone asking if you minded sitting at a table instead of a booth. 'Sure, that'd be fine,'" Nina parroted. Perri looked dismayed. Nina snickered, "Don't worry, I may not have done any better, but it was all I could do not to laugh right then."

They walked the rest of the distance to the car, Perri in thought. As they got in, Perri looked across the roof of the car at Nina, raised her hands in the air and said, exasperated, "So I carried a watermelon!"

Nina hooted with laughter at the use of their longtime euphemism for making a social blunder where romance was concerned and slid into the bucket seat of the Cooper.

Chapter 27

Nina was curled into the large overstuffed armchair absorbed in reading a mystery. Perri was sitting at the head of the bed, propped up by numerous pillows, and with her laptop on the bed in front of her. She had her notes next to her and was scrolling through city directories for Guthrie, Oklahoma, trying to find a clue to Jonathan Blackwell's business. She hit paydirt when she saw a listing in the 1894 directory: 'Blackwell's Water Company: Wells and Supply.' The owner was listed as Mr. Jon. Blackwell.

"I think I found something," said Perri. Nina looked up from her book inquisitively. "Looks like our renegade owned a water supply company."

"Water supply?" asked Nina.

"Mmm," Perri's fingers clattered over the laptop's keys as she did a couple of searches. Nina resumed reading until, nearly half an hour later, Perri said, "Ok, I think I see what he was doing, or did."

Nina put the bookmark back in her book and turned around to sit upright. "What did he do?"

"In a nutshell, back in 1889, Oklahoma land that had been the home to Native Americans was opened up for settlement by the federal government. There was a massive land grab on April 22, 1889, that started at noon with a pistol shot; more like a huge race of thousands and thousands of people to snatch acreage. Some greedy guts snuck in early, days or weeks prior, to cherry pick sites they wanted, some even hid and camped out. That's where the Oklahoma term "Sooners" comes from."

"Can you imagine what chaos that must have been?" asked Nina, amazed.

"No, I can't. They even had trains bringing people in to make the run. Hopeful land grabbers ran, rode horses, drove wagons, anything you can think of to get ahead of the others." Perri clicked through several tabs on her computer. "The University has an archive of old maps, plats, and other drawings. Our MIA Blackwell appears to have acquired some very prime real estate north of Guthrie, stretching from the current edge of town to the Cimarron River, including the area where Cottonwood Creek branches off the river and flows through Guthrie. His land also had large subterranean water resources." Perri looked at Nina, thinking.

"What does that mean?" asked Nina.

"Well...given the reports of food and water shortages in towns in Oklahoma immediately after the land rush, and also for some time afterward because of the massive increase in population, it would seem to me that Mr. Blackwell had a pretty firm grip on a water supply to the town of Guthrie. He would have made a killing since he essentially controlled the water supply."

"Couldn't people have dug their own wells?"

"Yes, but that takes time and it doesn't supply an entire growing city, including all the businesses and farms. He also controlled a section of the River and streams. Blackwell's Water Company not only dug wells, provided maintenance and supplies, but probably had a stranglehold on the larges sources of water in the area. According to this Guthrie City Directory, in 1894, Blackwell's occupied the entire top floor of a building on Oklahoma Avenue called the Adler Building. He was doing well enough by 1894 to have a large office."

"I see. He ran off, dumped his wife and kids, became a land and business owner, and never came back?" frowned Nina.

"Yep. And there's more. By 1910, Mr. B evidently was also in the oil business, because he is listed in the Directory for that year as owner of Blackwell Oil. I don't see anything that says if the oil was found on the same property, if he bought more land, or just bought into the business somewhere else, but he was doing a bang-up business out there."

"No wonder Patricia was interested in finding out more if she discovered her great-great-grandfather ran off to make a fortune somewhere else and never came back."

"If that didn't interest her, this sure did," said Perri.

"What's that?" Nina got up from the chair and sat on the end of the bed. Perri turned her laptop so Nina could see it. She clicked on a document, which opened and slowly came in to focus.

"This is a marriage certificate between Jonathan Blackwell of Guthrie, Oklahoma and a Miss Prudence Noble of Oklahoma City, Oklahoma, dated 1891."

"Oh wow, that scoundrel ran off and got married again, but, this would not be valid, would it?"

"Yes, because Susannah filed for, and got, a divorce in 1887 based on Jonathan's abandonment," responded Perri.

"That's right. Do you think he knew that or just went ahead and married someone else anyway?"

"I have no idea. He doesn't seem like the type to care and back then there was very little chance of being caught out if no one is looking for you anymore." Perri shook her head.

"What a creep!" Nina had a look of revulsion on her face, "Runs off and leaves his family and just goes on with another life like it never happened."

"The next thing I want to find out is if Mr. Blackwell had another family. He was thirty-five years old when he married Prudence, who was nineteen at the time. Chances are they had children. Jonathan could have had a second family."

"Oooo. Now *that* would be a real thorn in the side if Patricia knew, especially since her family had such a long history of difficulties. And it would also be..."

"…a reason for Amy to be removed if she was poking around in the records. Patricia may not have gotten this far without Amy." Perri pulled the laptop closer to her and said, "Let's check the census records for 1900, 1910, and 1920 and see if Jonathan is listed with a family. His mother died in 1901 and we know he was still in Guthrie then, because her Will placed him there. Unless the name is misspelled or not transcribed correctly, it shouldn't take long to check."

Nina sat cross-legged on the bed and leaned forward on her elbows. Perri first searched the 1900 census. "It's either ironic or a sick coincidence that Guthrie is also located in Logan County, Oklahoma." She bit her lower lip as she typed in the name to search and wait while the arrow circled round and round.

"Let's see, not too many Blackwells. There he is. Let's have a look at the actual image of the census record. The image appeared, there were numerous areas of scrawly writing that was crossed out and rewritten, and a couple of dark areas that looked like water stains. "At least it is legible, and this is the year they included the birth month and year. Awesome. Here they are, living on Warner Avenue. The Head of the Household is Jonathan Blackwell, his wife is Prudence, and there are three children: Edward, age eight, born April 1892; Phillip, age six, born May 1894; and Catherine, age two years and eight months, born October 1897. Jonathan's occupation is listed as Merchant," Perri looked at Nina and made a face.

Nina curled her upper lip, "He did have another family. What a jerk. It's one thing to divorce and move away, but to just abandon your family..." her voice trailed off Perri picked up her phone, "I need to call Sarah and let her know what I found. It's getting kind of late."

"Absolutely." Nina was thoughtful, "I wonder if we'll be able to find out how this turns out in the end. I mean, if they ever catch who killed Amy, and Rodney, if it was the same person. I guess it could have been someone else."

"I bet not, they happened too close together and Rodney was involved with the car used in Amy's murder." Perri dialed Sarah's number.

Chapter 28

Perri had just hung up from talking to Sarah when her phone rang again. She looked at the number but didn't recognize it. "Hmm, who's this I wonder?" She picked the phone up again and answered, "Hello?"

There was a brief pause, then, "Oh hi! Yeah." Perri stood up and walked to the window. "We are, yes." She touched the edge of the curtain, "Oh, well ok, I, let me check. I'll call you back, ok?" She dropped the curtain, "Alright then, I'll call you back." Perri ended the call. When she turned around a minute later, Nina was making an exaggerated silly grin, "Yeeees? Who, pray tell, was that M'lady?"

Perri sighed and plugged her phone in by the secretary. "Nick. He wanted to know if I'd consider coming back for the weekend."

"That's great! You are, aren't you?" Nina asked excitedly.

"Oh, I don't know. I said I'd call back." Perri sat in the rocking chair.

Nina got up and walked to the opposite side of the bed to sit in front of Perri. "Hey, I'm not sure why you are resistant to liking someone, or at least showing that you like someone."

Perri opened her mouth to protest, but Nina held up her hand, "No. Let me say this. I know Alan was a turd, a great big, smelly turd," Perri laughed. "I think you beat yourself up for not recognizing it early on, but who could have? That is something that happens. I know it took you a while to crawl out of the emotional hole you were in, but you still seem to feel like you have to be impermeable to anyone else's charms. You don't."

"Mmm, psychoanalysis your new hobby?"

"No...come on." Nina slapped Perri on the knee. "I just want to see you happy, you big goose. You like this guy, I can see that. He likes you or he wouldn't call you and ask you to come back."

"Yeah, that's probably the thing though, why do I have to come back down here? I just don't want to be the one to always put forth the effort."

"I get that, I do, but in this case, it might be because he is working, at least up until the day of the festival. And the festival is here, not in Vailsburg." Nina leaned back on her hands and raised her eyebrows.

"You're right. I know. Ok. I'll do it. I don't have to work in the next couple of weeks anyway and it'll be fun. Right?"

"You bet your hind quarters it will be fun!" Nina stood up. "Good, I'm glad you are going to come back for some, oh, R&R. Maybe not too much rest." Nina winked.

"I will be sure to keep copious and accurate notes to report back to you." Perri smiled.

"I gotta live vicariously through you girl. I'm too tired at night to have fun of any sort. I'm getting a bath and hitting the hay." Nina snapped her fingers as she headed for the bathroom. "Make your call."

Chapter 29

Wednesday morning breakfast was pleasantly shared with fellow Crow's Rest guests; two couples and a businesswoman. Alice kept the dining table supplied with fresh pancakes, waffles, sliced fruit with cream, fresh bread with butter and jam, and the sideboard warmers with eggs, bacon, and sausage.

The businesswoman was the first to leave, having a meeting appointment to keep, and Perri and Nina followed soon after. Their bags packed and loaded in the car, they checked out at the desk in the Parlor. "Alice, it has been a real treat staying here; I feel like we found a gem in your hotel," Perri gave praise.

"I thank you so much, it was wonderful to have you and I hope you'll come back again sometime. I'm sorry I don't have any rooms for this weekend, but the festival does draw people in and they reserve ahead of time," said Alice regretfully.

"Well, I think it's great your business is doing well," offered Nina. "Hopefully, we can come back down this way sometime again, and I would definitely refer someone here."

"I do hope so. You have a safe trip, now."

Perri and Nina walked through the creaky screen door to the Cooper, sitting in the shade of the trees. "Ready to get back home and your routine?" Perri asked Nina.

"I miss Aaron and Tom, but it has been really refreshing to be away for a few days. I can't say I'm looking forward to work, but then that's normal." Nina turned her face to the morning sun, closed her eyes, and took a deep breath. "The air smells like … corn field."

"I know exactly what you mean, that sort of dusky smell when the corn is close to harvest. I like that too." Both were seated and snapped in. Perri drove the Cooper past the grassy oval in front of the house, out to the county road, and began to retrace their route home.

***

Sarah Vines was at her desk in a small room at the station she shared with two of the other officers. Their work area was half of a larger room that had been sectioned off with an accordion style partition on a sliding track. The opposite end of the room, on the other side of the partition, was the dispatcher area. Emily was currently seated in front of the computer and radio, her mondo-sized coffee and two tiger tails at the ready to get her morning off to a start.

The desk phone rang and Sarah answered her first call of the day, "Good morning, Sarah Vines."

"Mornin' Sarah, Ted here. Got the results from the wrecker for you."

"Oh good, what have you got?"

"Nothing much. The cab was totally clean. I doubt anyone but Rodney was in the cab." Ted yawned.

"Keeping you awake Mr. Baker?" Sarah chuckled.

"Sorry, I'm not with it yet." Ted cleared this throat. "The only place we found anything other than Rodney's own fingerprints, or any other evidence, was on the winch cable. It looks like the person who strung him up got some of their own hair caught in the cable when it was being wrapped around the hands, because it isn't Rodney's."

"How do we know it was the killer; it could be anyone's, couldn't it?" asked Sarah.

"Sure, it could, but it isn't. At least I'm reasonably sure it isn't."

"Ok, Ted, you gonna tell me why?" Sarah let her hand drop down onto her desk.

"Yes, I am. The hair on the winch was a match with one of the hair samples we took from the old Chrysler. Neither sample had the root bulb attached. All we can do is compare, but the shaft of hair from the car is completely consistent with the hair from the winch. I feel fairly confident these samples are from was the killer since it seems very improbable that anyone else who was near the wrecker would have been in the car."

"Yes, that would be the clincher. Fantastic."

Ted blew out a long breath right into the receiver, "One more thing. There was a crowbar recovered from the periwinkle vines along the side of the road, probably went with the wrecker, but I found blood and hair on the end. Matches Rodney's hair and blood type. No prints on the cabling or framework, gloves again. But you are looking for someone with sandy blond hair, not cut too short; the sample was five inches long, wavy."

There was a pause and Ted continued, "And…we got a hit on a set of fingerprints from the Chrysler."

"You did? Who?" Sarah asked eagerly.

Ted read the results, "One Andrew Kratz, lives in Elkton, or at least he did when he was arrested for fraud in 2012. Owned a garage and was charged with fixing things that weren't broken. Did a little jail time, no problems since then."

Sarah scribbled down the information, "Where were the prints found, Ted?"

"Steering wheel, door handles inside and out, oil cap, air filter…"

"Anything else?"

"No, that's it.

"Thanks Ted. Good job." Sarah ended the call. She leaned over the arm of her chair and slipped the paper with the cemetery photograph from her briefcase. The man leaning against the car had blond hair, not sandy blond. "This photograph is forty-two years old. But, I wonder…" Sarah picked up the phone.

***

As the Cooper traveled down the last long stretch of highway toward Vailsburg, Perri's phone rang. She pressed the button on her steering column that would let her talk hands free. "Hello?"

"Hello? Perri, is that you? I can't hear you." Sarah found herself talking very loudly.

"Yeah, it's me. Sorry, top's down. What can I do for you?" Perri shouted. Nina pulled her sunglasses down to look over them and silently mouthed the words, 'What now?'

"Sorry to call you yet again, I really am. But I was wondering if, when you …"

"Sarah, I lost the last part of that."

"Ok. When you found Jonathan Blackwell's second family, how far down the line did you go? I mean like his grandchildren, or any further?"

"No. I stopped when I found that he had a second family. I only documented his children. I wouldn't be able to go too far down the line, not online anyway, because even census records are kept private for 70 years."

"Oh, I see."

"It could be done, but it would take a little longer and involve a few more resources, some I may not have access to."

"Ok, I understand."

"Are you interesting in finding Jonathan's descendants"

"That's exactly what I want to do," said Sarah.

"I tell you what, Sarah. I'm going to be coming back down there Friday morning."

"You are?"

"Yes, I …was invited to go to the Festival there this weekend. I'm taking Nina home and will come back Friday. If you still need help then, I can try to work on it for you."

"That would be a huge help. I hope I don't need it by then, but if I do, I'll appreciate your input. I'll let you go. Thanks."

"Bye." Perri pressed the disconnect button.

Nina gave Perri an exasperated look, "Tell me that you are not going to spend your weekend with Nick working on this stuff again?"

"No. Not all of it, at least."

"Perri, come on!"

"Nina, calm down, I'm not going to put off Nick to do it." Nina stared at her. She held up her right hand, "I promise!" Nina still stared. Perri held up two fingers, "Girl Scout's Honor?"

"Ok." She pointed at Perri, "I am going to check up on you. I am."

"Alright, ok."

The Cooper crossed the city limits of Vailsburg and Perri turned off the highway, toward Nina's house.

***

Perri unloaded her luggage, satchel, and the coffee cup and snack detritus from the last few days, then sorted her laundry and got the first load started. She took a look in the full-length mirror on the bathroom door after self-consciously noting that her jeans were a little more snug than they had been last week. Talking to her image accusingly, she asked "Did you think you could get away with eating

213

like a ravenous pig for four days?" She made a salad for lunch and planned to go for a long walk afterward, knowing that that part probably wouldn't happen.

After washing up her lunch dishes, Perri went to the bedroom to start on the plan for what clothes to pack for the weekend. 'Oh man, I don't have more than one really decent outfit,' she thought to herself as she flicked through the items in her closet. Scrubs, scrubs, faded jeans, old shirts. She made the decision to buy a new pair of jeans and a couple of shirts so she didn't look like a scruffy bum. "I hate shopping, but, gotta do it." She grabbed her purse and set off to get the job done.

Chapter 30

Sarah settled down in a booth at the downtown diner to eat the decent breakfast she didn't have the time to make for herself and drink large amounts of coffee while reviewing everything she had on the case. Periodically, someone would stop to ask about progress or if an arrest was imminent. She was glad she could reply that she wasn't able to discuss the case, since she would have had nearly nothing concrete to tell them. With the exception of the fingerprint match, which was being followed up on, the dearth of physical evidence forced her to rely on whatever possibilities she could squeeze out of the research Patricia and Amy had been doing. She took out a new notebook and started making notes on a fresh page.

After a three-egg omelet with toast and hash browns and at least four cups of coffee, Sarah had re-read all her notes from start to finish. She had the beginnings of a rough formulation for a possible solution. She rubbed her temples with her fingertips. Pretty shaky theory right now, but it was something. She decided to continue in her office, where she would have the privacy to make calls. She paid her bill, leaving an ample tip since she had once been a waitress and knew how tips sometimes made up the better part of a waitress's income.

Once back at the station, she separated from the pile the information she had received by fax that morning from the Guthrie public library and chamber of commerce. There was a Blackwell Oil & Synthetics in Guthrie, Joseph P. Blackwell listed as the CEO. The company had remained in its original city, Guthrie, since its inception, although it was now housed in a brand-new building in a business park on the west edge of town. This was the second new building the company had built and occupied over the years since the business began on Oklahoma Avenue during the booming growth of the city in the 1890s. Blackwell had diversified and branched out into plastics manufacturing in the 1980s and added synthetic fabrics to their product lines, in 2001.

The business reports showed its ups and downs over the intervening years, especially during the Depression when it nearly folded, but it had done quite well in the last fifteen years, exceptionally well since Blackwell Oil & Synthetics had obtained a number of lucrative government contracts that were renewed at every expiration date. It was the synthetics line that afforded Blackwell the military contracts, for anything from webbing for tarps and ammunition belts to wallets, pouches, duffels, equipment covers, and dozens of other items.

War could be a staggeringly profitable and rewarding business for those who didn't have to suffer the anxiety of having a family member deployed, lose a family member, need to close their business, or have to serve themselves. The Blackwell family had profited from their contracts quite well, the family members who worked for the company bringing home salaries in the millions. None of them appeared to have served in the military since WWII, when Nathaniel Blackwell had been in the Army Air Force.

There was a company phone number. Sarah dialed it.

"Good morning, Blackwell Oil & Synthetics." came the rapid, yet bored, greeting.

Sarah introduced herself and asked to speak with Joseph Blackwell. "I'm sorry, Mr. Blackwell is not available. May I take a message?"

"I understand that you probably give this standard answer to anyone who calls asking directly for Mr. Blackwell, but I'm calling from the Russellville, Kentucky Police Department. This is a police matter and I need to speak with him."

"I'm sorry," the voice repeated, "Mr. Blackwell is not available."

"Alright, I will take that to mean he would prefer the police come to your office in person to speak with him personally. I can go ahead and get that arranged." Sarah had the receiver halfway from her ear to the phone when the receptionist broke from her script.

"No. Don't do that." She hesitated, obviously trying to assemble her response in the best way she could to prevent herself from getting in trouble. Her voice lowered, "Mr. Blackwell is ill and he isn't in the office. He hasn't been for over a month. Look, I'm not supposed to let that out, but…you ARE the police, aren't you? Oh God."

"Yes, yes, I am who I told you I was. I'm sorry Mr. Blackwell is ill. Would I be able to call him at home, or perhaps talk to someone else in his family?"

"I don't know that. No. Can I just take a message? I'll just pass the message on." She seemed very agitated.

"Ok, but no, don't take a message. I'll go about contacting him another way. What is your name?"

"Do I have to tell you?"

"No, but if you don't I will find out anyway and it will be easier for both of us if you tell me yourself," replied Sarah.

"I'm Kim." She waited, "Kim Elhoff. Don't say anything. We aren't supposed to let anyone know he's sick."

"Alright, I won't reveal that you told me about it. Don't fret over it, there are other ways I could have found this out. Thanks, Kim. Goodbye."

Sarah replayed the conversation in her mind. Why was the receptionist all uptight about telling anyone the CEO was ill? Obviously, it must be a serious illness if he had been absent for over a month, but what was the reason for secrecy? "On to Plan B."

***

After getting all her bills squared away and doing everything she could do until time to leave, Perri found herself getting anxious about the weekend. It had been quite a while since she'd actually gone on a date. She considered what Sarah had said when she called yesterday, about maybe needing to call Perri if she needed some more research done, and decided to pre-empt having her weekend interrupted by doing the research that day. If she found anything worthwhile, she would go ahead and forward it to Sarah.

Making family connections and researching people who had lived more recently than the early 1900s, or who were still living, was sometimes much more difficult than those who had lived further in the past since restrictions were in place to prevent finding out too much personal information without some sort of official access. But Perri had an idea that might make it easy to at least get a general idea of the Blackwell family, if she could find it.

After eating a light lunch of steamed veggies and taking a walk, Perri felt justified in sitting down with a glass of sweet tea to nose around on the internet for the Blackwell bunch. She searched online trees on various genealogy sites and finally came up trumps with one she felt may be the same Blackwell family.

The tree allowed public viewing, so she was able to go through each generation. The more recent generations in this Blackwell Family Tree were not the same as Patricia's, but at the fifth generation, they converged; the tree was the same. It could have been a coincidence, but it seemed unlikely. There were too many matches. The sixth generation backward was Isaiah Blackwell, same birth and death years, as well as his wife, Judith Parr, same birth and death years. The fifth generation, their son, was Jonathan Blackwell, born 1856, just as Patricia's 2x Great Grandfather. This is where the similarity to Patricia's line ended. As Perri had found in the

Oklahoma marriage record, this tree showed Jonathan Blackwell married to Prudence Noble with the same three children that she had noted on the 1900 census.

The branches of the online tree continued down from Jonathan, through his son Edward and grandson Nathaniel. Beginning with Nathaniel's son, names no longer appeared and the next generation was designated only as "Living." And born in 1941. No personal information was viewable. Since the most recent census record available to the public was 1940, Perri wouldn't be able to find that information on a census. The next generation was of course also noted as Living, with a son being born in 1977. Again, no identifying information was available.

Perri saved a couple of screen shots of the tree, which included the tree owner's site ID in case Sarah wanted to contact them for information, then composed an email to her. She explained that since she was going to attend the festival in Russellville with Nick Silver on Friday night and would maybe see him again on Saturday, she had gone ahead and done some more checking in advance. Perri described what she had found and how to contact the person who created the tree. She attached the screen shot files, and sent it. She shut down her laptop and placed it on the desk in the second bedroom. She had decided not to take it with her, but to try to have a weekend as free from electronics as possible. Feeling she had done what she could at not-so-subtle hinting around that she didn't want to do research over the weekend, Perri got back to fretting about her date.

***

Sarah Vines opened Perri's email and the screen shots that were attached to it as soon as it popped up on her screen. She read the email and looked at the images with a cold creeping at her neck. At Perri's suggestion, she had immediately emailed the owner of the online Blackwell tree. She would check her email frequently until she got an answer.

Before she was finished in the office, Sarah had contacted the Guthrie Police Department and explained the situation in Russellville. She told them about the documentation she had concerning the Blackwell family, their possible relation to the incident, and her experience when talking to the receptionist at Blackwell Oil. She gave enough detail to ensure they understood why it was important she, or someone in their department, be able to talk to Joseph or a member of his family. Sarah had been told they would check on Mr. Blackwell and call her back.

After straightening up her desk and washing out her coffee cup, Sarah headed home with a sneaking feeling this might be the last full night's sleep she had until this was over. And she wasn't placing any bets on sleeping well tonight.

221

Chapter 31

Friday morning, Sarah checked her email while eating a bowl of cereal in the kitchen. Her stomach soured a little when she read the reply from the Blackwell tree creator, a woman named Laura Wyatt. The information from the tree was consistent with the idea Sarah had been forming the day before. She was eager to figure out the mystery and solve the murders, but she didn't like the direction it was going. In reality though, no direction was going to be good, so no point in wishing it was different.

According to Laura Wyatt, the first unnamed 'Living' person in the online tree, the one born in 1941, was Joseph Blackwell. This significantly bolstered Sarah's newly hatched idea. The other 'Living' person was his son, Jason, born in 1977. The creator of the tree was not a Blackwell, but a relative of the maternal side of Joseph's wife, Blanche Wyatt. Laura was a once or twice removed something or other. She couldn't tell Sarah anything about their personal lives since she didn't live in the same area and was not in contact with them. She said she only knew them through her family and hadn't met them in person before. However, she had been able to verify enough information about them that Sarah could confirm the Joseph Blackwell in the tree was the Joseph Blackwell who owned the oil company in Oklahoma, and it seemed certain that he was the descendent of the Jonathan Blackwell from Logan County, Kentucky. Laura had been instructed not to notify anyone in the Blackwell family that she had been contacted. Sarah shot a quick email to Perri to let her know who the two Living members of the tree were, and to thank her for checking.

As she was getting dressed after her shower, she took a call from the Guthrie police department. According to Officer Simms, they had been unable to interview Joseph Blackwell. He was not in his office and when officers had gone to his home and asked to speak briefly to Mr. Blackwell, his wife had refused, saying her husband was too ill to talk. Officer Simms had asked what illness Mr. Blackwell was suffering from, but she had also declined to comment on this. Officer Simms asked if Jason Blackwell was available for an interview, but Mrs. Blackwell had insisted the police mind their own business unless they had a warrant or planned to arrest her. The officer had been obliged to leave without obtaining any information, since, at that point, there was no firm information with which to secure a warrant.

Lacking any progress with the family, he had spoken with the neighbors on each side of the Blackwell home. The neighbors gave benign summations of Joseph, but their estimations of Blanche were not as harmless. Joseph was described as being a rather quiet man who was polite when they encountered him, but that it wasn't very often. The picture painted of Mrs. Blackwell was of an aloof, snooty woman who only cared to talk to people outside her social circle if she could be giving them instructions on mowing the lawn, caring for the gardens, or cleaning the pool. The neighbors hadn't seen Joseph for some time, but it wasn't all that unusual since the houses were situated on large lots and the Blackwells drove into their garage and closed the door without walking around outside where someone might speak to them. Jason was not an unfamiliar visitor to his parents' house, but the neighbors had not noticed him lately either.

Sarah guttered out a sigh of exasperation and finished getting dressed.

***

Perri hadn't slept very well Thursday night in anticipation of seeing Nick the next day. Contributing to her restlessness was that Nick had called her in the evening to say hello and, as he said, make sure she hadn't changed her mind about coming back to Russellville. She had known she was going to have difficulty getting to sleep, but she hadn't wanted to take something for fear she'd sleep like a corpse as well as feel like she had a hangover the next day. Instead, she drank two cups of chamomile tea which mainly caused her to get up to go to the bathroom during the night.

After what seemed like sixteen hours of fighting the covers, flipping the pillow over a couple dozen times to get to the cold side, and tossing like a jumping bean, Perri got up as soon as light peeped around the blinds. Her bag was already packed and the clothes she wanted to wear that day were laid out. She was eager to get on the road, figuring the tense apprehension she felt would get better if she could get the day started.

She was ready to go by 8:30 which was way too soon because she didn't want to get there so early that she looked like a stalker. Nick would be working the day shift anyway. He had asked her to come in to the Arrogant Rogue when she got to town, but she figured it wouldn't be a good idea to sit on a stool and ogle him for most of the day. She spent as much time as she could watering her flower beds, putting away the folded laundry, and anything else she could find to do to keep her busy.

Nina called close to noon to catch up and see if there were any developments. "No, I haven't heard from Sarah."

"No, you dope, I mean Nick. Have you talked to him?"

"Oh, yeah, I have. He called last night."

"Good. Spill!"

"He just called to make sure I was still coming, and to ask me to come by the tavern when I got into town."

"See, this is why I ask. I didn't know that and it's important for me to know. You know that I am living through you on this. Keep me in the loop." Nina laughed, then asked in a conspiratorial tone, "Soooo, where are you staying, hmm?"

"I did get a hotel room, come on now. It's just one of those generic places, right as you get into town. I was glad to be able to get a room at all. I'm not going down there without a place to stay. That would be pretty bold, wouldn't it? And what would Nick think then?"

"Yeah, I get it. I wouldn't do that either. I'm just a bit overzealous. I'm hoping you have a really great time."

"And that you will have a really great time by me telling you about it?" Perri laughed.

"You got it."

"Thanks, Nina, I think I will have a wonderful time. I'm nervous though. It's been a while since I was all nervous like this."

"Once you get there and get the ball rolling, you'll be fine." Nina's tone shifted gears, "Alright, I gotta go. I grabbed a break to call and see what was going on."

"Oh, sorry, that's right, you're at work. How's it going?" asked Perri.

"Same as usual, the case I would have been in on right now cancelled though, blood sugar sky high, too high for surgery. I had a few minutes before starting the prep for the next one."

"I'll call or text you when I can this weekend, ok?" said Perri.

"You bet! Have a good time, catch you later girl." Nina sung into the phone, and hung up.

Perri looked around the house. Everything was done, put away, or taken care of. "I'll make lunch and eat, then I'll go." Which is what she did.

Chapter 32

The drive back to Russellville calmed Perri's nerves a little bit. She kept the top up on the Cooper, but sang to the radio at the top of her lungs. Maybe she'd be a little hoarse when she got there. Wasn't it sexy when a woman has a husky voice? Her stomach wasn't churning like it had been since last night, at least not until she pulled into town. It was around 3:45 when she drove into the hotel lot and checked in. Her room was on the second floor, about as far from the elevator as it could be, but she wasn't going to complain about that since she had at least gotten a room.

After putting her bag in the room and freshening up a bit, Perri left the hotel and drove to the Arrogant Rogue. Her palms were sweaty on the wheel but not from the heat, which had mercifully let up and dropped down to the upper 70s. It was still only September 4, but the temps were starting to give way on some days. Perri looked forward to Fall, her favorite season, and the first day when the heat broke seemed like a signal to her.

After locking the car, she checked her image in the window of the driver's side door, which wasn't a good idea since it made her look squat and misshapen, then took a centering breath and walked toward the tavern. She couldn't resist looking at her reflection in the passing window fronts, decided she didn't look too bad after all, and even if she did it was too late to do anything about it. She pushed the door open and stepped into the cool interior of the tavern.

It was a quarter past four o'clock and there were a few tables of early diners and a handful of patrons at the bar. Nick was mixing up a cocktail of some sort in the shaker tin, his t-shirt sleeve sliding up and down with the motion. Perri could see the ripple of defined bicep and triceps muscles in his arm as he shook the canister back and forth. As he poured the drink into a martini glass, he caught sight of Perri still standing just inside the door and smiled. He slid the drink down the bar to the pick-up area and wiped his hands on a towel. Perri walked to the short portion of the L-shaped bar and sat on a stool, hanging her purse on a hook.

"Hey, look who's here! I'm glad to see you. Was your trip ok?" Nick asked as he spread his arms wide and leaned on the edge of the bar.

"It was, thanks. I'm glad to see you too."

"I've been looking forward to tonight all day, well, really since you left." Nick looked directly into Perri's eyes. "Are you staying out at the Crow's Rest again?"

"No, Alice didn't have any vacancies for this weekend, because of the festival. I'm staying at the hotel over on 9th Street." Perri grinned what she felt was a goofy smile.

"I know the one." Nick continued, "I'll be done here at five o'clock. We can go down to where the food booths are and get something to eat. Hope you're hungry, food is the biggest attraction at this festival. There's going to be a get-together out at a friend's place tonight too, bonfire and all that."

"That sounds great." Perri felt a little self-conscious under Nick's steady gaze and looked around the bar.

"You want a drink? Wow, I'm a bartender and I didn't ask you if you want something to drink." Nick shook his head.

"No, thanks, I think I'll wait, maybe have something later."

"Ok. Hang on a minute, be right back." Nick took a few long strides to the opposite end of the bar to fill a drink order for two beers. Perri surveyed the room and the other customers. Most people seemed to have just gotten off work and were eager to start their weekend. A couple of the people seated at the bar were alone. At the further end of the long section of bar was a woman who looked to be in her mid-fifties. She was dressed up, bleached haircut and styled, and keeping a close eye on the door. The other customer, at the near end of the bar, about three stools down from Perri, was a man probably in his late 30s, early 40s, his sandy blond hair combed with some sort of gel but still obviously curly. He sat stiffly on his stool, looking straight ahead or down into his highball glass. Nick came back to where Perri was seated.

"I should let you get back to your work," she laughed. When Nick looked like he was going to protest her leaving, she interjected, "I want to go back to the hotel and get cleaned up. Traveling, even for only a couple of hours, always makes me feel like I've been walking on a dusty road all day."

"I know what you mean," agreed Nick. "Are you free from doing work for Sarah Vines this weekend?" Nick turned around to get a soapy cloth to wipe a spill on the bar next to where Perri was seated. The blond man at the bar closely watched Nick and frowned at him. Nick stopped and said to him, "Can I get you something else?" The man shook his head and looked back down to the bar.

"I am work free, as far as I know. She called me when I was on my way home Wednesday and said she might need me to look up...well that she might need some more research done on Patricia's family, but she couldn't be sure yet. She just wanted to know if I'd be available if she did. I told her I was busy tonight, and probably tomorrow too, but that she could let me know."

"Let's hope she solves her murders without needing further assistance from you! I don't want to have to share you this weekend!"

"Why, thank you, I truly hope I don't have to be shared. I took preemptive action and did the research and sent it to her already." Perri took her purse from the hook under the bar. "I will go ahead back to my hotel and get cleaned up. I'll await your call."

"Sounds like a plan. I'll buzz you when I'm leaving here, ok? It'll only take me a few minutes to get to the hotel. Which room are you in? I can come up when I get there."

"I'm in 227." Perri stepped down from the foot rail. "I'll see you soon then."

"I'm looking forward to it," Nick smiled his dimpled smile again. Perri slid off the barstool and turned to leave, nearly colliding with the man who had been seated at the bar who had also risen to leave. He mumbled a quick "Excuse me," and left. Perri smiled back at Nick, then exited behind him. She continued to smile to herself walking back to her car, not even thinking about looking at her reflection.

Chapter 33

Sarah set the receiver back into the cradle. The hunt for the last owner of the Chrysler had been a laborious search of stored paper records by some unfortunate desk duty officer in Frankfort. His relief in finishing the task was obvious when he called Sarah just after three o'clock in the afternoon with the registration information. The car was last registered in 1997 to a Frank Quillen. The registration address was in Elkton.

Sarah checked the current property records for the address listed on the registration through the Todd County Assessor's Office, but unsurprisingly, the home no longer belonged to the Quillen family. In 1997, the house had been owned by a Mr. Walter Quillen who purchased the house new in 1969. The property was sold in 2004 and had changed hands twice since then. Sarah figured Walter Quillen was most likely Frank's father, or at least a relative. A check of three different online telephone directories placed a Frank Quillen in Needles, California. She thanked her lucky stars for the unusual name.

Sarah dialed the phone number. A woman answered who told Sarah in an annoyed tone that Frank was at work, not at home, but she did give her his cell phone number. Sarah called the cell's number. A man answered, "Hello?" he said loudly. She could hear a lot of traffic noise and sounds of machinery.

"Is this Mr. Quillen?"

"You'll have to speak up, can't hear you."

Louder, "Is this Mr. Quillen?"

"Yes, hang on a minute." Sarah could hear sounds of walking, as though on rocks, then steps, followed by the background sound being dampened to a manageable level. "Yes, this is Frank Quillen. Who's calling?"

"Hello, Mr. Quillen, my name is Sarah Vines, I'm a detective with the Russellville Police Department, in Logan County, Kentucky."

"Oh, my gosh, ok, what do you need with me?"

"I am hoping you can give me a little insight into the circumstances of a vehicle you once owned and last registered in 1997, a 1975 Chrysler Cordoba?"

There was silence on the other end, then, "Oh man, I forgot about that old car." He laughed, "What the heck is up with that?" He stopped laughing, "Am I in trouble for leaving it there?"

"No, not at all, Mr. Quillen. But what I do need, if you can, is for you to give me an idea of your history with the car, how long you have been in California, and why the car was last registered in your name and is still here in Kentucky when you aren't."

"Alright. Let me see." He exhaled slowly into the phone, "I'm originally from Elkton. I was eighteen years old when I got that car. It was right after I graduated high school, 1996, and I got my first job, for Lawson's Construction. I wanted to get my own house and car. I couldn't buy a house or a new car. I found a house to rent, on the south side. There were still residents in the house who had until the end of the month to move out. The landlord had that old car in a carport out behind the house and I saw it when I looked at the house. I asked about it because I was in the market for a car. The agent said he would check with the owner to see if he wanted to sell it. He did and I bought it from him for almost nothing."

"Ok, you bought the car when you still lived on Tulip Street, is that right? Was that your parents' house?"

"Yeah. I registered the car to that address because I did still live there at the time; I was waiting for the current tenants to move out. It was near the end of the registration year for 1996, so I registered it for the additional couple of months, through 1997. I never changed the address. By the time I needed to register it again I knew I was moving out here. I always wanted to live in California and had been hired at a construction company out here. I still work for them, I'm a Foreman now."

"I'm glad to hear you have done well in California. You didn't want to take the car with you?"

Frank laughed, "No, I was afraid it might not make it for one thing. It was 22 years old by then, older than me. And...I didn't have enough money to feed it gas every three or four hours all the way out here. It's a guzzler. I guess I shouldn't have just left it there, but I had a lot to do what with packing, trying to find a place to live, and then moving. I knew I wouldn't get much for it if I sold it and I didn't have time to do that anyway, so I just parked it back in the carport and left it there, then I forgot all about it."

Sarah then realized that when she made the request for registration information on the Chrysler, she hadn't asked for information regarding previous owners. "You said the car had belonged to your landlord at the time, what was your landlord's name?"

"Oh, what was it?" he asked himself. "It's been a long time. It was Joe something, I can't remember his last name. I never met him, he did everything through a rental agency. He didn't live in Kentucky."

Sarah felt the blood draining from her face. "Mr. Quillen, was your landlord's name Joe Blackwell, by any chance?"

"That's it! Yes, Blackwell. Now I remember. He lived in Kansas…no, it was Oklahoma. Some city in Oklahoma."

"Mr. Quillen, this is important or I wouldn't ask, can you remember the address of the house you rented? Or at least where it was located?"

"Sure, it was on Poplar, 619 Poplar."

Sarah hung up the phone. Her ear ached from having the receiver jammed into it all afternoon. She had made a lot of progress. It made up for the complete lack of progress over the last week, but her adrenaline level was inching upward by the minute as the pieces began to fit together and she realized her problems, their problems, were not over.

She snatched up the phone to again call the Todd County Assessor's office. She put in an urgent request for the deed or property ownership of 619 Poplar Street in Elkton, now and as far back as they could go, with instructions to call her on her cell phone as soon as the information was available. The reaction to her emergency request for property information late on a Friday afternoon was met with grudging verbal agreement which in no way promised actual results. Sarah definitely felt the prospect for a speedy result was pretty dismal. She called the Elkton PD and requested a little expediting assistance if possible. If what she thought was true was indeed true, she had to have something concrete to work with; acting on assumptions was never the best idea.

She then called the Guthrie police department again and asked to speak to the same detective she had spoken with earlier. When he came on the line, Sarah explained the developments of the afternoon and requested a photo of Joseph Blackwell as well as information on vehicles he owned. Detective Falls was amiable and promised to fax a photo as quickly as he could get one. It was 4:43 p.m. and that was really all Sarah could do at the moment.

She made a list of pending information in her phone to avoid shuffling through paperwork to find it. That was when she recalled that Perri had said she was returning to Russellville that day for the festival, which had started about an hour ago. Perri was in town and probably walking around downtown and elsewhere. She called

Perri's cell phone number, but the call went unanswered and Sarah was forwarded to voice mail.

Becoming more anxious than she had been, she scooped up her purse and phone. George Wilcox was manning the counter. Sarah barely slowed down as she went through the lobby and hurriedly told George that she was waiting on vital information either by phone or fax, or both, and asked him to forward calls to her cell phone, and if a fax came through to take a picture of it and send it to her phone. He nodded, "Ok, Sarah, sure, I sure will. But Sarah, do you need someone to go with you." As Sarah darted out the door she said, "George, I'll call you if I do, I'm not sure," and ran to her car.

Chapter 34

The hotel parking lot was nearly full when Perri got there and she had to drive around twice to find a space to park the Cooper. She muttered to herself, "Gee, I'm glad I'm not going to be driving again tonight; I might not get a spot."

She made sure she hadn't left anything valuable visible in the car. Crowds of out-of-towners to a large event tended to be a recipe for car theft in packed parking lots. As she crossed the parking lot, she saw streams of people flowing toward the downtown square, laughing and talking, ready for a night of fun. She walked through the crowded lobby, people were everywhere: checking in, pushing and pulling luggage into the elevator, kids running around.

There was a rapidly lengthening line at the check in desk; the couple currently at the head of the line apparently had some problem with their reservation and were arguing with the flustered desk clerk. The lobby was so congested that Perri had to sidestep and weave her way through. The elevators were on the opposite side of a throng of people standing in groups, talking, yelling at their kids, 'I think I'll take the stairs,' she decided.

It took Perri a minute to find the stairway door between a soft drink machine and a table displaying pamphlets for nearby attractions and coupons for local businesses. She tugged open the door, pulling against the resisting hydraulic arm that would shut the door after her. Every stair was a narrow slab of concrete seated in a metal framework that produced a brief metallic clang with each step she took. The stairway to the second floor was divided into two flights of stairs. As she reached for the handle to open the door on her floor, she could hear the door on the first floor open and close again followed by footfalls on the stairs. 'I'm not the only one who wants to avoid the crowd' she thought to herself.

The stairs were closer to her room than the elevator, but Perri was disoriented, having used the elevator when she checked in and she had to follow the signs to get to her room. The ice machine made a thumping noise as it dumped a new load of ice into the hopper when she passed the small room with vending machines, which was adjacent to her room. She marveled at the gaudy carpet. Hotels seemed to prefer these combinations of confetti-like geometric shapes in the most garish colors that were excellent at inducing vertigo while walking along a corridor. Once at her room, she had to insert the card key several times to get her door to open.

Perri closed the door with relief. She set her purse on the bed and pulled her phone out. There was a text she hadn't heard. It was from Nick, 'See you soon!' with a smiley face emoji. "At least I'm not the only one who is goofy." She smiled to herself as she set the phone on the dresser, next to the television, and opened her duffel bag on the luggage rack. She pulled out her zippered bag of shampoo, lotion, and other toiletries, tucked her hair dryer and curling iron under her arms, took the clothes for that night from the hangar she had hung them on when she checked in, and went into the bathroom to get ready.

The bath towels were a little rough and somewhat smaller than regular towels. Perri sniffed the towels. They smelled clean, but with the same kind of scent hospital linens had; a no-nonsense industrial detergent smell, nothing pretty or pleasant about it. She opened two of the towels, one for her hair and one to dry off with and laid them on the sink counter. She turned on the water and undressed while it warmed up. When it was steaming, she pushed the button in to send the water through the shower head. The curtain rod was curved, to keep the shower curtain from getting in the way, which she was glad of. She didn't like the thought of it touching her skin after touching who knew how many other people's skin.

She stood under the shower for a while just enjoying the hot water on the back of her neck, then stuck her head under the stream to wet her hair and shampoo first. Perri heard a thump and peeked out of the shower. The door was still closed and she saw nothing. 'With as many people as are here now, it was probably that ice machine again since it was against the shared wall of her room and the vending room.' She lathered up her hair with the bar of solid shampoo she had ordered and recently received in the mail. She loved this stuff and looked forward to using it.

***

Once in her car, Sarah tried Perri's phone again and still got voicemail. Sarah didn't know of any way Perri would be known to be helping with the research, but she couldn't be sure of it, and that is exactly what it seemed to Sarah had gotten Amy killed. She was trying to decide what her next move should be when her text message ring tone sounded. She pulled her phone out.

The text was from George and included two images from the Guthrie PD. The first image was of what looked like a glossy poster or sign. It announced the recipient of the local Business of the Year for the Guthrie Chamber of Commerce in 2013. The award had been given to Blackwell Oil & Synthetics. Pictured on the poster was a woman in a business suit presenting an abstract lump of acrylic mounted on a plaque to two men who were identified as Joseph Blackwell, CEO, and his son Jason Blackwell, Executive Vice President. The photograph wasn't great, but it did fully show their faces.

Joseph was a man who did appear to be in his mid-sixties, hair graying but the original blond color was clearly discernible. He appeared to be tall, he was taller than his son, and was slender and pale, almost a little gaunt. Sarah wondered if his health had not been good even in 2013.

His son, Jason, was slightly shorter than his father, not overweight but with a stockier build. His hair was sandy blond and curly. In an obviously posed, awkward stance, his father was smiling and holding the award with one hand while shaking the woman's hand with the other as they spoke. Jason was standing just behind his father and assertively smiling directly into the camera.

Sarah swiped the screen of her phone to the next image. It was a photo of a typed sheet of paper, clearly lying on the station counter when George snapped the picture. The lettering was quite small, so she expanded her view of it. It was a listing of the owners of 619 Tulip Avenue in Elkton, KY. There was no heading or salutation on the paper and it contained quite a few typos, indicating it had been hastily produced, but that didn't matter as long as it was readable. Sarah talked to herself, 'Not the time to be a spelling Nazi.'

Sarah scanned through the deed information. It wasn't hard because the last names were all the same, all the way back to the early 20th century. The house at 619 Tulip Avenue had initially belonged to Judith Blackwell, Jonathan's mother. Judith's house had been transferred to the ownership of Jonathan Blackwell in 1902 and had remained as such until 1929, when it passed to Edward. Ownership of the house followed the lineage through Edward and Nathaniel, down to Joseph, the current owner.

Sarah's anxiety instantly multiplied. When she called Perri's phone again and there was still no answer, she got back out of the car and headed toward the Arrogant Rogue. Perri had said she was going to the festival with Nick. Since she was yards away from it, she'd check for them in the tavern first. She hoped against hope they weren't already milling around in the hordes of people downtown.

Although, that might be why Perri didn't answer, either she couldn't hear the phone or had turned it off.

Chapter 35

Perri was just about finished luxuriating in the shower when she thought she heard her phone. She realized she had left the phone on the dresser. She was suddenly afraid it was Nick calling to say he was on the way and here she was in the shower. The light shining into the shower dimmed briefly, not more than a flicker. She turned her head and saw the top of the door, now visible over the shower rod, closing. Adrenaline shot through her body making her heart pound and her breath catch. The curtain was a coffee brown color, so she couldn't see through it. Facing the curtain, Perri stood stock still and listened. Surely Nick wouldn't have come on into her room and he didn't have a key. And even so, he wouldn't have barged into the bathroom. She couldn't hear anything but the water and the rushing of blood through her ears. She realized she was breathing through her mouth, water running in at the corners then dribbling back out down her chin. She closed it.

In a sudden burst of movement, the shower curtain hurtled into Perri. She could feel arms closing in around her through the wet plastic. She struggled against the gripping embrace as the curtain was wrenched away from the rod. The attacker pushed her against the tiled wall at her back and pinned her arms at her sides. Her feet were slipping on the bottom of the tub. Now loose, the top of the shower curtain collapsed and folded over her head.

Perri tried to think of the best response, but the attacker was pulling her downward and her feet were almost against the side wall of the tub in her struggle to remain upright. She tried to grab the plastic of the shower curtain between her thumbs and forefingers in an attempt to pull it down, to see her attacker and hopefully get out of the plastic bag she was now in. That was hopeless. The curtain didn't budge with the little amount of grip she could get.

Without warning, the attacker's head rammed into her face. Sharp pain shot upward from her nose and into her skull, her eyes watered and she pinched them shut. In that moment of distraction, the attacker overlapped the sides of the curtain around her back, fully enveloping her. She lost her footing and went down sideways, her head smacking the knob of the faucet as she fell. The curtain served as some cushion, but it was still extremely painful since her ear was the main point of contact. Panic started to win the struggle and she began kicking wildly, as much as was possible with the curtain tangled up in her legs. The man, it had to be a man, climbed in and sat on her abdomen, pinning her arms down at her sides to the bottom of the tub with his knees.

Perri took a huge breath and launched into what she hoped was a far-ranging blood-curdling scream, but it was cut off by an object being shoved into the opening of her mouth from the other side of the curtain. She gagged, but the hand held the object in place.

She heard the shower head being shut off and in the next second, the water came from the faucet which was directly over her forehead; she could feel the water hitting the curtain full force. The next sound she heard was the tub stopper. Perri was engulfed with the hot, horrifying realization that he was going to fill the tub.

***

Sarah pushed through the door of the Arrogant Rogue without apology for pushing aside several patrons trying to leave. Andrea was the bartender behind the bar and was emptying a large plastic bucket of ice into a hopper.

"Andrea, where is Nick? Has he left?"

"Hi, Sarah."

"*Has he left? Is Nick still here??*" Sarah's voice rose.

"No, he's in the back. He finished his shift and went to the back to clock out."

"I need to talk to him right now, this instant," Sarah headed toward the employee door.

"Sure, go on back…" but Sarah was already through the door behind the bar. The back of the tavern was a warren of small rooms: kitchen, bathroom, employee area, store rooms, closets. Sarah didn't see Nick. She poked her head in every room and called his name. The cook looked at her with surprise. Sarah was headed back toward the bar area when she noticed the rear exit. "Crap." She ran through the door. Nick had backed out of his parking space and was shifting to drive forward out of the small parking area behind the building. Sarah ran in front of the car.

"Nick, stop, stop." She was out of breath, more from fear than exertion.

He stomped on the brake and rolled down the window. "What's up, Sarah? What's wrong. Something happening in the bar?" He put his hand on the door handle to exit the car.

"No," she took a breath, "Are you on the way to meet Perri? Have you seen her?"

"Yeah, I saw her about an hour ago, maybe less. Why?"

"Do you know where she is now?"

"She was going back to her hotel to get ready for the festival. Why? What's wrong?" his curiosity had turned to alarm at the sight of Sarah's stricken face.

"Do you know where she is staying?" Nick nodded affirmatively. "Take me there. Right now." Sarah ran around to the passenger side and got in, "Go."

"What's going on?"

Sarah didn't answer him. She rustled through her purse frantically and finally came up with her phone, hitting speed dial. She nervously bounced her hand on the arm rest. "George, George. Sarah here, right now, send a car and at least two officers over to the 9th Street Hotel, send more if you have them," she swung back to Nick, "Do you know what room?"

"Yeah, um, 227."

"Room 227, have someone call the manager now so they can be ready to let you in if they need to, if there's no answer."

"No answer? What the hell is going on?" Nick continually swiveled his head between the road and Sarah.

"Yes.... now. This is an emergency. Ok. I'm on my way there."

"Sarah, you have to...."

Sarah held up her phone with the photograph of the two Blackwell men where Nick could see it. "Recognize anyone in this photo?"

Nick was repeatedly glancing at the photograph, "I can't look at it long enough to..."

Sarah grabbed the wheel, "Look at it!"

Nick leaned in and looked at the photograph while Sarah held the wheel. "Yeah, I've seen this one guy a few times."

"When?" Sarah relinquished control of the steering wheel to Nick.

"I've seen him in the tavern a couple of times over the last, I don't know...couple of weeks. And I saw him this afternoon, he was at the bar."

"When? How long ago?" Sarah shouted.

"Ok!" Nick turned onto 9th Street. "It had to have been around 4:30 because I saw him when I was talking to Perri, he was sitting a few stools down."

"And?"

Nick's brow furrowed and he stared ahead as he drove. Sarah urged, "Did he say or do anything?"

"Well, I was talking to Perri. I had turned to pick something up, a rag, and I noticed the guy kind of scowling at me. I thought he might want another drink and was mad that I was talking to a customer. I asked him if he needed anything and he said 'No' and looked away."

"What had you been talking about, I mean when you noticed him scowling at you?"

"Geez, I don't know..."

"Think!!"

"Ok, ok, I guess it was when I asked Perri if she was going to be free for the whole weekend or was going to have to do some more work for...well, for you."

"Damn it! How long was he there?" Sarah asked.

"I'm sorry, Sarah, I…"

"No, no, no, that doesn't matter. How long was he there after that?"

"Let me think. I told Perri I was going to be off work at five o'clock and said she was going to go back to her hotel and get cleaned up, you know, after the drive. I asked her where she was staying."

"And she told you?"

"Well, yeah. I told her I would call her when I was finished here and would come to pick her up."

"Anything else?"

"I asked her what room she was in and she told me."

"Drive faster, we're almost there, you won't get a ticket, I promise." Sarah waved ahead of her, then said, "You said you told her you would call when you were finished, did you call her?"

"Yes, I did, but I didn't get an answer."

Chapter 36

A black and white was already parked by the lobby doors. Sarah directed Nick to stop just behind it. She flung her door open and called over her shoulder for him to park and wait in the lobby. She disappeared inside. Nick backed the car away from the police car but left it crossways behind two other cars, blocking them into their spaces. He ran into the lobby behind Sarah. He didn't see Sarah or the officers, but the guests standing in the lobby were looking around them in surprise.

Ignoring Sarah's instructions to wait in the lobby, Nick said under his breath, "Like hell I will," and ran for the stairway door leaping between two startled ladies who were chatting in the hallway. He bounded up the stairs two at a time, the railing screeched as he used it to swing around the turn to the second set of steps. He yanked open the second-floor door, looking for a sign to indicate which hallway to take. He could hear pounding and shouting. He headed down the left hallway, toward the disturbance.

Nick slowed down and stopped twenty feet from the doorway. Sarah turned to look at him and set her lips in a thin line and shook her head, but didn't say anything. Nick stood his ground and watched. The hotel manager was approaching the door with a key card, but Officer Harper got a fistful of his suit coat and pulled him backwards, "It's busted. Get back."

There had been no answer to loud knocking. The level style handle did not turn and the lock had been broken. With weapons drawn and everyone away from the door, Joe kicked the door. It swung open and banged against the interior wall. After checking and seeing no one, the officers entered the room one by one.

Sarah was sweating. She could feel rivulets of sweat coursing down her spine and being absorbed into the waistband of her pants. Her underarms were sweaty and the fabric of her shirt was plastered against her skin. The bathroom door was closed, but they could hear water running and splashing. "Get in there!" Sarah ordered.

The uniformed policemen stood on either side of the bathroom door; Joe Harper on the interior side, in front of the mirrored closet, and Brett Maddux on the hallway side. Officer Maddux tried the bathroom knob, which was locked. As Joe withdrew his hand from the knob, a gunshot sounded and a hole appeared through the door. The splashing and thumping from inside continued.

Brett motioned that he would break through the door. Joe and Sarah remained in place, ready to act. Brett kicked the door just beneath the handle. It made a crunching sound; Brett returned to his position. A few more seconds and he kicked again. The cheap resin molding around the latch bolt gave way and the door was open, but all three held their positions, weapons aimed at the doorway.

Another shot was fired from within the bathroom; this time it was accompanied by a man running headlong through the door with a gun in his hand.

Sarah shouted, "Stop. STOP!" He didn't. Instead he fired again, not taking time to aim, just getting off a shot by pointing the gun over his shoulder. It hit just left of Sarah and struck the mirrored door of the closet which shattered into thousands of shimmering, knife-sharp pieces that floated through the air and settled to the floor. She instinctively threw her right arm in front her face to protect her eyes, raising the barrel of her gun with her left hand. Officer Harper fired a shot at the man as he headed through the door into the hall then followed him out.

Sarah shouted, "Brett, go with Joe, get that guy!" She holstered her gun as she crunched over the broken shards of mirror and raced into the bathroom. The water was running full blast, the tub was nearly full and there was water all over the floor and walls. Sarah braced her knees against the outside of the tub and put her arms beneath the gasping, struggling mass of plastic inside it; water sloshed over the edge in waves, soaking Sarah's shirt and slacks. She called out, "Perri, Perri, it's Sarah, we're here to help. Calm down, stop thrashing."

***

Brett looked around the corner of the door to see the wounded man shambling down the hallway; he had been hit in the right arm, which hung limply, and he had transferred his gun to his left hand. 'Good,' thought Brett.

As the shooter was about to reach the T of the hallway, he man looked back over his left shoulder. As Brett and Joe both raised and aimed their guns, Nick lunged forward from the right side of the cross hallway and used the butt end of a fire extinguisher to clobber the escaping man in the head. He then stepped back, taking the extinguisher with him, and was no longer visible

The shooter reflexively threw his left arm out, the right arm still hanging uselessly at his side, and dropped to his knees. As the man kneeled, he raised in his left arm and shuffled to turn to face Nick. Officer Harper shouted, "Nick, you get out of here, now!" A couple of seconds later, the fire extinguisher came flying through the air from right to left and hit the wall just next to the shooter. The policemen heard the stairway door open and hush closed.

A door opened from another guest's room between the attacker and the officers. Officer Harper bellowed for the guest to shut and lock the door and get away from it. The door shut promptly with no protest.

Officer Maddux gave warning, "Drop that gun right now. I will shoot if you don't drop the gun now." The man was nearly standing again, making for the corner.

Last warning, "Drop your weapon NOW." The man continued and was about to disappear around the corner. A shot echoed through the hallway. Joe Harper had aimed for the left calf and squarely hit the target. The shooter dropped to the floor, the gun bouncing out of his hand.

Officer Maddux reached the man first. He kicked the gun away and stood over him with his weapon solidly trained on the man's chest. Brett Harper applied the handcuffs and turned him face up on the floor. The shooter had gunshot wounds to the right arm and left calf, and a bloody circular abrasion on his right forehead courtesy of Nick and the fire extinguisher.

***

Sarah supported Perri's upper body while she opened the plug on the tub to drain the water. She wasn't going to be able to get her out with the tub while it was full. Perri was coughing, gasping, and twisting inside the plastic curtain. Sarah kept talking to her in as soothing a voice as she could muster.

With Perri in a near seated position in the tub, Sarah flipped the top of the curtain back and maneuvered her into a position where she could grasp one of the edges of the curtain and pull it away. "Perri, hold still, ok?" but Perri was as terrified as a trapped animal. One arm came through the opening and grabbed at Sarah, catching her hair.

"Calm down, stop, hold on, I've got you, stop, I'm getting you out of here." Perri relinquished her grip on Sarah's hair. She was naked beneath the shower curtain. Sarah pulled it away from her face but left it covering her body. When the water had drained away. Sarah grabbed two towels that were on the closed toilet seat and placed them on the floor right outside the tub. "Ok, Perri, I'm going to help you up, but I just want to get you out of the tub and have you sit on the towels." There was a lot of broken glass on the floor between the bathroom and the bed; Sarah didn't want to attempt to move Perri.

With assistance, Perri was able to stand and step over the tub onto the towels. Sarah eased her to the floor. Perri's face was blotchy and her mouth was beginning to show signs of bruising around the lips with a small amount of blood where her teeth had scraped against the inside of her lower lip. She was hiccoughing and sputtering.

"Are you able to breathe alright?"

Perri coughed a couple more times and said, "I think so. I feel like I have water in my lungs that I can't cough up, but I can breathe. It's getting better."

"I know you are cold and uncomfortable, but I don't want to move you again until paramedics have a chance to look you over."

As she reached for her phone, Nick's voice came from the entryway to the room. "Oh, my God, is she ok?"

Sarah turned, "Nick, call an ambulance." His face was taut and pale as he pulled his phone from his back pocket and dialed. Sarah motioned for him to back away from the bathroom, which he did.

Perri sniffed and coughed, "I left my phone on the dresser. I thought I heard it ring once and I was afraid maybe Nick was already headed to the hotel. That's when I saw the bathroom door closing and..." She shuddered once and started to shiver. "The water was coming in under the curtain and I couldn't move." She was breathing anxiously, "But there was a little pocket of air. If it hadn't been there, I don't know."

"Try to just sit and don't talk, get your breath."

Nick stepped back into the room, "The ambulance is on the way."

Sarah replied, "Good. Nick, go get blankets off the bed please."

Nick reappeared with two blankets and a pillow. Sarah took them from him and, pulling Perri forward toward her, placed the pillow between her back and the tub. Sarah turned again,

"Is it ok if I stand out here?" Nick asked tentatively from outside the bathroom door.

"Oh, my God," Perri moaned and looked at Sarah.

"What's wrong, what's happening?" came Sarah's urgent response. She rapidly looked over Perri and the floor, half expecting to see a pool of blood forming or some other catastrophe.

"Nothing, I just…" A bedraggled Perri looked forlornly up at Nick.

Nick tentatively stepped into the frame of the doorway. "Don't concern yourself with anything right now. You just went through something terrible. I'm not afraid to admit that I was scared to death, so I can't even imagine how you felt."

Sarah grinned and said, "We were both scared to death, Nick." She turned back to Perri, "While I absolutely don't condone it, Nick didn't stay where I asked him to. He was supposed to stay in the lobby, but here he is."

"There is no way I was going to lollygag around the lobby. I got a good chop in on your attacker."

Sarah whirled around to look questioningly at Nick, "You did what?"

"I just happened to have a fire extinguisher in my hand when he was hotfooting it down the hall. I couldn't let him evade capture. How would I feel about myself if I stood by and watched him run away?"

"Are you saying our fine city police officers wouldn't have caught him without your 'help'?" Sarah asked.

"Nope. Just saying I'm a helpful, concerned citizen."

Sarah gave a resigned shake of her head.

A bedraggled Perri looked up at Nick with a wan smile, "This isn't exactly how I planned on starting our date."

The rattle of an approaching gurney came from down the hallway. The paramedics left the gurney outside in the hallway and brought their kit from the gurney into the room. Nick stepped out of the bathroom. Sarah lightly squeezed Perri's arm and said, "I'm going to be right outside."

As she exited the door, Perri called out to her, "Sarah, who was the guy? Who did it turn out to be?"

She sighed and looked at the floor, then up at Perri, "I'm so very sorry, Perri. I tried to call you as soon as I realized that you were also at risk. I tell you what. Let's get you checked out first and when we're sure you're alright and things have calmed down, I'll explain the whole thing to you. I have a lot of paperwork to do and couple of things to verify, but rest assured, I will let you fill you in on the entire picture."

***

Nick sat in one of the chairs by the window that looked out to the parking lot. Sarah sat in the other and called the station to apprise George of the developments.

Less than ten minutes later, one of the paramedics stuck his head out of the bathroom, "Can someone bring a pair of shoes? She's going to need them to walk out of here with all this debris."

Shortly, Perri emerged from the bathroom, gingerly walking across the jagged pieces of mirror glass. She was still swaddled in the blanket which was mostly wet by now, having soaked up water from the floor. The second medic spoke while the first packed the kit back onto the gurney, "She doesn't want to go to the hospital, says she's ok. She has a few contusions and abrasions, her nose is a little swollen but it isn't broken, probably going to have some bruising around the nose and eyes. Will someone be able to stay with her for a while?"

"Definitely!" piped Nick, "I will."

The same medic asked Perri, "You will go to the ER if you have any headaches that worsen, you are unusually sleepy, or have significant increasing pain other than general soreness?"

"Yes, I will. I think the fright was the worst of it."

He nodded and left the room. The sounds of the gurney retreating down the hallway faded away.

Nick left his chair and walked toward Perri. "You sure you don't need to go have an x-ray or something?" he asked uncertainly.

"No, I don't think so, I'm ok. But I will say I don't want to be alone. I appreciate you staying with me, Nick."

"Are you kidding me? This is not a chore, I want to stay with you."

"Our date night is ruined, I hate that." She smiled apologetically, "I guess I'm a wet blanket."

"Ugh!" Nick hugged her, wet blanket and all, "It isn't ruined."

Perri shivered again, "I guess I need to get into something dry."

Nick released her, his shirt now wet down the front and the inside of his arms. Sarah walked past the two, "Perri, we need to move you from this room. You can't stay here, obviously, and we need to keep the room off limits until the investigation of this whole incident is complete."

"No objection from me; I don't want to stay here. Can I get dry clothes out of my duffel and put them on? The ones in the bathroom are soaking wet and I'm freezing."

Sarah considered, "Yes, you have to have something to wear, but we need to leave the rest of your stuff here, just until we're finished. Once you are changed, we need to leave."

"Ok, can I take my phone? It's just sitting right there on the dresser?"

"Yes, you can take your phone. And I'm holding Nick responsible for keeping an eye on you," Sarah fastened a meaningful gaze on Nick who nodded in agreement. You promise me you will go to the ER if you feel at all worse?" Perri nodded.

"Ok." Sarah picked the duffel up from the luggage rack and set it on the end of the bed. Perri rummaged through it and pulled out a handful of clothing then looked awkwardly at Nick and Sarah. "Right, you can't use the bathroom here. We'll step out into the hallway. Sarah walked toward the door looking back at Nick expectantly.

Perri said to Nick, "You promise you'll be right outside the door? I'm still a little nervous, I know they took him away, but…"

Nick held Perri by the shoulders and said gently, "I will be right on the other side of the door. I can talk to you while I'm out there, will that help?"

"Yes. Thanks. It won't take me long." Nick placed a tender kiss on Perri's forehead and walked toward the hallway. He passed through the broken door behind Sarah. As he started to pull the door as close to closed as it would get, Perri said, "I'm never again going to poke fun at someone for having shower fright because of the movie Psycho."

Nick laughed, "You still have your sense of humor. That's a good thing."

Chapter 37

Saturday morning was brilliantly sunny and seventy-five degrees. Perri woke to a breeze through the open window and the smell of something yeasty baking. She looked around the bedroom, confused at first. After a fleeting moment of alarm, she remembered she was at Nick's house.

She relaxed against the fat pillow and sank further down into the dark gray cotton sheets. There had been no carousing through the festival last night for either of them, no bonfire party. She recalled sitting on the couch with Nick for what must have been several hours, just talking. Nick had called for pizza delivery so Perri didn't have to leave the house. They had eaten pizza with a soda. Perri declined a beer. She was pretty sure she was fine, but didn't want to risk a beer or three masking any change in her condition. She had turned out to be ravenously hungry and had to hold herself back from gobbling down three-fourths of the pizza. Her nose was sore and her ear felt tender where it touched the pillow.

She would need to call Nina today and bring her up to date. Perri knew she would be livid and worried at the same time and decided that task could wait a while. She sat up; there was a man's robe across the foot of the bed. She didn't remember much about the layout of the house from last night. Perri put the robe on over her underwear and turned the brass knob on the three-panel door of the bedroom, which opened directly onto the living room. The kitchen was a straight shot through the living room and she could see Nick standing at the counter wearing a pair of jeans and no shirt. As she padded through the living room, Perri looked at the couch with its pillow and rumpled afghan and realized he had slept on the couch. She walked into the kitchen. "It smells like a bakery in here."

Nick startled and spun around, sloshing some orange juice on the counter. "You're up, great! How do you feel this morning?"

"Stiff, sore, but not terrible. Do I look like a raccoon who lost a boxing match?"

"You look great to me."

"Oh, come on, we both know that's not right." Perri laughed and sat down at the small table set with two plates and napkins. "Thank you, Nick, for letting me stay here, and for … giving up your bedroom last night. You had to be uncomfortable on that couch."

"It isn't bad. You needed to sleep, and sleep well. Did you?"

"Yes, I think I did. I don't remember waking up through the night. I was exhausted."

"I was too. I'm sorry we didn't get to go to the festival last night, but I thoroughly enjoyed just sitting here and talking. Besides, it isn't over; the festival is still on the rest of the weekend if you feel like going."

The oven timer buzzed and Nick grabbed an oven mitt. Perri tried to look around him as he pulled a pan from the oven. "What do you have in there? It smells delicious."

"Just some of those canned cinnamon rolls. I'm definitely not a pastry chef."

"They smell perfect to me." Nick set the pan on a folded towel on the table followed by the glasses of juice. "There's some coffee too; I know you like your coffee but I don't know if you will like *my* coffee."

"Can I stand a spoon up in it?" she asked.

"Possibly," Nick answered warily.

"Then I'll like it." Perri sipped the juice and stared at her plate. "Nick, I'm not trying to be a drama queen, but if Sarah had missed you, or you hadn't been able to tell her where I was…"

Nick took each of Perri's hands in his, "It didn't happen that way though."

Perri smiled ruefully. "You're right. I won't dwell on it. I'm glad it's over and I'm glad they shot the stupid guy. I just wish they'd shot him in the head. I can't wait to hear the details. Two weeks ago, I thought I was coming down here for three days of fun and relaxation with some research and grave spotting mixed in. You never know, do you?"

"Nope. But I'm glad you are here now." Nick's dimple appeared. He pointed to the pan of rolls, "Dig in, while they're still hot."

Nick watched her grab three of the cinnamon rolls. Perri notice. "You may as well learn now that I'm not a dainty little woman who eats like a bird. It was all I could do to not grab that last piece of pizza out of your hand last night. You know those women who push away a half-finished plate of food and say how full they are, couldn't eat another thing? That's not me. If you ever see me do that, I'm sick."

"Good. I like a real woman!"

Perri bit into a roll, chewed and swallowed, then said, "You told me last night you lived in Nashville for a few years, but we got to talking about me and didn't get back to that. What did you do there, and why did you come back to Russellville?"

"Yeah." He took a swallow of juice. "I didn't want to live in a small town. I moved down there for a while to try to work in the entertainment business. That sounds pretty tired and cliché, doesn't it?"

"Do you play music?"

"No, good lord no. I manage sound systems, well, I did manage sound systems. I'm a tech geek, not a musician."

"Why'd you come back?" Perri sipped the strong coffee and started on her second cinnamon roll.

"I did pretty well down there, and I enjoyed it. Well, I thought I did." Perri waited while Nick formulated what he wanted to say. "Even though I was doing well financially and was in the career I believed I wanted, it wasn't really what I thought it would be."

"What do you mean?"

"I guess it got to be automatic and, well, boring. It's exciting at first, but the social and political antics of the entertainment business were a big disappointment to me. Not that it affected my job so much as I just hated seeing the phoniness of the people I thought I respected and admired."

"What about the Nashville social life? It didn't make up for the disappointing work aspect?" Perri asked.

"Nashville has an endless social life, that's for sure. I had a couple of relationships that I thought could work out. They didn't. Both times, there was an agenda; it turned out to be a hopeful 'in' for them. Basically, I was a rung on the ladder."

"What do you mean?"

"Sometimes, people think that the recording booth techs can get them an audition, or even a contract. That isn't how it works. I couldn't have gotten myself one, much less them. After a while, I didn't trust anyone's motives. I didn't want to live that way."

"I'm sorry it didn't work out for you." Perri's eyes lit up when she smiled at Nick. "Ok, I'm not totally sorry."

"I'm glad you aren't sorry, because I'm not either. A couple of years ago, my Mom and Dad decided to sell up and move into one of those condo villages where Dad wouldn't constantly be having to fix things on the house and do hours of yard work every week. They wanted to travel a little bit and just enjoy themselves. This was their house, our house, my sister and I grew up here. When they told me there were putting the house up for sale, it gave me the motivation to make a decision. I bought it from them and moved back."

"Are you happy with your decision?" asked Perri.

"Yes, I really am. I enjoy being a bartender at the tavern. I don't feel limited. I missed the small-town environment while I was gone. I still do contract technical work, but it isn't my full-time employment anymore."

"Does your sister live in Russellville?"

"No, she lives in Massachusetts. I don't see her much." Nick gazed at the wall behind Perri, unfocused. "We used to play in the little creek that runs through the woods in back of the house. Those were good times. I didn't want to see the house go to someone else. Is that silly?"

"Not at all silly." Perri looked into Nick's eyes, "Your home and family meant something to you."

They enjoyed the shared silence while Perri finished her third cinnamon roll and Nick ate his in two bites a piece.

Chapter 38

Perri was dressed in the same clothes she had worn from the hotel and hoped she could get the rest of her belongings soon. It not, she would have to make a trip to the store. She showered and did the best she could just drying her hair, which meant it was straight as a stick and kept falling in front of her eyes. She didn't have anything to cover the bruising with, so she pretended it wasn't there.

It was ironic that she had been overly concerned with planning her wardrobe for this weekend and ended up spending it wet and wrapped naked in a plastic sheet or wet blanket, bruised, wearing Nick's robe, and then having to wear the same clothes two days in a row. It didn't seem to bother Nick at all and that meant something to her.

Nick had asked her if she felt like walking around downtown, driving somewhere, or just staying in the house. She wanted to get out into the sunshine and be around other people before she started to get weird. She knew it was best to get back to normal as much as possible after a crisis like the one yesterday.

While Nick was getting showered and dressed, she called Nina, wanting to get that hurricane over with. And it had been a hurricane. Nina exploded with fury at the shooter, at Perri for being alone, and everyone in the world for not preventing it, but mostly at herself for not being there. Then she calmed down, as Perri knew she would, and was sympathetic and worrying and clucking like a hen. That was the eye of the hurricane. It was followed by the opposing wall of the storm where Nina got mad again at the police for not having caught the culprit before he nearly drowned Perri.

Perri reassured Nina repeatedly that the man was not only shot and beaten, but had been arrested and that Nick was serving as her protector while she was there. She swore a solemn oath that she would definitely call before she left Russellville to come home on Sunday and would check in halfway through the trip. Satisfied for the time being, Nina had reminded Perri that she required details of her time spent with Nick and finally hung up. Perri puffed out her cheeks and blew out a long breath.

***

Nick and Perri walked around the central square of Russellville, amidst crowds of people, Nick holding on to Perri's hand. The food booths lined both sides of the street of the square and continued down one of the side streets. So far, Perri had consumed a bowl of Kentucky Burgoo, a funnel cake, fried pickles, and was finishing up some fried ice cream. "Oh, my gosh, I'm full, but I don't regret my actions. It was really good. Grease and salt are too of my favorites."

Nick was polishing off a plate of fried mac n' cheese, he nodded and agreed with an "umph," through a full mouth.

Perri's phone rang. She tossed her napkin in a trash barrel, and answered. "Hello?" It was Sarah.

"Perri? How are you doing today?"

"I'm good, Sarah. I slept great last night and I've already eaten enough today to last me a week. Nick and I are walking around the square."

"I'm glad to hear that. Since you are close to the station, would you mind stopping in for a little while? I have your purse and duffel bag and thought you might want to hear the explanation for this whole mess."

"You bet I would. Thank you, we'll head right over there." Perri hung up and stuck the phone back in her pocket.

***

Sarah was in the lobby waiting for them. She walked them back to the same combo kitchen / conference room where Perri and Nina had reviewed documents with Sarah last week.

"Have a seat, would you like anything to drink? I can make coffee if you like."

"Lord no, I'm full as a tick." Perri said, Nick laughed.

Sarah gathered her thoughts while she took a chair at the end of the table and placed an accordion file in front of her. "Our prisoner agreed to fill in some of the blanks for the sake of cooperation; he is hoping it will help him in the end. I'll try to summarize this and not make it too lengthy, but I will start from the beginning."

"I don't mind if it is lengthy or not. I can't wait to find out what happened."

Nick added, "And I don't mind, because I don't know most of it."

"As we knew, Patricia had been working on her family tree. I don't know motivated her to start, probably never will know now. She dug around enough to find evidence that her 3X Grandfather, that's how you say it right, had run off and left his family, and that he had not died somewhere out there but, instead, started a new life and family."

"As you found out, Jonathan cornered the water market during the Oklahoma land rush and got rich. He switched from water to oil, added other products, and so on. His second wife, Prudence Noble, came from an immensely wealthy and influential family from Boston, which is probably why he zeroed in on her. They married and had children. The Blackwell family company continued to grow, with a few bumps here and there. The position of head of the company was traditionally passed from father to son, all the way from Edward down to Joseph Blackwell, the current CEO."

Perri nodded, knowing this much already. Nick said, "Ok, I'm following you."

"I tried to talk to Joseph Blackwell. I called the company and was told he was not there; finally, the receptionist admitted he was ill and had been out for quite some time. The local PD sent an officer to the Blackwell home to talk to Joseph, to make sure he was really in town. Mrs. Blackwell refused the officer admittance or to talk to

Joseph at all. She wouldn't any information about her husband's illness and told him to come back with a warrant if he had questions. The neighbors hadn't seen him in a while either."

Nick spoke up, "Wait, you are saying that Joseph Blackwell and Patricia both descend from the same man, this Jonathan guy?"

Sarah explained, "Right, Jonathan was Joseph's Great Grandfather." She shifted in her chair, "The problems began when Patricia called Blackwell Oil on August 13 to talk to Joseph. Of course, she didn't talk to him but she left a message. And she continued to call and leave messages, which were ultimately given to Jason. Evidently, Jason knew enough of the family history to realize this could be true, and he called Patricia back. Patricia demanded money from Jason."

Perri asked, "But why would Patricia feel she had any leverage to ask for money? It was over a century ago and Susannah had been granted a divorce from Jonathan. He wasn't married to her anymore when he married Prudence Noble."

"You and I can see that, but Patricia wasn't necessarily realistic. She had a history of being delusional and uncontrollable at times. She had a lot of problems, both psychological and chemical. When Jason refused, she became enraged. She spouted off about telling everyone the story about how the Blackwell family patriarch was a loser who abandoned his family and took up with another woman. She had enough details, and she convinced Jason Blackwell that she had proof, which she may have had at the time because she had enlisted Amy Barrow's help. She may or may not have gloated to Jason about Amy helping her. The Blackwell family values their position in society quite highly and have touted their self-defined old-world values and honor for a very long time, even incorporating it as part of their public company image. They have held Jonathan Blackwell up as a gleaming gem in their crown as a patriarch who helped settle Guthrie, Oklahoma. They didn't want his reputation to be tarnished and his true actions to be known. They were disturbed enough by Patricia's threats to want to prevent it."

"What happened then?"

"Oddly enough, Joseph Blackwell already knew about Patricia and her part of the family line."

"Ahh," Perri said in realization. "Know thy enemies?"

"Yes. Joseph had known most of his life, was probably told by his father. We didn't comprehend it at the time, but we both saw a photo of Joseph Blackwell last week...a photo from 1976. Remember the photo that was taken in the cemetery when Patricia's grandfather died? That was Joseph Blackwell leaning against the door of the same car used in the murder of Patricia and Amy. The car was his at the time, purchased new the year before. It was eventually sold to the renter of the Elkton property in 1997. Joseph may have been in Elkton and seen the obituary for Noah Blackwell in 1976 or someone may have told him about it. We know he came back a couple times a year to check on the property. He showed up at the cemetery, out of curiosity maybe, to have a look at the family."

Perri nodded at Sarah, "I do remember. You thought you recognized the car but I forgot about it because it seemed unlikely."

"Right. I'm not sure how Jason missed that when he went through Patricia's paperwork, but I'm glad he did."

"Anyway, Joseph was never told about Patricia contacting Jason, and Jason had decided to put a stop to it before his father returned home, if he returns home. Joseph truly has been ill with cancer and isn't even in Oklahoma. He has been in a treatment hospital in Dallas for a month. The family didn't want anyone to know he was ill and they didn't want him to find out about Patricia. I'm not sure if they were afraid Joseph might give in to her or if they thought he was too weak to deal with Jason's solution to the problem. At any rate, they never told him."

"Jason left Oklahoma during the middle of the night Friday, August 14-15, in a black SUV was normally driven by his wife. He drove west into Arkansas, stopping in Fayetteville to steal a license plate on Saturday night. It was discovered on Sunday and reported, but it wasn't spotted because it wasn't being used yet. Jason then drove to Elkton, bringing the plate with him."

The direction of the events was now dawning on Perri, but Nick was still out of the loop. "Why did he go to Elkton?"

Sarah proceeded, "Because his family still owned a house there. The house was originally owned by Jonathan's mother, Judith, and has been passed down every generation since she died in 1901."

"Good grief, they hold on to things, don't they?" asked Nick.

"Yes, they do, including their money. Joseph started grooming his successor early, not just in running the company. The house in Elkton isn't the only rental property they have. Once he was old enough, Joseph took Jason with him on his rounds of the properties they owned. Because of that, Jason had been to the house numerous times. He knew there had always been an old car parked in a carport behind the house and it was still there. It wasn't in working order but he spent three days and paid a substantial amount of money to a mechanic to get the car in running order and to keep his mouth shut about it."

"Jason wore gloves when he was in the car, but the mechanic left his prints all over it. Jason didn't think about that. Mr. Andrew Kratz admitted to being paid very handsomely by Jason Blackwell to expedite repair of the car, although he wasn't told why. Jason also paid Mr. Kratz to deliver his car to him in Kentucky when, as Jason told him, the Chrysler broke down. The tenants living in the rental house knew the car was gone, but they hadn't been home when it was removed; they just assumed the owner had it towed off and that it wasn't really their business."

"What happened next is something we tragically misinterpreted, until now. Patricia died near midnight on Wednesday, August 19, when she drove over a concrete culvert and down an embankment while intoxicated; her blood alcohol concentration was more than double the legal limit. There were no indications that she had been forced off the road. Jason had spent the first part of the week here, in Russellville, watching Patricia. She wasn't hard to find since he had her real name and her address was available in the internet directories."

"Jason had gone through Patricia's apartment before she died. He saw her in the Rogue. She looked settled in for an evening of drinking, so he went to her apartment. Burglary wasn't his normal line of work. He was probably afraid of being caught and wasn't very thorough. He didn't take all of Patricia's notes, just the documents he thought were relevant, those that listed his family's names and relationship to Patricia. We don't know if she kept the information in separate places or if he simply didn't realize until after Patricia was dead that Amy Barrow had been helping her. Patricia didn't report a theft; she probably hadn't noticed. She had found the information she needed and may not have referred back to it once she began calling the Blackwells. Jason spent a lot of his time here sitting in local bars, that's where he picked up a stockpile of information. He didn't talk to people directly, but listened closely."

Nick sat up quickly in his chair, "I knew I'd seen him before! He was in the Rogue when you came in town yesterday, Perri! Remember, he was sitting a few stools down from you?"

"Oh yeah, he was staring at you and you asked him if he wanted anything else."

"Right. Oh God…right before I asked you what room you were in? That's how he found out how to find you!"

Sarah held up both hands, "Before you get all worked up about it, Nick, he would have found out anyway. All he had to do was follow her out of the tavern and back to her hotel. You asking for her room number made no difference. He already knew who she was. He was also in the Rogue the night Rodney came in and made a big scene over Perri and Nina filing a complaint against Milton. It wasn't you." Nick's face was twisted with remorse, but he tried to let that go and listen to the rest of what Sarah had to say.

When the car was ready, on Wednesday afternoon, Jason went to Elkton, left his car parked behind the mechanic's shop, and drove the Chrysler to Russellville with the Arkansas plate on it. There are a lot of older model vehicles around here; no one paid any attention. He never had to make contact with Patricia's car to run her off the road; we would have caught that. She was impaired enough, and her reactions were probably exaggerated enough, that he was able to force her off the road by intimidation. There were no markings on the car, no skid marks, nothing. And with Patricia's history, it looked like what it was meant to, an accident."

Sarah got up to get a glass of water and took a drink. "Now, instead of being able to go home, Jason decides he has to take care of Amy too. It takes him another week, but he kills Amy in the cemetery with one of the guns he brought from home. Jason is a gun lover and has a sizeable collection; both the rifle and the pistol were his own."

"Amy is now dead, but Jason has wrecked the Chrysler enough that he can't drive it back to Elkton. The radiator was leaking from the impact, not enough to disable it on the spot, but it wouldn't have made it back to Elkton. He drives it north for a few miles and ditches it and calls Andrew Kratz to bring his car to him.

Andrew was sitting in the passenger seat while Jason worked out the deal with Rodney Sauer. He paid Rodney $1,000.00 to hide the car and tell no one. His choice of Rodney for that job was a major mistake.

"Jason drove Mr. Kratz back to Elkton and returned to Russellville. Because there were a lot of cars from other states in town that weekend because of the car show out at the fairgrounds, he didn't stand out. He hadn't counted on Rodney being too lazy to get rid of the car. Instead, Rodney just parked it in Alex Freighley's old barn; right next to the Sauer property. He told his Dad about it, but when Milton got suspicious and wouldn't stop asking him about the extra money, he told him the real story."

"That's where you and Nina come in, Perri. You came into town on Friday and did your own research at the Clerk's office. You ate at the Rogue Friday night, right?" Perri nodded. "You heard the story about Amy's death not only while you were in the Clerk's office, but in the bar from Emily, our dispatcher. On Saturday, you went to several different cemeteries, even stopped by Whippoorwill at the start of the day. By the time you were in the cemetery on Mr. Freighley's property, Milton knew about the car in the barn. He was all worked up about it and scared Rodney would go to jail. You spooked him and he threatened you with the shotgun."

"I learned about your experience in doing that type of research when you made the police report about Milton early Saturday evening and it came up again later that night after Rodney threatened you in the bar. I managed to involve you further when I visited you at The Crow's Rest on Sunday and asked you to help me out by doing research on Patricia's family at the Clerk's office on Monday, August 31. You found enough information there to warrant me asking you to continue in Todd County on Tuesday, September 1."

"In the meantime, Rodney's body was discovered, hanged, up at Lake Inola. Rodney was too visible, shooting off his mouth and threatening people in public. Jason realized then he had made a bad choice and had to get rid of Rodney."

"I let you know about Rodney when I called to ask if you could continue researching in Todd County the next day. It sent Jason over the edge when he saw you heading for Elkton. He could tell where you were headed, but he didn't know why. He followed you there. He was relieved when you didn't go to the rental house, but became agitated when you did go to the Clerk's office there."

"Damn." Nick pursed his lips together.

Perri felt a chill run up her spine. "Nina was right to insist we not walk around town or eat out anywhere. She was unnerved after you called to let us know about Rodney being killed."

Sarah responded, "Well, she was right to be concerned. I'm glad you two were cautious. I certainly had no idea it could lead to this, and I'm sorry for involving you."

"When you returned from Todd County, you filled me in and that was it, as far as you were concerned. And that probably would have been it. Unfortunately, since Jason did spend a significant amount of time sitting around the Rogue, he heard Nick ask you to return when he called you Tuesday night. He knew when you were returning and that you would stop in at the tavern when you arrived."

"Me again! I'm an unwitting informant for the criminal and I don't leave anything out." Nick shook his head and looked at the floor, exasperated.

"Nick, how would you know that? You were at work when you called her, it was nothing that you would have thought to keep private." Perri put her hand on Nick's arm. "It isn't your fault."

"Not purposely, but it is my fault." Nick looked stricken. Perri took his hand and squeezed it.

"You pretty much know how the rest played out, since you were there."

"What I don't know is how you knew for sure that it was Jason Blackwell?" Perri asked.

"Honestly, I didn't know it was Jason until we had him at the hotel. I was a little misled by the fact that Joseph Blackwell hadn't been seen for a month. Yesterday, I received an image of Joseph and Jason from the PD in Guthrie, so I knew what they looked like. The first time I saw Jason was after he attacked you, and that's when I knew it was him.

It took time to connect all the pieces of the puzzle. What helped put me on the right track was talking to the last registered owner of the Chrysler. He told me he rented the house in Elkton when he graduated high school in 1996 and purchased the car from the owner of the house at the time. He left the car when he moved to California. I got confirmation that the property belonged to Joseph

Blackwell from the property deed information and this was another link from the car to the Blackwells. Jason knew the car had been abandoned there and wanted to use it, thinking it would be untraceable to him since the registration was in someone else's name and the plate was from a different state."

"Blanche Blackwell, Jason's mother, has also been arrested as an accomplice. She knew what Jason came here to do, and he kept her up to date. She encouraged him to get rid of anyone else who might sully their name. They are a cut-throat family; Jason didn't hesitate to explain her part. Joseph Blackwell's prognosis is not good. Jason wanted the title of CEO and an unblemished image so badly that he was willing to murder someone to make sure he got it.

Perri said sadly, "All of this killing and general mayhem was for fear of losing their public image. What a mess it turned out to be. In the end, they lose not only their image, but their freedom too. What's wrong with people?"

Nick answered her question, "Money and social status can make people do some strange things."

"You're right. It does." Sarah agreed. "Well Perri, again I thank you and Nina both for your help with all this. I regret it put you in danger though. Between us, I'm still a little new at being a detective and...I should have known better."

"Sarah, I will say that while I'd rather not have been wrapped up like a burrito and half drowned, I don't blame you at all. I'm glad you and Nick popped in when you did," she smiled.

Sarah gathered her papers and said, "One more thing, I nearly forgot. Alice Wooldridge called me this morning, from the B&B you and Nina stayed in?"

"Oh yeah, Alice." Perri said.

"She heard about the goings on and wanted to know if you were ok. I told her that you were pretty shaken and banged up, but doing alright. I wanted to let you know she was concerned."

"Thanks, Sarah, that was nice of Alice." She and Nick stood up, "I guess we'll be on our way. We can have our Friday night date tonight maybe."

"Have fun!" Sarah shook their hands and escorted them to the lobby. They said goodnight and walked out into the sunshine.

Nick and Perri walked back through the downtown area, music was playing and there were more people than before. "I think there is a watermelon seed spitting contest," Nick laughed, "You wanting to hang around for that?"

"I'll pass, thank you. What I'd like is to have that date we didn't have last night."

"That's what I was hoping you would say."

Chapter 39

Nick drove Perri back to the parking lot of the hotel. He put her duffel in the trunk of the Cooper. "I'm so glad you came back for the weekend. Friday night was a nightmare but Saturday and this morning were awesome. That's silly, they were fabulous, amazing."

Perri giggled. "I know, it's hard to say it without sounding like a line from a bodice-ripper isn't it?"

"Yes, it is. But you know what I mean."

"I do know, Nick. Thank you so much for rescuing me and for making the rest of my weekend awesome and fabulous and amazing."

Nick slipped his tanned and tattooed arms around Perri and pulled her into his chest, his t-shirt smelled of sun and warmth, like it had been hung on a clothes line. He kissed her, long and lusciously. "You will call as soon as you get home, won't you?"

"That I will do." Perri held up two fingers, "Girl Scout's Honor."

"You were a Girl Scout?"

"Don't say that so disbelieving. Of course I was. I didn't say I was a good one. You are coming up to Vailsburg in a couple weeks?"

"I wouldn't miss it for the world," Nick assured her.

"Goody! I better get going."

Nick kissed her again. "Ok, be careful and call me!" Perri kissed him back and got in the Cooper. She looked back at Nick in the rearview mirror as she drove away, he waved.

***

Perri wanted to make one stop before she headed for the interstate that would take her home. As she drove the now familiar county road 102, she called Nina to let her know she was on the way. Perri pulled into driveway of The Crow's Rest and parked in the same spot she had eleven days before. Alice opened the door as she climbed the stairs. "Perri, my stars, I heard what happened to you. Sarah Vines told me about it. I can't believe all this murder."

Perri walked into the cool interior of the house. Alice invited, "Come on in to the parlor and sit down. You want something to drink?"

"No Alice, I just wanted to stop by and say thanks. Sarah told me you called to check on me. Nina and I really enjoyed staying here. I'm heading home now."

"Well, maybe you'll be back to the area sometime, I hear you have made a new friend here." Alice tried to sound innocent.

Perri laughed, "Word does get around in a small town, doesn't it?"

"You bet it does." Alice got up and said, "Hold on just a minute. There's something I want to show you."

"Ok, Alice, sure." Perri leaned back on the brocade settee and looked out the window at the swaying willow trees.

Alice was back shortly with a photo frame in her hand. She sat on the settee next to Perri. "Like I said, Sarah told me the gist of the saga of the Blackwell family and what led up to all this. I thought it might interest you to look at this photo again. I know you admired the old photos on the wall upstairs when you stayed here." She handed Perri the frame photo of the men standing in front of the Rogue's Harbor tavern.

"Yes, I did." Perri studied the faces of the men captured in that moment more than one hundred years ago. "This place really was a Rogue's Harbor, wasn't it?"

"More than you realize." Alice pointed, one at a time, to three of the people in the photo. "This one, the man holding the shotgun, that's James Blackwell, Jonathan Blackwell's younger brother. This woman, the one half in and half out of the doorway, that's Emma Crawford Blackwell, James's wife."

"Oh, my gosh, Alice, how incredible that you have a photo of them. How interesting!"

"Perri, that's not the most interesting part. This one," Alice indicated the frowning man, the man James was pointing his shotgun toward, "This is Jonathan Blackwell."

"Oh, wow. So…that's the scoundrel!"

"Yes, but what makes this photo important is that this was taken in March of 1889."

"How do you know that?"

Alice turned the frame over and took the photo out. She held it out to Perri. "Their names and the date are on written on the back."

Perri took the photo carefully, "They sure are. Wait, March of 1889. Jonathan Blackwell ran off in 1887. He did come back once!"

"He did. And I think that's why James is laughing, because someone was taking a photo and Jonathan didn't like it. It's probably the same reason Emma has such a disapproving expression."

"The court documents I read did say there had been some 'proof' submitted that Jonathan hadn't died after he ran off."

"Yes, and this may be it. But even that isn't the best part. This was in a box of old photos we were given when an older home was being cleared out, remember I said that's how we got a lot of them?"

"Yes, I do."

The name of the person who took the photo, and who recorded the names of the people in the photo, is on the back too. Look in the lower right corner, after the list of names.

Perri turned it over again. She read the name cramped beneath the other writing. She looked at Alice, then back at the name, "Zachariah Silver!" She looked at Alice.

"That's one of Nick's grandpas. Some of the photos we were given came from the Silver's old place. I thought you'd be interested."

"I am! I'm glad you showed me this." Perri reached out to hand the photograph back to Alice.

Alice gently refused, lightly pushing Perri's arm away, "You should keep that photo."

"Oh Alice, I couldn't."

"Yes, you can. Take it. I want you to. And you show that to Nick, ok?"

"Thank you, Alice, I will."

***

The Cooper zoomed down the interstate, the top down, Perri's hair blowing and whipping wildly in the wind. Despite her bumps and bruises, she felt sunny and hopeful. "I knew this family tree stuff would be a good diversion." She smiled bigger than she had in ages and turned up the radio.

THE END

About the Author

My interest in Genealogy first reared its head when I was around twelve years old. I started asking the oldest family members questions about the past after seeing some old photos, including my Great-Great Grandfather's Civil War portrait. I was fascinated. Being a history lover, my interest has continued to grow over the years and I've spent the last couple of decades searching for information, documents, headstones, anything I can find to learn more about who my ancestors were and where they came from. There are many great stories in our family trees; ferreting them out is just part of the fun.

Perri Seamore Series:

Poison Branches
Buried Roots
Drawing on the Past

Read the Author's Interview at Smashwords:
https://www.smashwords.com/interview/CRaleigh
Webpage: http://www.cynthiaraleigh.com
Goodreads Author Page:
https://www.goodreads.com/author/show/15251249.Cynthia_Raleigh

Notes and Acknowledgements

Thank you for reading Poison Branches! I truly hope you enjoyed it.

All reviews are appreciated. If you would like, please take a moment to leave me a review at your favorite retailer.

If you would like to be notified when the next Perri Seamore book is available, please either sign up for the email list at www.cynthiaraleigh.com, visit me on Facebook, or send an email to CRaleigh@cynthiaraleigh.com.

I want to thank the people who helped me during the writing of this book. My husband, Greg, who repeatedly made sure I had time to write and offered support in every way. Debby Prow, my best friend from five years old onward, thank you for being my inspiration and support. Colin Lawson, the creator of the marvelous Poison Branches book jacket and the close friend who patiently endured a bombardment of questions from me concerning HTML and many other publishing subjects. Chad Parson, the cousin I didn't know I had until I traced my family back to the mid-1800s. It has been a true reward to find a relative who shares my enthusiasm for genealogy.

Made in the USA
Lexington, KY
04 August 2018